*I*nside the world of humans is the world of imagination, and the only way you can go there is through the door of your mind.

A girl called Tuesday asked her mother, "Who made the place that stories come from?"

Her mother thought for a moment, then said, "I think it began when the first person ever looked at a cloud and saw a wild beast. Or perhaps the first time a girl bent over a pond and saw a heroine in the reflection there. Or maybe when a boy first imagined himself walking into the forest and finding a feast. I know that long before stories were written down, they were spoken as whispers in the dark of winter, as tales at the fireside under a full moon, as songs to lull children to sleep.

"And I think it's been going on for all this time, ever since then, world after world being created, growing, expanding until we could never know the scale of it all. It's rather like the universe: the more we seek to find the boundaries, the larger it grows. Because the place stories come from holds everything we have ever feared or hoped or lived for, and when you think of how many people there have ever been, all of them hoping and fearing and living . . . well, that's quite something."

The Tuesday McGillycuddy Adventures

>>>> BOOK TWO <<<<

A WEEK
without
TUESDAY

Angelica Banks

with illustrations by Stevie Lewis

SQUARE
FISH

HENRY HOLT AND COMPANY ✳ NEW YORK

For BAFFIX,

May your ideas be your wings

**SQUARE
FISH**

An imprint of Macmillan Publishing Group, LLC
175 Fifth Avenue
New York, NY 10010
mackids.com

A WEEK WITHOUT TUESDAY. Text copyright © 2015 by
Heather Rose and Danielle Wood. Illustrations copyright © 2016 by Stevie Lewis.
All rights reserved. Printed in the United States of America by
LSC Communications, Harrisonburg, Virginia.

Square Fish and the Square Fish logo are trademarks of Macmillan and
are used by Henry Holt and Company under license from Macmillan.

Our books may be purchased in bulk for promotional, educational, or business use.
Please contact your local bookseller or the Macmillan Corporate and
Premium Sales Department at (800) 221-7945 ext. 5442 or by e-mail
at MacmillanSpecialMarkets@macmillan.com.

Library of Congress Cataloging-in-Publication Data
Banks, Angelica, author.
A week without Tuesday / Angelica Banks.
pages   cm
Sequel to: Finding serendipity.
Summary: Real and imaginary worlds are colliding so Tuesday and Baxterr, at the request
of the Librarian, venture to find the Gardener—the one person who can stop this
catastrophe—but will they be able to save the land of story?
ISBN 978-1-250-10422-9 (paperback) — ISBN 978-1-62779-543-2 (ebook)
[1. Adventure and adventurers—Fiction.   2. Books and reading—Fiction.
3. Magic—Fiction.]   I. Title.
PZ7.1.B365We 2016   [Fic]—dc23   2015011993

First published in Australia by Allen and Unwin, 2015.
First published in the United States by Henry Holt and Company
First Square Fish Edition: 2017 / Book designed by April Ward
Square Fish logo designed by Filomena Tuosto

1 3 5 7 9 10 8 6 4 2

AR: 5.6 / LEXILE: 870L

Chapter One

Vivienne Small lived in a tree house. It was quite new, her previous tree house having been destroyed by pirates, as some of you may remember. The new house had beautiful canvas awnings and a deep veranda. Through the veranda's carved railings, Vivienne had trained a length of pikwan vine.

A pikwan is something like a mango crossed with a horse chestnut, and one morning as the forest came to life in shimmering shades of green, Vivienne plucked a ripe one from the vine. She split open the hard, spiky shell with her pocketknife, but before she had even managed one bite of the sweet flesh on the inside, she heard a ferocious cracking, rushing, breaking noise from above. She dropped the pikwan in alarm, and its two halves rolled off the veranda, falling a very, very long way to the ground.

Vivienne looked up to see a huge brown blur hurtling toward her through the forest's canopy. She flared her wings and made a desperate flying lunge to

get clear of it. She wrapped her arms around a branch and hung on tightly as whatever it was crashed into one side of her tree house, taking with it her canvas awnings, a large part of the veranda, the kitchen wall, and a dresser full of crockery and cutlery. Vivienne was left clinging to the branch, her feet dangling above the ruins of her house, as a thunderous noise rose up from the forest floor. She watched in dismay as her remaining furniture, books, and ornaments vibrated with the impact, then settled untidily back to their respective places in the ravaged tree house.

Vivienne fluttered down on outspread wings to land on what was left of her veranda. Above her, where there should have been branches of all sizes and leaves of infinite shades of green, with only tiny pinpricks of sunshine and sky peeping through, there was a huge hole, and Vivienne found herself staring up into a pinkish dawn. Far, far below her, in the deep gloom of the forest, she could just make out the shape of the thing that had caused all this damage. For the briefest of moments, she allowed herself to feel heartbroken and cross about the devastation of her beautiful new home. Then her thoughts turned to questions.

What on earth was that thing? And had it really been *furry*?

Gliding down branch by branch through the layers of the forest to its floor, Vivienne landed deftly beside what was, indeed, an animal. It was a dog, but not like most of us are used to. This was a gigantic dog, bigger than any you have ever seen. Also, it had wings.

Once, and not all that long ago, Winged Dogs had been a common sight in the skies above the Peppermint Forest. Vivienne remembered the days when dogs such as these had lived in packs in the Winged Mountains, making dens in the highest of the mountain caves, flying above towering waterfalls, and fledging their pups from craggy outcrops. Vivienne had loved to watch the parent dogs hover as their little ones practiced the use of their wings. Sometimes the puppies would fall into the lakes below and face a long dog paddle back to shore. Then they would shake themselves off, and their parents would urge them up into the sky to try again.

Those days were gone: the Winged Dogs had vanished. Not one by one, as is so often the case when rare creatures leave the world, but all at once, and quite mysteriously. Vivienne had heard it said—though she didn't know whether or not it was true—that all of the Winged Dogs had flown right out of her world and into another.

And yet, here was a Winged Dog, its fur glowing in the bright shaft of light that shone into the deep green of the forest. Its head had come to rest between two giant tree trunks. Its body crushed an entire stand of enormous ferns. One of the dog's wings was wedged in a myrtle tree, while the other was pinned awkwardly beneath its body. All around and underneath the creature were shreds of canvas and shards of railings and floorboards. Vivienne also saw two of her chairs (now broken) and several plates and cups.

The dog's breathing was slow and shallow. Blood dripped from one of its nostrils, and its tongue lolled—huge and pink and wet—on the ground. Making soft crooning noises, Vivienne reached out and stroked the dog's face. Carefully, she pulled back one of the dog's eyelids. The pupil did not contract. As she inspected the length of the animal's huge body, she found what appeared to be claw marks on its underbelly. There were deep wounds on the dog's sides, too, and bloodstains on its thick pelt.

A white crescent moon marked the fur between

the dog's huge eyes. And when Vivienne checked more closely, she saw by the narrowness of the muzzle that this was a female, and quite an old girl, judging by the silvering around her eyes. If only Vivienne knew the dog's name, she might be able to call her back to consciousness.

"Moonthread?" she guessed. "Moonborn? Crescent Moon? White Moon?"

The dog did not stir. Her breathing was slowing still further. Vivienne thought more widely.

"Windseeker? Weathereye? Stormwing?" Vivienne said, but the dog lay silent and unmoving. Vivienne's brow furrowed. "What kind of creature has done this to you?"

Vivienne knew of beasts that were large and beasts that were vicious, but she knew of no creature that was both large and vicious enough to inflict such terrible wounds on a Winged Dog. Even if two Winged Dogs were to clash, which was unheard of, their claws were not sharp enough to make the awful gashes this dog had suffered.

Vivienne studied the place, high above, where the falling dog had torn a hole in the forest's leafy ceiling. She shuddered as if a cold breeze had suddenly blown, although none had. What was out there? She had to know.

With the ease and speed of someone who has flown through forests her whole life, Vivienne spread her small, blue, leathery wings and made a series of flying leaps up, up, up, past her broken tree house and into the tree's very highest branches. From where she stood, sharing her weight between two leafy limbs, she saw two salt eagles flying north and a flock of derry birds down on the shore. Wrens and swallows darted about. Otherwise, the sky was empty. Whatever creature had savaged the Winged Dog and caused it to fall was no longer in sight.

Vivienne sighed and felt troubled. In the distance, the morning sea was the color of the inside of an oyster shell. To the east, a bright sun was climbing into the day. Beams of light threaded in and out of long slender clouds. Vivienne also spied the wide mouth of the River of Rythwyck emerging from the depths of the Peppermint Forest. To the south, as she twisted around, she saw the snowcapped ridgeline of the Mountains of Margolov, bright against the horizon. But no, she didn't. Vivienne rubbed her eyes. Although she could see the *slopes* of the Mountains of Margolov, she could not see their jagged peaks. The mountains had . . . grown.

"Not possible," Vivienne murmured to herself.

Was this a trick of the light? Vivienne blinked several times and looked again. Still the mountains blocked out the entire southern sky. And with a shiver that went all the way out to the tips of her wings, she saw that at their very tops, the mountains seemed to pierce the firmament itself. The sky puckered and folded around the shoulders of the mountains as if they were outgrowing the world itself.

Vivienne's adventures had taken her high into the Mountains of Margolov on several occasions, through foothills tangled with lush jungle, and into the upper reaches where the trees and plants grew stunted and sideways in the constant wind. She had ventured up past the snow line, where the air thinned and nothing green grew, and she remembered how it felt to stand at the top of the very highest peak and see the entire world stretched out at her feet. The Mountains of Margolov that Vivienne knew were immense. So how had they become larger still?

Vivienne's heart raced. She realized she was experiencing a very rare thing: she was afraid.

Chapter Two

A very long way from the Peppermint Forest, Denis McGillycuddy was in his tartan dressing gown making pancakes. It was Sunday morning, and the McGillycuddy house, the tallest and narrowest house on Brown Street, was in the special variety of chaos that comes only at the end of the summer holidays. The fridge was papered with sticky notes on which had been scribbled potential names for characters (Lydia Bottle, Maple Hartigan, Volker Fink). On the windowsill was a procession of shells and fossilized sea stars (banded trochus, purple linckia, marbled fromia) and other mysterious maritime objects that

Denis had shaken out of pockets and bags while unpacking from the family's three-week escape to a faraway island with palm trees and warm, aqua-blue water.

Since the McGillycuddys' return to Brown Street, meals had been taken at erratic hours and in all parts of the house, so that cups and plates and forks and spoons had migrated to bookshelves, chairs, mantelpieces, and even the bathtub. Abandoned board games and half-finished crossword puzzles cluttered every surface in the kitchen, while striped beach towels and gritty bathing suits languished in the laundry. No matter how many times Denis swept, he couldn't get rid of the crunch of fine-grained tropical sand on the floor.

It was a quarter to eleven, and although Denis could hear no movement from the upper floors of the house, he was not surprised. Last night on his way to bed, when he had looked in on his daughter, Tuesday, he had found her still sitting up at her desk, tapping away on the keys of her baby-blue typewriter. It had been nearly midnight.

Tuesday was working on a story, the same one that she had been working on for every spare minute of her holidays. During the weeks they had spent on the remote island, Tuesday had barely been separated from her typewriter. She had written while sitting on the beach, while drifting in a kayak, and while lying under a mosquito net. She had written while sipping coconut milk and while hermit crabs crawled over her toes. And then, after returning to Brown Street, Tuesday had written at her desk in her bedroom, and under a tree in City Park, in the local library, and at the kitchen table before and after (but never during) breakfast, lunch, and dinner. Very late nights had become something of a habit.

But while Tuesday was sleeping in, the other writer in the house had risen early, roused by the sound of a summer rainstorm on the roof. Since before dawn, Serendipity had been in her writing room on the top floor of the house, sometimes rapping urgently on the keys of her typewriter and other times simply sitting with a blanket about her, her elbows on her desk, staring out through an open window at the morning clouds. Serendipity had once told Denis that it was hard to say which was more important, making words on a page or staring out the window, having ideas. Both were essential for a writer.

Downstairs in the kitchen, Denis set his pancake mixture aside to rest, checked the clock again, and resolved to give Tuesday and Serendipity until eleven o'clock before disturbing them for breakfast. To fill the time, he folded a load of clean washing, rustled up Tuesday's school uniform from the bottom of the ironing basket in readiness for Monday morning, and then went to fetch the Sunday paper from where it had landed on the front steps.

He shook the newspaper open quite casually, but what he read on the front page made him sit down on the top step, which was wet from the rain, stand up again, turn around, and turn around again. Then Denis did something very unusual, something quite unprecedented, in fact. He burst back through the front door and ran noisily up four flights of stairs and barreled into Serendipity's writing room. She sat at her desk wearing the vague expression she always wore when she was daydreaming.

"Thank goodness!" Denis said, but his relief was only fleeting.

He swooped past Serendipity, his dressing gown

billowing out behind him, and pulled the window shut, banging the clasp in place rather more forcefully than was necessary. And then, as if to be doubly cautious, he hastily drew the curtains, dimming the room almost entirely.

"You have to stop immediately!" Denis said. "No writing! No thinking! No imagining! You have to stop it right now."

Serendipity blinked, flicked on her desk lamp, and stared at Denis, who, breathing hard from having run up the stairs so quickly, was waving a newspaper around. She appeared to observe his unusual behavior as though from a long way off until at last her eyes focused and she took in the panicked expression on Denis's face.

"Darling, what on earth is going on?" Serendipity asked.

"Here, here!" he said, thrusting the newspaper at her.

The headline read EXCLUSIVE! SEVEN WRITERS ABDUCTED.

"Abducted?" Serendipity asked.

"So the story goes. For now, at least."

Serendipity read the article aloud: *"Crime might be*

her career, but J. D. Jones, one of the world's most admired writers, never imagined she would be part of a real-life global mystery. Jones was found wandering in the streets of Abu Dhabi last night. She is reported to have no memory of how she came to be there or how she sustained a broken arm. Jones is not alone. In the past five days, six other famous writers have been abducted from their homes, only to reappear in distant locations with no memory of how they got there or of their kidnappers. There have been no demands for ransom. Police are seeking any information that might indicate a motive for these increasingly bizarre disappearances."

Serendipity stared in alarm at the photographs of the writers who had turned up in all manner of places. One from France had turned up in Alaska. Another from Sydney had been found in Cape Town. Two British writers had been discovered in Kansas, and a Chinese writer had been rescued from high in the mountains of Argentina. All of them claimed they had gone to bed, and when they had woken up, they found themselves half a world away from home, without money or a passport, and with no way of contacting their loved ones. Some had broken bones; others had suffered burns, cuts, and bruises.

All the color drained out of Serendipity's face.

"Denis," she said, "where is Tuesday?"

"Asleep, I imagine. She was still writing at midnight, so I thought I'd let her sleep as long—"

"Midnight? But where is she *now*? Denis!" Serendipity grasped her husband by his elbows.

He said, "You don't think . . . surely not? These are published writers, famous writers. Tuesday's just—"

"Denis, was she *writing*? When you checked on her? What was she doing?"

Before Denis could reply, Serendipity had flown past him, out the door, and down the stairs to Tuesday's room.

Tuesday woke to shouts of "Tuesday! Tuesday!" and the sound of rapid footsteps on the stairs outside her room. She lurched upright. Her strawberry blond hair looked as if it had fought with a cat in the night.

"Sweetheart," said Serendipity in relief, sweeping Tuesday into an almost violent hug.

"What? What? I'm right here," Tuesday said.

"I have never been so pleased to see you. Well, perhaps I have. When you were first born. And then, a little while ago, when you got back from being *there*. Well, I was very pleased then too, but I still think that—"

"Mom, you're blathering. Could you stop squashing me?"

"Thank goodness you're *here*!" said Serendipity, letting go at last.

"Where else would I be?"

"Who knows, darling? Belize? Afghanistan? Japan?" said Serendipity, handing the newspaper to Tuesday.

Tuesday pushed herself upright and rubbed her eyes.

"Here, let me," said Denis impatiently, and he plucked the newspaper out of her hands and read aloud the headline and the text below. He turned the newspaper to Tuesday and showed her the photographs.

A feeling of dread washed over Tuesday. This was not, she realized, only news about other people. This was news about people like her mother.

"What's happening?" Tuesday asked. "Mom?"

"I don't know. I really don't know."

"They weren't abducted, were they?"

"Not a bit, darling," Serendipity said. "But the fact that it's a lie doesn't make it any less worrying."

What Serendipity knew, Tuesday knew too, as did Denis, of course. The writers who had been found thousands of miles from home—some with broken bones, all with injuries—had not been kidnapped. Nor had they been asleep when they'd vanished, as they claimed. They had all been quite awake.

"Something's wrong *there*. Isn't it, Mom?"

There. It was the only word Tuesday could bring herself to use for the world of story that existed on the other end of a silvery thread of imagination—a magical place that was the collective secret of every writer who ever lived. Tuesday had been *there*. Serendipity went *there* all the time. And these writers on the front of the newspaper had been *there*. But instead of coming safely home again, as usual, to sit down at their desks and transcribe all the things they had seen and smelled and touched and tasted and lived and imagined, something had gone horribly wrong. Somehow, on their journeys homeward, they had been knocked off course.

But no writer would ever tell the police, let alone the media, exactly what they had been doing before they were discovered in Madrid or Melbourne or Minnesota. Everyone would think they were mad.

"What do we do?" Tuesday asked.

"Well, I know what we don't do," said Denis.

Denis was at Tuesday's desk, shoving pens and pencils and notepads and scraps of paper into his dressing-gown pockets. He tucked Tuesday's little blue typewriter into its matching case and snapped the latch.

"No, Dad! Not my typewriter," Tuesday begged, but her father was unmoved.

"Until further notice," said Denis, "we do not *write*."

Tuesday and Serendipity looked at each other. He might as well have told them not to breathe.

Chapter Three

V ivienne Small could do many things. She could sail a boat, tie a knot, sharpen a knife, whistle a tune, solve a riddle, read a map, light a fire, hit a target with a speeding arrow, scale a cliff, swim through a wild sea, make an ice cave, tap a cactus, and survive a sandstorm. She could run fast and walk quietly. And with the help of her blue, leathery wings, she could leap small, dangerous distances.

Vivienne could speak and write fluently in several languages, including Xunchillese, Formosan, and Sandshuck, but she had never learned the tongue that might have helped her to talk with the great Winged

Dog who lay on the forest floor at the base of her tree. She wanted to know where the dog had come from, and where it had been going, and whether or not it knew anything about the Mountains of Margolov and what had made them grow. And while Vivienne had some art as a healer, she knew that the cure of the Winged Dog's terrible injuries was beyond her skill. Still, she was determined to do all she could to help.

Leaping from branch to branch, Vivienne made a swift descent from the top branches of her tree to the ruins of her house. Gingerly, she entered what was left of her kitchen, stepping over broken beams. She saw that the tree house was now so unstable that what remained of it was likely to be blown out of the tree in the next high wind.

Luckily, Vivienne kept her favorite weapons on the kitchen's back wall, where they had not been harmed. Thinking of the unknown beast that had felled the Winged Dog, she slung her bow across her body, swiftly counted her turquoise-feathered arrows, and secured her quiver neatly between her wings. Next, she tucked her blowpipe into her belt and gathered a pouch of poison darts.

Then, from underneath her partly shattered kitchen

bench, Vivienne extracted a wooden box. It was rather like a toolbox, but with a top tray full of buttons and needles, a pair of small silver scissors and a thimble, a length of twine, a set of playing cards, and a few scraps of leather. With a click, Vivienne released a hidden clasp at the side of the tray and lifted it away to reveal a compartment filled with small bottles of remedies that she herself had brewed and concocted from plants that grew all about her in the Peppermint Forest.

"No, not that one. No, no, no," she muttered to herself, lifting out and then replacing small glass bottles labeled ZINNOBER EXTRACT, INFUSION OF JESSAMY, INCARNADINE, WILLOWISH POWDER. At last Vivienne found what she was searching for.

"Yes!" she said, snatching up a small bottle labeled TINCTURE OF GOLDEN RHODELIA. The medicine was made from the stamens of tiny, glossy yellow flowers that bloomed for only a day or two each year. It had extraordinary healing properties, and Vivienne hoped a dose might keep the dog alive long enough for her to seek help from somebody with greater healing powers. She held the bottle up to the light to check the level of the liquid and saw with dismay that it was

only half full. A drop or two of the powerful medicine would be a sufficient dose for Vivienne herself,
but would the amount she had be enough to help an
animal the size of a Winged Dog? She didn't know.
Even so, the golden rhodelia was her best hope.

Taking the branches two at a time, Vivienne dashed
down to the forest floor where the dog lay, barely
breathing.

"Here you go, beauty," Vivienne whispered as she
carefully dripped the golden rhodelia onto the dog's
tongue, one drop at a time. The pinkish flesh of the
tongue glowed brightly as the potion was absorbed.
Vivienne watched the stricken dog intently. It stirred,
retracted its tongue into its mouth, and twitched its
gigantic paws. The dog tried to flex her upper wing
but—finding it still caught fast in the branches of the
myrtle tree—gave a whimper of pain.

"Easy, easy," Vivienne said. She laid a hand on
the dog's muzzle.

Just then, Vivienne heard another noise. From high
above her came a loud buzzing sound, and Vivienne
looked up to see two creatures spiraling downward
through the column of tattered forest. She didn't
know what these creatures were; she had never seen

their like, and they moved so fast that at first all she could see was the haze of whirring wings and the long, insect-like shapes of their bodies. She took cover beside the dog's face, whipped her bow off her shoulder, and fitted an arrow, focusing her dead-eye gaze. As the creatures came closer, Vivienne saw no sign of the sharp claws or jagged teeth that might have injured the dog by her side. Her instincts told her that these otherworldly beings were gentle, not dangerous. When they landed on the forest floor, Vivienne lowered her bow. She realized that there were not two beings, as she had first thought, but four.

The winged creatures were steeds, rather like immense dragonflies with bodies covered in close-cropped, velvety fur that was mottled cream and white. Saddled upon their backs were people, and they, too, were of a kind that Vivienne had never encountered before. They were about her own size and dressed in tight-fitting suits made of a near-white leather or suede, with golden embroidery at the wrists and ankles. On their bare hands and feet, in place of skin, were small, pearlescent scales. Their heads were encased in large, creamy-white helmets that were ridged in the manner of seashells. The narrow openings in the front of these helmets showed large eyes, gleaming darkly in the place where the whites ought to be, yet with irises of an intense, clear white.

They stepped down from their saddles and removed their helmets, revealing the fine fur that grew all over their faces. Their noses and mouths were small, their narrow lips shimmering and pale. The two were very like each other—their bodies exactly the same size and 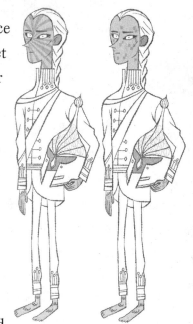 shape, and their long hair was identically fixed into neat, snowy braids—but the fur on their faces was patterned quite differently. One was marked with irregular checkers of cream and white, while the other had darker stripes radiating out from the nose to the edges of the face.

The pair held their helmets beneath their arms and bowed deeply to Vivienne, who gave a small, suspicious nod in return. The buzzing of the steeds' wings settled to a low hum as the creatures lowered their heads to the forest floor to graze on the moss. Vivienne raised herself up to her full height, slung her bow back across her body, and said, "I am Vivienne Small."

The one with the checkered face stepped forward and spoke in a clear and musical female voice.

"I am Harlequin."

"And I am Tarquin," said her stripe-faced companion, his voice lower though equally melodic.

It took Vivienne a moment to register that when she heard their voices, it was both through her ears and right inside her mind.

"My sister and I were chasing the vercaka who attacked this great beast," said Tarquin, gesturing to the dog.

Vivienne shook her head, unaccustomed to this unusual way of hearing. She heard him clearly inside her head, even though he stood a distance from her. It felt like having a fly in her ear.

"You saw what caused this?" she asked. "What was it? I don't know anything that could bring down a Winged Dog in this way."

"*Dog?*" Tarquin inquired of Vivienne.

"Yes."

"Dog," Harlequin repeated, as if committing the word deliberately to memory.

"Yes, dog," said Vivienne, a little more impatiently than she meant to. "What did you say attacked it?"

"Vercaka," Tarquin said bitterly.

Harlequin looked into Vivienne's face through large, pale eyes.

"You know nothing of vercaka?" Harlequin asked.

"No. Nothing," Vivienne admitted, though it pained her to do so. There were few places she had not been and—so she had thought—no creatures that were foreign to her. "What is this vercaka?"

"Vercaka are monsters on the wing, both stupid and cruel. They have sharpness of claw, and of beak, and the way they speak their words poisons the heart," Harlequin explained. "This is how they brought down the dog. They have some way of seeing your greatest fears. Once they have this knowledge, they use words to stop your courage, to kill all your hopes."

"That sounds dreadful. Where are they from?" demanded Vivienne. "I've never heard of such an animal before."

Harlequin turned to her brother, and it seemed to Vivienne that the two spoke to each other within their own minds, so that she could not know what they were saying.

Tarquin said, "The vercaka are the enemy of our people, and they prey on us and our farouche whenever they can." He gestured to the pale, insect-like creatures nearby. "They come from our world, which we can no longer find."

The music in Tarquin's voice changed to a minor key, and Vivienne heard in it a great sadness.

Harlequin went on. "We have flown and flown but can find nothing that is familiar. Our world has great sand plains, and for all time, they have been wide and flat and endless. But lately, and without warning, they have changed. Slopes rise up and fall away in places they have never been. Winds rush across these plains with terrible force. We were caught in such a storm. Instead of being buried by sand, we fell through into your sky. And the vercaka must have come through too, from our world to yours. It is a curse that we would not have wished upon you."

"Strange things are happening everywhere," Vivienne said. She thought again of the Mountains of Margolov and felt deeply unsettled. If faced with the need to duel with a pirate or battle a fire-breathing pyronelle, Vivienne would know exactly what to do. She could outsmart a two-faced fortune-teller, and tie a purple-banded sea snake in knots, and make a flying fox out of two lengths of Hartaxian poison ivy, but she didn't know the first thing about how to fix a world that was suddenly and perilously unpredictable.

"It's not only your world," she said. "Winged Dogs such as this one have been gone from our skies for some time. And yet one has returned."

"It is difficult to know what may be done," Tarquin said. "We have lost our weapons in our fall and can only hope we find something here that will slay this creature and any others that may follow."

"What do you need?" she asked. She indicated her bow.

Tarquin shook his head. "Their bodies are tough. We have a poison that kills them. It runs in small rivers on our plains."

Vivienne then drew out her Lucretian blowpipe. "This has poison darts that can make any creature sleep," she said.

"Sleep will not be enough," Harlequin said.

"You might try Lucretia," Vivienne said. "It is far to the south, a group of islands, and they have many poisons . . ."

The dog gave a low moan. One of its big amber eyes flickered open, then closed again.

"The drops I have given the dog are having some

effect," Vivienne explained, tossing the empty bottle to Harlequin. "This mixture works to soften the pain and begin the healing, but I doubt that the little I had will be enough to cure a creature so large and so badly hurt. I must go for help."

"May we look to your dog? We know much about the vercaka, and we have ways of seeing," Harlequin said.

Vivienne hesitated. She knew nothing of these people. But the dog needed help, and it couldn't wait. Besides, she thought, the dog was not hers to command or control. She stepped away to allow Tarquin and Harlequin to come closer.

The two inspected the wounded dog, walking all around its great body. Vivienne observed the unusual way that the siblings moved: as if they had extra elbows in their arms and more than one knee in each leg. It was strange, yet graceful. From time to time, Harlequin and Tarquin looked at each other, and Vivienne knew they were again communicating in their silent, secret way. At length, Harlequin returned to where Vivienne stood waiting. Harlequin reached out and took Vivienne's hands in her own, and she was surprised that the pearly scales that covered them were warm and soft to the touch.

"Vivienne Small, the dog is dying," said Harlequin. Her voice was as low as a lullaby, and its soothing notes echoed inside Vivienne's mind.

She pulled away crossly.

"It can't die. We need to heal it!"

"It is beyond that," said Tarquin. "You must understand, Vivienne Small, that the wounds the vercaka inflict are not only to the body. There is also the damage that has been done to the dog's mind."

Vivienne kicked at a tree root in frustration. "But the drops! I gave her all I had. It might work yet—"

Tarquin said, "The time for healing had passed."

"There has to be something we can do!" said Vivienne.

"No," said Tarquin softly. "And you know, in your deepest heart, that this is so."

"Before she goes, Vivienne Small," Harlequin said, "we must learn what we can from her. Do you not think, as we do, it is possible she knows something of the strange events in your world, and in ours?"

Vivienne looked searchingly at Harlequin, and then at Tarquin. Their faces showed little expression, but their eyes were full of sorrow.

"Will it cause her pain?"

"None at all," said Tarquin. "Together, we are able to sense her thoughts, and her memories."

Vivienne nodded sadly, and Tarquin and Harlequin each placed a pearly hand upon the crescent moon between the dog's closed eyes.

Vivienne waited.

"Well?" she said.

"Patience. When life is this close to death, it's not easy to find a memory," Tarquin said.

Vivienne waited a little longer.

"Can you see anything yet?"

"More patience, Vivienne Small," said Harlequin.

Vivienne wandered over to where Tarquin and Harlequin's farouche lay dozing at the base of her tree. Their long, fluffy antennae trembled in time with the soft, sighing sounds they made in their sleep.

"The dog carries something," said Tarquin at last.

"What?" asked Vivienne.

"Quiet," said Harlequin, a note of command in her voice.

"Her destination is a place of stone and mist," Tarquin said.

"The mist is thick, and the way is closed to all but some," Harlequin said.

"There is a code, carved into the stone," Tarquin added. "It is written in runes that we do not know, but we will remember it."

"The way is guarded by beasts," Harlequin said. "With great heads—"

And then she broke away and brought her hand to her chest. The dog took a shallow, rattling breath and then sighed for the longest time. Vivienne, Harlequin, and Tarquin all gazed at her, and despite the differences between them, each of them knew that sound. It was a last breath. A breath that carried away memory, smell, sound, and thought.

Tears filled Vivienne's eyes.

"Peace," said Harlequin.

"Farewell," said Tarquin.

For a time, the three stood in silence.

And then Tarquin spoke. "Have you a tool for making runes?"

The question roused Vivienne from her silent sorrow. Her eyes still wet with tears, she watched as Harlequin searched about for a small stick and, finding one, drew in the earth a series of lines.

"The place we have seen in the dog's thoughts bears this sign, Vivienne Small. What does it say?"

ΙΠΛϹΙΠΣ

Although Vivienne looked long and hard at the seven characters, they meant nothing whatsoever to her. She tried reading them upside down and backward, to no avail.

"This is not your language?" Tarquin said.

Vivienne bristled. "It is not any language I know. And I know many, thank you very much."

She was about to suggest that Tarquin might have written the letters down incorrectly, but before she could say anything more, Harlequin's voice broke into her thoughts.

"Look to the dog, Vivienne Small!"

The dog was changing. No longer did its fur glow golden-brown; instead it shimmered in silvery gray. The animal's great body was becoming less substantial, as though fading from being. It became less and less solid until at last, the sparkling particles that composed the dog's colossal shape collapsed onto the ground in a sudden shower of golden dust. There remained nothing of the great dog other than a faint sparkle to the leaf litter and moss of the forest floor, and a circlet of fine rope. Vivienne picked it up and examined it.

"A collar!" she said, cross with herself for failing to discover it when she had examined the dog. The rope had a silver medallion affixed to it. The medallion was the size of Vivienne's palm. It was engraved on one side with an image of a dog in flight, but the other side was blank. Vivienne knew better than to expect the dog's name to be etched upon its reverse side, for a Winged Dog's name is always a secret part of its magic.

"What is this 'collar,' Vivienne Small?" Harlequin asked.

"It means that this dog has a companion. It means that somebody, somewhere, will be heartbroken."

Running her fingers around the medallion's rim, Vivienne found a tiny latch, and when she released it, the disc sprang open like a locket. Inside lay a small scroll of paper.

"A note," said Vivienne, unrolling it.

"This is the thing she carries," Tarquin said.

"What does it say, Vivienne Small?" Harlequin asked.

Vivienne peered intently at the words; they were

written with green ink in shaky, spidery hand-writing.

"It says, *My great love.*" Vivienne grimaced. She didn't have much time for things to do with love. "*I cannot hold the worlds apart much longer. Have you found our answer? G.*"

Harlequin whispered, "*Cannot hold the worlds apart much longer . . .*"

Vivienne wondered what would happen if worlds got too close. Might worlds crumple at their edges, pushing mountain ranges up into the fabric of the sky? Might dangerous beasts slip from one world to the next? And strangers too? Worlds were worlds for a reason, Vivienne thought.

"*Have you found our answer?*" she repeated.

"This message must be delivered," Tarquin said.

"Yes," Vivienne agreed. "But to whom?"

"To this great love," Harlequin said, "who dwells in the place of stone and mist, where the beasts guard the way."

"Yes. And this person will know who sent the dog," said Vivienne. "We must find them also. Tell them what has happened. You'll come with me?"

"No, Vivienne Small. We must hunt down the

vercaka," Tarquin said. "We must find a poison so that these creatures cannot take hold in your world."

Harlequin said, "And you will deliver this message, Vivienne Small. I know that you will. I see you have a great power of determination within you."

Harlequin stared at her with steady eyes, and Vivienne smelled something then. Something sharp, like gunpowder and sea salt. It was the unmistakeable scent of adventure. And adventure, to Vivienne Small, was like a mosquito to a frog or an egg to a snake—it was the most delicious thing imaginable.

Have you ever noticed how smells can remind you of things? Even of things you thought you'd forgotten? Well, when Vivienne Small caught that whiff of adventure, a memory came to her. It was the memory of a dog. A golden-brown dog. And of someone else—a girl or a ghost? Vivienne tried to make her mind grasp hold of this picture, but it was light and shadow like a dream. It drifted out of her mind's eye and away. She scrunched her eyes tight and concentrated as hard as she could.

"You are troubled, Vivienne Small," said Harlequin.

"It's a memory," Vivienne said. "I can't quite . . . Oh!" Vivienne, in frustration, smacked herself on the side of the head as if she might jolt it into place.

"We could look to your thoughts, Vivienne Small," Harlequin said gently.

Vivienne took a step backward, not quite liking the idea of two people poking around in her mind. But the memory she had glimpsed was such a tantalizing mystery. She wanted it solved.

"It would be as it was for the dog. There would be no pain," Harlequin offered.

Vivienne snorted. "Do you think I am afraid? Well, I'm not."

"Then will you sit?" Tarquin said. "And close your eyes."

Vivienne crossed her arms and scowled a little. And then, after a moment, she sat. The siblings' hands on the center of her forehead were gentle and soft. Her mind felt soothed. Vivienne became aware of a humming sound and of a sound like distant bells chiming.

"We see a dog," Tarquin said, after a time. "A dog very similar to this one who has fallen."

"There is a name, but your mind will not give it to us," Harlequin said.

"There is a word that comes in its place. Not quite dog. More like 'dog-o,'" Tarquin said.

Dog-o. Doggo! Yes, this reminded Vivienne of something, of someone! And now, for no apparent reason, she sneezed violently, and that seemed important also. And then she thought of *Vivacious*, her little red sailing boat. She could picture it quite clearly, pulled up high out of the water upon a pebbled shore. And there! The dog, gamboling on the shore. And there had been somebody else too. A girl. A girl with gingery blond hair and sea-green eyes and freckles across her nose. But an odd, ghostly kind of girl, much less real than the dog that was rolling on its back on the scrunching pebbles. Even as Vivienne stared at the image that had settled into the center of her mind, she could not tell if this was a real girl or only an imagined one.

For this is how it is in the world of imagination: when writers return home, they take their characters with them and never forget them. But it is not the same for characters. Writers fade quickly from their minds. But every now and then, a writer is lodged so deeply within a character's heart that they cannot be entirely forgotten.

That girl, Vivienne thought to herself, what had she been called?

"Tuesday," said Harlequin.

The word fitted like a key into Vivienne's mind, and all of a sudden, she remembered everything.

Tarquin and Harlequin removed their hands from Vivienne's forehead, and her eyes sprang open, shining with excitement and resolve.

"I must find Tuesday and her dog. That's what I have to do! They will help me deliver this message," Vivienne said.

"She is a friend to you, this Tuesday?" Harlequin asked.

"I think so," Vivienne said. And then, "Yes. Yes, she is. A very fine friend."

"She lives near here?" Tarquin asked.

"Not even close," Vivienne said. "But I shall find her."

Vivienne caught another whiff of sea salt and gunpowder. Finding things was an essential part of an adventure, which meant that Vivienne was very good at it. If there was someone she needed, Vivienne had an instinct for knowing on exactly which stretch of river, up which cobbled laneway, or in which distant tavern she was likely to find them. When she had seen Tuesday and her dog, Baxterr, last, they had been flying in the direction of the Hills of Mist, which lay beyond the eastern edge of the forest. Might these hills even be the place of mist toward which the great dog had been traveling?

Vivienne leapt to her feet.

"I must get going," she said.

"We, too, must hurry, lest the vercaka travel too far beyond us," Tarquin said.

"Once our task is accomplished, we will seek you, Vivienne Small," Harlequin said.

Vivienne watched as the two climbed astride their farouche and rose vertically from the ground, up through the forest to the beckoning sky. It was after the pair had left the treetops behind them and disappeared from sight that Vivienne heard Harlequin's voice inside her head, chiming with delicate harmonies.

"Go well, Vivienne Small," it said.

Chapter Four

Tuesday and Serendipity sat opposite each other at the kitchen table, which Denis had swept clean of a half-finished game of Scrabble and several incomplete crossword puzzles. Both, he insisted, involved writing of a kind. Along with Tuesday's small and relatively new typewriter, Denis had confiscated Serendipity's big antique one, and he'd collected up all the notebooks, exercise books, ballpoint and felt-tipped pens, and colored pencils that he could find throughout the house.

Denis was whistling as he cooked pancakes, as if a cheerful enough whistle could somehow counteract the disconsolate moods of his wife and daughter, who couldn't take their eyes off the newspaper that lay on the table between them. He slid a pancake onto Serendipity's plate and then—before she could crack pepper all over it—whipped the grinder out of her hand and replaced it with a bottle of maple syrup. The next pancake went to Tuesday, and the third to Baxterr, who polished it off with his usual gusto, even though—if pushed—he would have had to admit that it was not up to Denis's usual lofty standard.

Absentmindedly, Serendipity pulled a pencil from behind her ear and began doodling in the margin of the newspaper. But before she could make more than a few curly lines, Denis snatched the pencil out of her grasp.

"No writing," Denis said, gesturing at her with the pencil.

Serendipity and Tuesday gave a simultaneous sigh. Denis put Serendipity's pencil into the bin, which was already full of writing implements he'd emptied from various pots and jars throughout the kitchen. He broke the cord that tied a whiteboard marker to the fridge.

"Absolutely *no* writing. Promise me?"

Denis glared at his wife, then at his daughter. "What if . . . what if you went *there* and ended up in Antarctica, and you froze before anyone could help you? Or roasted to a crisp in Death Valley? I'm serious. What if you landed in the middle of the Atlantic Ocean? No writing, my loves. It's not safe. Please?"

"You realize, of course," said Serendipity, "that it may not be that simple."

"What do you mean?" Denis asked.

"I mean, think of Sleeping Beauty!" said Serendipity. "Her parents banned spindles from the entire kingdom, but that didn't stop her from pricking her finger, did it?"

Serendipity waved her hands at the seven faces staring up at her from the newspaper.

"Stories don't happen only when you have a pen in your hand or a typewriter under your fingers. They can sneak up on you in the shower or when you're climbing the stairs. They can come to you in dreams, and they can arrive while you're hanging out the laundry. Remember that time when I was stirring the soup? Completely ruined that pot! If you hadn't come home and found it, the house might have burned down."

Denis's eyes narrowed. "Yes, but actually sitting down to write makes it more likely to happen, hmm? Sitting and staring out windows increases the chances, doesn't it? It isn't a perfect solution, but it's the best we can do until we find out what's happening. Yes?"

"Denis—" began Serendipity.

"No, no, no. I won't hear a peep of protest. No writing. Not a word. From either of you. I want you to promise. Serendipity?"

"Oh, all right then."

"Tuesday?"

Before Tuesday could say a word, Baxterr let out a growl that was not especially unfriendly, but meant that something was happening on his turf. Baxterr usually growled in this particular way about thirty seconds before the McGillycuddys' doorbell rang. This time there was no doorbell. Instead there was a sharp rap at the kitchen window, and they were all surprised to see Miss Digby, Serendipity's long-serving assistant, peering in at them across the hydrangea bushes with the morning paper rolled into a tight scroll in her hand and a panicked look upon her face.

Miss Digby was neither old nor young. She was neither fair nor dark. She wasn't tall, but neither was she short. Her nose wasn't big or small. Her eyes weren't blue or green, and neither would you have said they were gray. Miss Digby had a way of dressing that made her almost entirely forgettable. She was a very mild woman who spoke precisely, who was never flustered or in a rush, and who, if you got close enough, always smelled of dried flowers. Today, as usual, Miss Digby was wearing clothes in shades so colorless they didn't really even have names. Her shoes were flat, with laces, and her hair was caught back in the sort of arrangement that stayed neat yet showed no clips or pins.

Miss Digby was not married, had no children, and had been Serendipity's assistant for as long as Tuesday could remember. Tuesday could not imagine Miss Digby as a girl, or what she might have done before she came into their lives. She was both as familiar and unknown to Tuesday as the moon. But one thing Tuesday did know was that Miss Digby never, ever came to their house on Brown Street, and that was because Miss Digby was just about the only person, other than Denis, Tuesday, and Serendipity, who knew the truth about Serendipity's double life.

As Miss Digby was so often seen with the public Serendipity Smith—the famous writer who had long red hair and wore outlandish glasses, velvet coats, and knee-high boots—it was very risky for her to be seen with the private Serendipity, the one who had short dark hair, wore comfortable black clothes, and allowed people to think that her name was Sarah McGillycuddy. Tuesday knew that if anyone should put two and two together, it would ruin everything. If fame followed Serendipity to Brown Street, her family would never be able to go anywhere or do anything normal ever again.

This is why Tuesday scowled, just a little, at the sight of Miss Digby at the kitchen window. But Denis, being famously hospitable, leapt up to let Miss Digby in through the back door. For a moment she stood with her hands clutched together in front of her chest, as if she were about to sing. Instead she spoke at what was, for Miss Digby, an unusually fast pace.

"I am so very sorry to intrude this way, and believe me, I did very carefully weigh the potential risks against the likely benefits of coming here to your home and, after careful consideration, decided that it was imperative we discuss the present state of emergency, especially after I heard the news about Dame Elizabeth Coventry. Hence my use of the rear entrance."

Serendipity's mouth fell open.

"No! Not poor, dear Elizabeth?"

Tuesday pictured the dame: a majestic woman with a large, square jaw and hair dyed the color of an Irish setter's fur.

"I'm afraid so," Miss Digby said, nodding earnestly.

"She's more than eighty years old!" Serendipity protested.

"And Flynn McMurtry, found nearly dead in the Mekong Delta, a million miles from where he lives. He's not regained consciousness yet," Miss Digby said. Tuesday's thoughts rushed to her friend, Blake Luckhurst, also a writer of adventure stories and almost as famous as Flynn McMurtry, though half his age. She would have to call Blake as soon as Miss Digby was gone.

Denis invited Miss Digby to breakfast, which, she protested, must surely be lunch at this hour: it was one o'clock. Since the pancake mixture had been used up, he made for their guest his famous toasted ham-on-cheese-on-more-cheese sandwiches, and Miss Digby ate them with a knife and fork, cutting each mouthful into a perfect square before raising her fork delicately to her mouth. Tuesday had never seen anyone eat a toasted sandwich with a knife and fork, and she found it hard not to stare.

"I think we must thank our lucky stars that it hasn't happened to you already," Miss Digby said to Serendipity.

"Perhaps it's because I've been on holiday," suggested Serendipity.

"You were expecting, were you not, on Monday to resume your usual schedule?" Miss Digby asked.

"I was thinking I might stay home," said Serendipity.

"But reporters will be all over the hotel trying to get interviews. How will I explain your absence if they're expecting you back? I simply won't be able to reassure them that you're not caught up in any of this unless they actually see you in person."

"Hmmm," said Serendipity.

"Well, perhaps you could go to the hotel, but no writing," said Denis, eyeing his wife sternly.

"Yes, Denis has made me promise not to write," said Serendipity.

"Probably wise," said Miss Digby.

Denis and Serendipity exchanged a glance.

Although Serendipity knew that Miss Digby must have observed some strange things over the years, working so closely with a writer, she was certain Miss Digby did not know about *there*. Miss Digby, being entirely practical and pragmatic, would never have imagined, not even in her dreams, that while she sat in the McGillycuddys' kitchen, there was—in another place entirely—Vivienne Small, the world-famous heroine of the Serendipity Smith books, hurrying along a narrow path through the Peppermint Forest, her mind on the business of finding Tuesday McGillycuddy and her dog, Baxterr.

Chapter Five

The path Vivienne walked was narrow, its surface cabled with the twisted roots of trees and vines. It led to the eastern edge of the Peppermint Forest and, in turn, to the Hills of Mist. Vivienne almost never went this way, in part because the Hills of Mist held little draw for her. The hills were quite pretty, with their gentle grassy slopes and occasional rocky banks of sparkling white stone, but nothing ever happened there (well, nothing of interest to Vivienne Small), and the persistent mists that clung about the hills had the effect of making Vivienne feel sleepy and distracted.

There was another reason that Vivienne Small rarely went this way, and as she emerged at last from the shelter of the forest, she remembered what it was. Between the rim of the forest and the beginnings of the Hills of Mist was a swamp. It stretched out before her, beneath an unfriendly gray sky, smelling of sulfur, rotting fish heads, and death. Across its forbidding surface were gurgling, plopping pools of mud, between which rose small islands covered with harsh, spiky reeds.

"Urgh," Vivienne said, wishing that her path lay anywhere but here. There were other ways, but this was the quickest by far, and Vivienne felt it in the tip of her one pointed ear that there was no time to lose in delivering the Winged Dog's message. She patted her pocket and remembered the words written on the slip of paper within. *My great love, I cannot hold the worlds apart much longer. Have you found our answer? G.* Then Vivienne, trying to breathe through her mouth rather than her nose, set out grimly to cross the swamp. The small reedy islands were big enough to stand on but slightly too far apart to easily jump between, so Vivienne used her small wings to help her spring precariously from one muddy outcrop to the next. Luckily, she was wearing her trusty long boots, so her feet stayed dry, even if her hands were being cut and scratched by the reeds.

This was one of those occasions on which Vivienne Small cursed the smallness of her wings. Usually she told herself that small wings were better than no wings at all. Sometimes, though, she got frustrated that her wings were too small to keep her airborne more than a few moments at a time. And, deep down, she wished that she could truly fly.

Since flying was not an option, Vivienne made her way erratically across the swamp, trying her best to avoid the clouds of gnats that rose up around her and the mosquitoes that landed on her hands and neck. Her hurriedly packed satchel banged against her side with every leap.

As she went deeper into the swamp, the light became gloomier and the mud more putrid-smelling. And then, quite suddenly, the swamp came to an end. One minute Vivienne was leaping across a murky expanse of water, aiming for a particularly tiny clump of reeds—her cheeks burning with mosquito bites—and the next, she was standing on rocky ground within a shroud of drifting, swirling mist.

She moved carefully ahead, one hand outstretched to avoid walking smack into any obstacles. After a time, her hand came into contact with something solid and cold. It was a wall of white stone, its surface striated in shades of chalk and shimmering quartz. She peered up through the mist to see the wall that rose up and up, forming a formidable cliff face.

She took a step back, crossed her arms, and glared at the stone wall before her. There were fissures and ledges in it, as if water regularly flowed down over, and Vivienne supposed they would do as handholds and footholds for the climb. But how great that climb would be, she couldn't tell.

Using her wings for balance, and once again cursing their smallness, Vivienne began. She climbed, and she climbed. It was impossible to get a sense of how far she had gone. Several times she had to stop and rest, and each time she did so, she realized how completely alone she was. There were no other beings in sight: she saw not a single bird, nor a fly, nor a bee, nor a moth, nor a grasshopper—not even a mosquito straying from the swamp. It was almost as if the world had temporarily stopped all activity. Vivienne felt a sense of impending doom. But being Vivienne Small, mostly fearless and always formidable in a tight spot, she took a deep breath and continued to climb.

After what seemed like hours, she noticed that the mist was becoming a little thinner. She glanced up and was immensely relieved to see that the sky above was tinged with blue and the lip of the cliff was only a few more scrambling moves away.

Once she was clear of the mist and on horizontal ground at last, Vivienne lay on her back and gazed up at the sky. After the dismal swamp and the eerie mist that had seemed to seep out of the cliff, the blue sky was a welcome sight. But there was no more time to waste, so she sprang to her feet and took in the view. Beyond the mist, the distant Mountains of Margolov still pierced the sky. She had not considered that the sky might have limits, but clearly it did.

She turned away from the cliff, and there was a bright green field. In the center of it on a small hilltop was a single, enormous tree. It wasn't enormous in the same way that Vivienne's home tree in the Peppermint Forest was enormous. Hers was very, very tall. This one was immensely wide.

Vivienne bounded toward the tree in excitement, using her wings to buoy herself up with each stride.

The girth of the tree was so great that it would take a minute or two to walk all the way around its base. Vivienne touched the ancient bark and peered up into the spreading branches above. They were thick and twisted, and their timber gleamed, dark and rich, as if polished. This tree was so beautiful that Vivienne couldn't help thinking about building a tree house in it.

Now, what Vivienne Small did not know was that it was extremely unusual for anyone who was not a writer to find this particular tree. You see, for writers, the tree was something like the landing platform, or the doorway, or the welcome mat. For as long as any writer could remember, it had been there for them, supplying wet-weather gear, umbrellas, sleeping bags, suitable walking shoes, matches, candles, towels, and even a hot-air balloon on one occasion. So the tree was a little bit surprised to find a very small person, clearly not a writer, standing beneath its boughs. Odd things had been happening all day, and the tree could feel it from deep in the earth, through the tips of its roots. Things had been groaning and moving and unsettling. Something was wrong, and the tree did not like it. It decided to be very quiet and see what the small person had to say for herself.

"Hello, you wonderful tree," Vivienne said.

The tree remained silent, but it was impressed by the small person's manners. Trees like to be flattered.

"Oh, you don't need to be shy," said Vivienne. "I have known a lot of trees, and I know that you can hear me. And you are really the most beautiful tree I have ever seen."

The tree couldn't help rustling. In truth, you cannot flatter a tree too much.

"It's lovely to meet you too," said Vivienne Small.

The tree let its leaves shiver.

"I'm looking," said the small girl, "for a person called Tuesday McGillycuddy, and for . . . um . . . her dog as well."

Vivienne would never say Baxterr's name out loud in company—not even if that company was a tree—because the true name of a Winged Dog is sacred.

"I don't suppose you know how I might find them?"

Now the tree faced something of a dilemma. It knew that writers came flying in from every direction, day and night, pulled by their stories. From time to time, the tree knew, stories went flying off to get a writer. At nighttime, stories in search of writers looked like shooting stars arcing across the sky. And sure enough, soon a writer would come tumbling into the world, asking the tree for a thermos of coffee or a compass. But the tree had never before had a *character* ask it for help to bring a writer to them.

The tree considered this request. Would it do any harm to help this small person? The tree certainly had plenty of thread to spare. Beneath the ground, it felt the waves of uncertainty that were spreading through the deepest parts of the world. Perhaps helping this small person was required. Perhaps the tree might be about to play an important part in a story itself.

"Please, could you tell me if you know them? If you know how I can get them to come here?" Vivienne Small asked, her hand upon the tree's dark, furrowed trunk.

A single heart-shaped leaf drifted down from the branches above, and Vivienne caught it in the palm of her hand.

Inspecting it closely, she saw that on its underside, the veins had curled into elegant writing. There were two words upon the leaf: *Call them.*

"Call them?" Vivienne asked the tree. "Just call them?"

The tree's leaves danced.

Vivienne walked out from under the wide branches. Taking a great breath, she called as loudly as she could, "Tuesday! Doggo!" Then again she called, "Tuesday! Doggo!"

As Vivienne's voice rang out into the sky, the tree did not hold back. It launched a ball of thread from deep in its branches high into the sky. Vivienne herself did not even see it, but nevertheless, the thread flew, one end fixed in the tree, unraveling a line of the finest silver as it went. It rose high above Vivienne Small and the tree and the world below, and on into immense and infinite blueness.

Chapter Six

Miss Digby, Serendipity, and Denis talked. They went over the details of the disappearances again, and then they made more cups of tea and turned up the volume on the radio for the next news update. Tuesday looked out the window and noticed what a very lovely day it was outside. It occurred to her that she would much prefer to be taking Baxterr for a walk than sitting about in the kitchen and wishing she had not been forbidden to write. She jumped up.

"I'm taking Baxterr to the park," she declared.

"Shall I come too?" Denis offered.

"Or all of us?" Serendipity suggested.

"No, it's fine. Really, you all keep on with your . . . plans." Tuesday waved her hands around vaguely. "We need a walk, don't we, Baxterr?"

Baxterr had already trotted off to retrieve his leash from the hall table. He was an eminently sensible dog, who never embarrassed himself by appearing overexcited at the delightful prospect of going for a walk. He waited patiently by the front door as Tuesday fixed his lead to his collar and took her bright red jacket from the hallstand. Before she left, she ran quickly upstairs to snatch up an opened letter from a drawer in her desk.

Coming back downstairs, she heard her mother telling Miss Digby, "Of course she'll be fine. Baxterr is wonderful. And much fiercer than you'd think."

"Back soon," Tuesday called out, and then she closed the front door behind her. Tuesday had no reason or desire to lie to her parents, and yet those two words proved to be entirely untrue.

It was a perfect day to be walking with a dog in City Park, and Tuesday was far from the only person to be doing it. She was amused by how much some of the human beings around her resembled the dogs at their sides. Tuesday wondered whether anybody would think she and Baxterr were particularly alike. Certainly they both had hair of almost every shade of gold and brown, though Baxterr's eyes were golden-brown while Tuesday's were blue-green. Tuesday thought that if she did look like her dog, then there was no nicer dog to look like than Baxterr.

Not far from the fountain at the center of City Park was a stand of public telephones. Each telephone was fixed on a short pillar inside an ornate wrought-iron sculpture that protected it from the wind and rain. One of the sculptures was a mermaid with long curling tresses, and the next was a lion with its mouth fixed in a fearsome roar. The phones within each of these were in use, but the third phone, the one encased by a sculpture of a prancing horse, was free.

Tuesday fished out the letter she had tucked into her pocket. It was from one of the world's most famous young writers, Blake Luckhurst, and she smiled as she thought of him and of the adventures they'd had together. Blake had published his first book when he was only twelve, and there were action figures of his characters, and the first film of his books was about to premiere on big screens around the world. All this had gone to his head, and he had a dreadful habit of teasing Tuesday, but despite all of that, she liked him.

Tuesday entered the shelter of the horse, put a coin in the slot of the telephone, and dialed the number Blake had written at the top of his letter. The phone rang two times, three times, four, and as she waited for him to pick up, she scanned the words he had written.

Madness here with interviews. I'm just so famous. Talk to me if you're going _there_. (This word was underlined several times.) I am going _there_ again very soon. It could be cool to hang out. Maybe. Say hello to Baxterr.

Yours, Blake Luckhurst the Glorious.

"It's your money. Talk fast," said a voice on the other end of the phone.

"Blake, is that you?" said Tuesday.

"Maybe," came the voice.

"It's Tuesday."

"I don't think so," he said.

"Really, it's _Tuesday_," she repeated.

"No, today is definitely Sunday," he said.

"Stop it," Tuesday said.

"Okay," Blake said.

"Have you heard about J. D. Jones and Flynn McMurtry and all the others? What on earth is going on? Do you know?"

"Yeah, no. Weird, hey? I haven't been *there* in weeks. The new book is causing chaos. You would think, being a writer, that people might leave you alone to write, but instead they want to put makeup on you and drag you in front of a camera and ask you questions—"

"Which you love—"

"Which sells books. Especially when you're as good-looking as I am."

"Really," Tuesday said.

"That's right, getting more handsome every day. So how's the book coming along? Is it finished?"

"Of course not," said Tuesday. "I've only just started. How do you manage to do it so quickly?"

"Natural genius," he said. "But listen. Don't be going *there* anytime soon, okay? It's not safe."

"Why? What's gone wrong?" Tuesday asked. And as she said this, she heard someone calling her name. She spun about expecting to see a friend. But she saw nobody that she knew.

Blake said, "Just stay home, paint your toenails, okay?"

And while Tuesday was busily wondering why Blake was talking about toenails, Baxterr barked. He stood very upright, with his tail wagging, as though he could hear someone calling his name too.

Again it happened. Someone was definitely calling her name. And then Tuesday heard a voice yell "Doggo!" and from the look on Baxterr's face, Tuesday was certain that he thought the call was for him. Tuesday peered at the people strolling across the large square and throwing coins into the fountain. She couldn't see anybody familiar, even though the voice had sounded so close.

And then something in the sky caught her attention. There was something high above the fountain, coming toward her in a streak of silver—and Baxterr was watching it too and barking excitedly. Maybe it was a thread of water catching the light? Or maybe . . . maybe it was actual thread. Tuesday felt the skin on the back of her neck prickling.

"Um, Blake, is it possible for a story to come and get you?"

"Sure. Happens to me all the time. I'm dead asleep

and then I'm yanked awake and dragged into some war zone—"

It *was* thread, and it was diving toward Tuesday, coming closer and closer. She reached her hand out to catch it, fascinated. It landed in her palm, wrapping swiftly around her wrist and looping through her fingers. As it did so, she felt a fizzy sensation in her

hands and feet. She knew she shouldn't be doing this. She knew she ought to push the sparkling thread away, but she didn't. Instead she let it gently and persistently tug her away from where she stood.

"I think I'm going," Tuesday said to Blake as first one foot, then the other, lifted off the ground. "I think I'm going *there*!"

"What? Now? No, you can't . . . Wait!"

"Bye, Blake!" she called out, then dropped the receiver. She called urgently to Baxterr, and he leapt into her arms, and the thread pulled them high up into the air, away from the phone box and the fountain, right out of City Park and into the sky. Nobody noticed—nobody except a small boy in a stroller, who would one day be a writer himself. He pointed and called out to them, but Tuesday couldn't hear what he said because they were above the trees, above the mirrored lake, and going higher still.

Tuesday could see Brown Street and the roof of her own home far below her. She felt a twinge of guilt that she was doing precisely the thing she was not supposed to do. She had allowed herself to be completely swept up. A story had come to get her, and she had simply taken flight.

Chapter Seven

From high in the air, Tuesday caught sight of the hillside and its single tree. Baxterr barked with delight and wriggled in Tuesday's arms.

"No!" called Tuesday in alarm, as Baxterr launched himself into thin air.

The distance to the ground was much too great for an ordinary dog to leap, but in this world, Baxterr was anything but ordinary. He opened up a pair of golden-brown wings that were all covered on their outer side with short, shaggy fur. Tuesday watched in awe as Baxterr transformed into a gigantic dog, flapping his way up into the sky above her, and then turning to soar, swoop, and loop-the-loop his way to the hillside, where he landed with perfect grace.

Tuesday felt as if she were flying too, zooming along at the behest of the silvery thread that was wrapped around her hand and her wrist, pulling her toward the tree. Tuesday continued to hurtle down, and just when she was certain that she would slam into its branches, the thread went slack and unwound itself from her arm. Tuesday fell out of the air like a stone and landed on the ground in an ungainly collection of elbows and knees. Baxterr bounded over to her, his wings partly folded, and stood beside her, grinning widely.

"Well, I'd probably land beautifully too, if I had wings," she said, scrambling to her feet. It was wonderful to watch Baxterr frolic in his proper size across the hillside, sniffing with his wet black nose at every last blade of grass he passed. Tuesday was expecting to see evidence of chaos, but everything was much the same as it had been when she was last here. There was the beautiful old tree, and the hillside rolling down to a moat of white mist, and a lovely, serene sense that she was standing on top of the world, which—in a way—she was. Everything was quiet and calm, and there was nothing at all to suggest that this was a place where anyone might be in danger.

"What's been happening, tree?" Tuesday inquired, but the tree only whispered to itself in a green sort of language and dispatched out of a hollow in its trunk Tuesday's thread, neatly rolled into a ball about the size of a tangerine. It rolled to a stop at her feet.

"Oh, thanks," Tuesday said, and put it away carefully in a pocket of her jacket. And then she squealed as something hairy fell from the branch right above her head and brushed creepily across her face. As she jumped away, swatting at her face in alarm, Tuesday heard a giggle that she recognized. She looked up, and there, hanging by her knees from a branch, was Vivienne Small, with a huge grin on her cheeky, upside-down face. Vivienne swung herself down and landed delicately on her feet in front of Tuesday. She was a good bit shorter than Tuesday, though they were about the same age.

For a moment, the two girls stood and beamed at each other. Tuesday wanted to hug Vivienne, but she wasn't exactly sure that Vivienne was the hugging type. And Vivienne wanted to pull a hank of Tuesday's hair, out of pure happiness to see her

again, but she wasn't sure that Tuesday would understand.

"I'm glad you came," said Vivienne. "I really need your help."

"Well, here I am," said Tuesday. Then Baxterr bounded up the hill with his tail waving like a furry banner, clearly delighted to see his old friend Vivienne.

"Doggo!" Vivienne said.

At his full size, Baxterr towered over Vivienne, so in order to greet her properly, he flung himself down onto his belly beside the tree and rested his muzzle on the ground. Vivienne reached up and scratched one of his huge ears.

"I really hate to tell you this, doggo, but you can't be this big. And you can't go flying about, either." Vivienne turned to Tuesday. "It's not safe for him. There are horrible, dangerous things flying around out there. They've already killed a Winged Dog."

"What?" said Tuesday.

"Hurrrrrr," said Baxterr, shrinking himself back to his compact size. He kept his wings, though, and folded them in close so that they were quite invisible.

Vivienne nodded. "So, are you ready?"

"For what?" Tuesday said.

"We have an urgent message to deliver. C'mon, let's go."

"What message? From who? Where? *What?*"

Without wasting words, Vivienne told Tuesday everything she knew about the Winged Dog that had fallen through the roof of the Peppermint Forest. She walked her to the edge of the white cliff and pointed to the Mountains of Margolov and told Tuesday about meeting Harlequin and Tarquin and about the vercaka that had fallen through the sky from another world. She handed Tuesday the dog's collar and the scroll of paper that had been concealed in the medallion.

"*My great love,*" Tuesday read aloud. "*I cannot hold the worlds apart much longer.* What do you think it means?"

"I think it means that worlds are coming together in dangerous ways," Vivienne said. "I mean, you only have to look at the mountains to know something is terribly wrong. How else did Harlequin and Tarquin get here? And the vercaka?"

"Dangerous for writers too," Tuesday murmured.

"For writers?" said Vivienne.

"Oh," said Tuesday, and bit her lip.

It never felt right to Tuesday to tell Vivienne that

she was a character in a book. Tuesday hadn't the first idea how Vivienne would react if Tuesday were to tell her that back in the world that she came from, Vivienne was one of the most famous characters of all time. Not only were there the five books in the Vivienne Small series, written by none other than Serendipity Smith, there were also films and stage plays and radio dramas. There were Vivienne Small soft toys and Vivienne Small cups and jigsaw puzzles, bookmarks, and pencil cases. There were posters and a theme park and . . . the list went on. But standing in front of Tuesday was the real Vivienne Small: the one who had saved Baxterr's life and helped Tuesday find her way home. And Tuesday felt it would be all wrong even to mention the cups or jigsaws or pencil cases to *this* Vivienne Small.

"What do you mean about the writers?" Vivienne asked again.

"Well," said Tuesday, "there have been people getting injured in my world. Perhaps the same sorts of things are happening in each of our worlds."

"Are your mountains growing? Are there vercaka?"

"No vercaka, luckily," said Tuesday. "And so far

the mountains are fine. Hang on, I didn't think the Winged Dogs lived here anymore?"

Tuesday had once asked her mother what had become of the Winged Dogs that, in one of her books, had mysteriously disappeared. Serendipity had said, "Oh, I think they've gone someplace rather wonderful. What sort of place do you think Winged Dogs would like to live?"

Tuesday had said, "Maybe a place where there were long sandy beaches and the breeze was always blowing a little bit to keep them cool. I think they'd love a place where there were waterfalls, like in the Winged Mountains, and lovely, shady trees. A place where there were holes in the ground, and instead of hot water coming out of them, every few minutes balls would pop up and fly about so the dogs could chase them."

Tuesday wondered whether or not she should tell Vivienne any of this. Probably not, she decided.

"Are you listening?" Vivienne said, snapping her fingers impatiently in Tuesday's face.

"Sorry."

"The Winged Dog. The one that died on the forest floor. There is somebody, somewhere, who is waiting for that dog to come home, just as you would wait if Baxterr had gone out to deliver a message. This dog was someone's eternal companion, and that person will want to know what has happened. We must find them, don't you see?"

"And this person is the *G* in the note?"

Vivienne nodded vigorously.

"Who do you think *G* is?" asked Tuesday.

"How should I know?" said Vivienne sharply. "Clearly it's somebody who is worried that they can't keep the worlds apart. Don't you think it all sounds rather *important*? We have to deliver that message."

"We?"

"Yes. You're meant to be here to help!"

Tuesday said, "There's only one problem. I can't stay long. I've only gone for a walk, supposedly, and I have to get home again before my parents realize I'm missing."

Had Tuesday been wearing a watch, she might have checked it. Since she wasn't, she looked up at the sky. The sun was getting low and casting a golden-syrup light over the green leaves and polished branches of the ancient tree.

"If I'm not home by dark, they'll panic."

"So you're going to be no help at all?" asked Vivienne in frustration, and for a moment, Tuesday fancied smoke was coming out of Vivienne's right ear—the one with the pointed tip.

"I want to help. Really I do . . ." Tuesday was torn. She thought of her mother and father at home on Brown Street, and how worried they must be. She thought of Dame Elizabeth Coventry. And Flynn McMurtry. And J. D. Jones, and all the others. She knew that she should throw her thread in the air immediately and have it speed her all the way home. But perhaps even that wasn't safe. What if she asked her thread to take her home, and instead she got caught on the Mountains of Margolov or it landed her back in her own world in some remote quarter of the Southern Ocean or the Simpson Desert? And to complicate matters, here was Vivienne Small, the *real* Vivienne Small, expecting her to help deal with things that were unfathomably daunting. And extremely interesting at the same time. Tuesday read the note again, then absentmindedly slipped it into her pocket.

"Tell me again about the dog's memories," she said.

And Vivienne, trying hard to control her impatience, told her.

"A place of stone and mist," Tuesday pondered aloud. "Guarded by beasts."

Something stirred in Tuesday's memory.

"And there are runes, you say? Somewhere on or near this place?"

"So we think."

"You do remember them?"

"Of course," said Vivienne, with a slight sniff.

"Okay then, write them on my arm," Tuesday said. Vivienne traced onto her inner arm the seven characters that Tarquin had seen in the memory of the Winged Dog.

Ι Π Λ Ϲ Ι Π Σ

Tuesday stared at the invisible letters.

"Do it again," she said.

With a sigh, Vivienne sketched out the marks a second time.

Ι Π Λ Ϲ Ι Π Σ

This time, when Vivienne finished, Tuesday grinned. Perhaps it was going to be easier to deliver this message than she had first thought. Perhaps she could even be home in time for dinner, without anyone ever having noticed she'd been *there*—which, of course, had now lost its *t* and become *here*.

"IMAGINE!" Tuesday announced excitedly. "It's IMAGINE!"

"What?"

"That's what your runes say. They say IMAGINE."

"IMAGINE? How does that help?" Vivienne said.

Tuesday reached out and tweaked one of the small braids that dangled down amid Vivienne's messy black curls, and Vivienne's cross expression transformed into a smile.

"Come on," Tuesday said. "I know exactly where we have to go. It's not far."

Chapter Eight

Baxterr knew too, and he dashed down the hill toward the fog. He checked that Tuesday and Vivienne were following, then plunged into the whiteness and disappeared from sight. Vivienne, reaching the edge of the fog, stopped in her tracks and began anxiously searching her pockets.

"The message . . . ," she said.

"It's all right, I've got it," Tuesday said. "Stay close."

So thick was the mist that when Tuesday looked down at her own feet, she could barely see them padding along on the path made of uneven paving stones. If she held her arm right out in front of her, she could only just make out the star shape of her outstretched hand. This was a mist of an entirely different kind from any that Tuesday had ever encountered at home. The sort she knew and understood was damp and chilly, but this was quite dry and not cold at all. As she breathed it in, she was reminded of the fug in the kitchen at Brown Street when her father was baking with spices like cinnamon and nutmeg and cloves. Tuesday thought it rather lovely, but Vivienne was not impressed.

"Will this last long? I've had quite enough of mist for one day," she grumbled.

"It's not far. At least, I don't think so," Tuesday said.

"Ruff," agreed Baxterr, who had doubled back to Tuesday's side.

They walked for a few more moments before Tuesday saw two great white shapes materialize in the fog: they were marble statues, a matching pair of larger-than-life lions, each one with an impressive carved mane.

"There you go!" said Tuesday.

"Here I go . . . what?"

"They're the beasts from the dog's memory. Lions."

Vivienne peered into the mist, bewildered, and Tuesday knew that if her father had been with them, he would have said that Vivienne was *mystified*.

"Where? What lions? Are you sure you're not—"

Then Vivienne stopped, midsentence. She didn't only stop speaking—she stopped altogether, as if someone had pressed a pause button.

"Vivienne?"

Tuesday shook Vivienne by the arm, but she was quite immobilized. Her eyes were half shut and her mouth half open. Tuesday felt panicked.

"Vivienne? *Vivienne?*"

"She will be quite all right," said a familiar, steely voice from somewhere within the mist. "I must say, it was foolish to attempt to bring her here. I thought you would know better, Ms. McGillycuddy."

"Madame Librarian?" asked Tuesday, spinning about. The mist parted like a pair of fluffy white curtains, and there, standing on the path flanked by the two stone lions, was the Librarian. She was dressed from head to toe in her customary purple, but today, instead of wearing an outfit that most people would wear only if they were heading off to the opera, the Librarian wore a rather chic purple tracksuit with a patterned silk scarf at her neck.

"Vivienne cannot come here, Tuesday," said the Librarian. "You have forgotten the most important rule of all. This Library is for writers only. She cannot see the Library. As you have discovered, she cannot even see the lions. Frankly, I'm rather amazed she was able to meet you at the tree. It goes to show how peculiar things are becoming around here."

"What have you done to her?"

"Nothing serious. I promise you that she will be waiting right here for you when you get back. Come along, please. I admire your courage in starting a new story at this time, but you'll need to take some extra precautions. So come along, and we'll get you organized."

Tuesday reached out to touch Vivienne's cheek. Her skin was quite warm.

"Are you sure she's all right?" Tuesday said, worried.

"Come along, come along," the Librarian said, clapping her fingers briskly against her palm. "We have vastly more important things to worry about than the feelings of Vivienne Small."

Tuesday was about to argue, but the Librarian's piercing gaze made her knees tremble. The Librarian, although short, somehow managed to appear very tall. Tuesday straightened herself up, and she noticed that Baxterr was standing with his head held high, as if he too felt he must be on his best behavior.

"Good," said the Librarian, then turned on her heel. She set off up the path at a rapid clip, and as Tuesday followed, she noticed that the Librarian's usually perfect cap of silvery hair was a little out of place at the back. And although both her shoes were a very similar shade of lilac, they were definitely not a pair. Tuesday thought it best not to mention this.

"Madame Librarian," Tuesday called after her, somewhat shakily, "I think you may be getting the wrong idea. I should tell you that I'm not here to write a new story. I haven't even finished the first one yet. I'm here because a thread came to get me and—"

The Librarian stopped in her tracks and whirled around to glare at Tuesday.

"Oh, goodness gracious, Tuesday McGillycuddy. It seems to me that every time you come here, you are *not* writing a story. And yet a story came to get you, did it not? Hmm? In my capacious experience, I find it often happens this way on second visits. A story comes to get you, sometimes before you feel ready. But whether or not you felt ready, you did say yes to this story, didn't you? You allowed it to bring you here, didn't you?"

"I've just come to deliver a message, which I thought might have been for—"

"A message, hmm? What is a story if not a message of sorts? A message that you deliver not only to one person, but to all people who care to open its covers and receive it? A message to all people, for all time? What could be more wonderful than that?"

"I don't have time for a whole story—" Tuesday began, but the Librarian interrupted her again.

"Time!" she said, indicating to Tuesday to follow along quickly. "Nobody has time to write a novel or paint a picture or pen a song. Can you *make* time, Tuesday?"

"I don't think so, but—"

"No, we cannot, Ms. McGillycuddy. Time is simply there, and we choose how to fill it up. We sleep. And we eat. And we take baths and read books and visit with friends and have parties and—"

"Go to school," said Tuesday. "*That* takes up a lot of time."

"Ruff, ruff," added Baxterr.

"Ah, yes," said the Librarian, "and we frolic in the park, Baxterr. Good point. So, where, in amongst all of that, is the time to write stories, Tuesday?"

"Well, in between everything else?"

"And is that how you managed to write all you have? Did you fit it in between everything else?" asked the Librarian.

"Sort of," said Tuesday.

"But not really," said the Librarian, "because if I'm not mistaken, you got up early, and you stayed up late. You turned down offers to do all sorts of other things, and you *wrote*. Did you not?"

"Yes," said Tuesday.

"So, you might say that although you didn't make time, because the day was still as long as it was and the weeks exactly the same length, you made time *for writing*."

"Yes," said Tuesday. "But—"

"Do not tell me that you have to go home, that you don't have time, because this is the time you've made, Tuesday, for this story. You have to live it. There's no going back. There is only going forward."

There was definitely an unsettling tone to the Librarian's voice. She reminded Tuesday of Serendipity when she was at the end of a novel and hadn't had enough sleep, and everything was difficult and confusing. The Librarian stared intently at Tuesday. They had arrived at the bottom of the great stone steps that led to the Library's front doors.

The tinkling sound of a fountain reached Tuesday's ears, and she caught the scent of roses. She noticed, however, that the Library's gardens—which had been entirely manicured the last time she was here—were now a little disheveled and unkempt. As they climbed the stone steps to the front door, Tuesday saw the word engraved across the lintel: the word that Tarquin and Harlequin had glimpsed in the fallen dog's memories. An enormous seven-letter word.

IMAGINE

Tuesday took a deep breath.

"Madame Librarian, I promised my parents I wouldn't come here. Back at home, writers have been going missing. Writing has become . . . dangerous."

"It is! Oh, it is! Make no mistake about that. It's chaos!" The Librarian waved her short arms about wildly. "I've got a Library full of writers too frightened to even attempt to return home. I've not a single tea bag left, the Confidence Food ran out yesterday, and the bandage supply will be quite exhausted by this time tomorrow if things don't improve."

"Dad made me promise not to write. He made Mom promise too. We were trying to be normal."

In front of the Library's huge front doors, the Librarian stopped.

>>>> §§ <<<<

"*Normal?*" she said, turning to frown at Tuesday. "What in the dictionary did you think you were doing? Normal is not what writers need. Regularity, a set time to write, that can be very useful. But normality? No, there's no adventure in normal. There's no surprise or mystery, no villains or great love affairs, no tragedies or victories in *normal*. Normality is highly overrated, Tuesday. Eccentricity. Impulsiveness. Passion. Surprise. Joy. This is what a writer's heart requires. And that most important thing of all—curiosity. Aren't you *curious*, Tuesday, about the story that has brought you here? Don't you want to know what happens next?"

Tuesday felt the Librarian's deep violet eyes boring through her. She summoned her courage and reached into her pocket.

"What I do want to know," Tuesday said, "is whether or not this is meant for you."

At the sight of the scroll of paper on Tuesday's palm, the Librarian gasped. She hovered one small wrinkled hand over the message. At last, she made up her mind to take it, unroll it, and read it.

Tuesday watched the Librarian's face closely as she read the note. Once she had finished reading, she held it to her chest.

"Where did you get this?" the Librarian asked.

"Vivienne Small found it," said Tuesday, drawing out the circlet of fine rope. "In the collar of a Winged Dog."

"Where is the dog now?" the Librarian asked, taking the collar and inspecting the medallion with its engraving of a dog in flight.

"I'm sorry, Madame Librarian . . . the dog died."

"Oh!" Tears sprang into the Librarian's eyes. Still holding the collar, she extracted a lilac handkerchief from inside her sleeve and held it to her eyes.

Tuesday spoke gently. "So, the message. It was for you?"

"Yes, dear," the Librarian said. "Yes, it was."

"And do you? Do you have the answer yet?"

The Librarian tucked her handkerchief back into her sleeve. Without warning, she took a firm hold of Tuesday's chin and turned her face this way, then that. She gazed deeply into Tuesday's eyes. Then she glanced down at Baxterr, standing to attention at Tuesday's feet. A shrewd expression came over her wrinkled face. She carefully returned the silver collar to Tuesday.

"Why, yes," she said. "I believe that, at last, I do."

Chapter Nine

Perhaps you didn't know this, but parents are made partly of elastic. When a person first becomes a parent, the elastic is quite firm and doesn't stretch very far at all—hardly even from one side of a room to the other. Then, after they've been a parent for a while, and their children have learned to walk and talk, brush their teeth and do up their shoes, that elastic becomes more pliable, capable of stretching quite incredible distances: the length of several city blocks, the width of whole suburbs, and across entire countries in some cases. Even so, there is always a point at which the elastic goes *ping!* and the parent starts to feel that the child has gone too far, or been gone for too long.

And this is precisely what happened to Serendipity Smith at five o'clock that Sunday afternoon, a couple of hours after Tuesday had gone for a walk to City Park with Baxterr. Serendipity was sitting at the kitchen table, and although she was mostly listening to Miss Digby—who was finalizing the very long list of things to do that they had spent the afternoon preparing—she was also listening for the sound of Tuesday coming in the front door. *She's been gone too long,* said one part of Serendipity's brain. Another part answered back, *Nonsense! It's a beautiful sunny afternoon, and she's at the park with her dog. Relax.*

Denis was experiencing much the same thing, so at half past five, he filled Miss Digby's teacup yet again and excused himself from the conversation. He went out the front and looked up the street, fully expecting to see Tuesday and Baxterr ambling toward him. Old Mr. Garfunkle from next door was walking along with his ancient cocker spaniel, Dougal, who dragged his toenails on the footpath with every step. Denis greeted them both, then called to Serendipity that he was going to meet Tuesday, and started out in the direction of City Park.

The sun was getting lower in the sky, and the trees and houses and cars and people that Denis passed were throwing out long, streaky shadows. There was the reassuring hum of a great city at work, and Denis couldn't help thinking how, in all the restaurants across the city, white tablecloths were being smoothed over tabletops, cutlery was being polished, and glassware was being shined. In the kitchens of all those restaurants, he knew, potatoes were being peeled, peas shelled, cucumbers sliced, carrots shredded, and fennel slivered. But that did not help him feel better about not yet seeing Tuesday and Baxterr on their way home.

Denis crossed the street into City Park. Mothers and fathers, their clothes crumpled from lazing on the lawn and their hats a little awry, were pushing strollers out through the park gates. At their sides were older children who dawdled along, some yawning, others looking decidedly dejected, as if they wished they could magically be back at home again without having to walk.

Farther into the park, the ice-cream trucks and hot-dog stands were closing up for the day. Several wedding parties were posing for photographs near the fountain in the slanting late-afternoon light, and

Denis noted the pinks and lemons, the creams and grays and blues of their outfits. One bride had a fluffy white dog tucked under her arm, and that only made Denis even more acutely aware that though there were several dogs accompanying their owners as they departed the park, none of them was Baxterr. A newspaper boy slung his satchel over his shoulder and picked up the wire cage that held the day's paper, which read SEVEN WRITERS ABDUCTED in very large letters. Denis began to get a bad feeling.

He called out, "Tuesday! Baxterr!"

Several people stared at him. "I'm looking for my daughter and her dog," he said. "Have you seen a girl in a red jacket with a smallish brown dog?"

Nobody had. He searched for another hour, scouring every inch of the park, checking at every statue he knew Tuesday liked, at every swing and slide and at every green, daisy-spotted slope. He climbed the park's small knolls and stood atop its rocky outcrops. He peered into every boat pulled up on the shore of the lake, thinking that perhaps Tuesday and Baxterr had curled up inside one of them to take a siesta and were still asleep. But every boat was empty.

He called. He asked. He searched. But there was no Tuesday and no Baxterr. The day was fading. The people walking across the park were dressed for dinner; their clothes had the polish and color of evening. They were on their way to the tablecloths and glassware and vegetables that Denis had imagined earlier.

Perhaps Tuesday and Baxterr had gone home another way, Denis thought, somewhat desperately. Perhaps they'd been hungry and stopped by a café and he hadn't seen them. He stood again by the fountain. He noticed the three public telephones with their sculptured custodians: the mermaid, the lion, and the horse. The phone from the horse was hanging off its hook, swinging a little, as if in a breeze. He walked across to it and replaced the phone on its hook. Much tidier. Then a sudden feeling swept through him that Tuesday had stood right here, right where he was standing. Then what? What had happened after that?

A story got her, he thought. He knew this with every fiber of his being. He knew it as well as he knew how to make blueberry pancakes. A story had taken hold of his imaginative daughter and whisked her away.

"Oh, dear," he gasped. "That means she's gone *there*. She's gone *there*, and *there* isn't safe at all. Not even a little bit."

Denis knew he had to get back to Brown Street. He had to talk to Serendipity, and quickly. But he did not run. Instead he strode, because once, a long time ago, Denis had been the maître d' of the finest restaurant in the city. This meant that he had the stride of a man who could carry twenty old-fashioned champagne glasses stacked one upon the other. He could juggle twelve plates and still manage to save a napkin from falling to the floor. He could assuage the bad humors of rich guests and remember the names of poorer ones. He had a natural instinct for what people would like, or not like. He was never wrong about who might choose the lemon tart over the crème brûlée, or the white chocolate mousse over the dark chocolate layer cake. He had once served quail in a raspberry sauce to one hundred guests in five minutes flat. At his restaurant they'd catered eighty elegant weddings each year, and one hundred civilized birthday parties. Denis had a highly attuned sense of what was so. And he understood how to be calm when everything about him was madness. But as he made his way across the final intersection to Brown Street, he broke into a trot and then a jog. By the time he reached his own front gate, he was sprinting.

Serendipity was on the steps, watching out for him.

"No sign?" she began.

"I think she's gone . . . ," he said. He tried to catch his breath, but he couldn't. A cramp was starting above his ear.

"Gone?" Serendipity said. "Gone where?"

"*There* . . . ," said Denis. His voice sounded wheezy.

"Oh my goodness," Serendipity said, and then, "Denis, sweetheart, are you all right? You look terrible."

"Yes," he said. "I'm fine, really."

But Denis wasn't fine. He thought he might faint, so he sat down on the top step. Serendipity sank down beside him and took his hand. They looked at each other and saw reflected in each other's face the utter despair that comes with losing control of the most precious thing in your life.

"She can't have gone *there*. Not after everything we said," said Serendipity.

"What do you mean *there*?" said Miss Digby from the open doorway behind them. "Where on earth has Tuesday gone?"

Serendipity had thought Miss Digby was leaving, but now it seemed that she was not. She clearly felt it was her responsibility to stay with Serendipity and assist her, in whatever way was necessary, until Tuesday was found. For many years Miss Digby had regarded Serendipity Smith's problems as her own. So Miss Digby remained with Denis and Serendipity, and it was she who made the tea and filled everyone's cups while Denis and Serendipity made very boring small talk. Denis understood that Miss Digby could never know about *there*, and Serendipity understood that Denis knew this. They both hoped they might eventually bore Miss Digby into leaving the house, but the more relaxed they appeared, the more Miss Digby worked herself into a froth.

"You must call the police," Miss Digby said to them for the umpteenth time.

Denis and Serendipity shook their heads.

"Why am I the only one of us who thinks this is a very good idea?"

"Because we think she'll be back," said Denis. "You have to trust us. I know it seems strange to you. Really, you just have to trust us."

"Does she have a habit of flitting off in the middle

of the afternoon and not coming home until—" Miss Digby spun about and checked the clock on the mantelpiece. "Until eight thirty! I mean, look how dark it is! It's not safe out there."

"No, it's really not," said Serendipity vaguely, and then she shook her head. "Yes, it is safe. It's perfectly safe. Why, Denis and I often take an evening stroll. And we encourage Tuesday to, as well. There are people about. It's a very safe city."

Denis smiled in agreement.

"No, it's not," said Miss Digby.

"The crime rate has dropped remarkably in the last few years," said Denis.

"It's the new mayor," said Serendipity. "She's done wonders."

Miss Digby stared at them as if they'd both gone mad. "What you seem to both be missing entirely is that your daughter has disappeared. She must be *somewhere*. Possibly with *someone*. Someone dangerous!"

"She might have fallen asleep," said Denis.

"In a tree," said Serendipity.

"Yes, in a very large, comfortable tree," added Denis.

"Or a boat. She might have taken a boat out onto the lake in the park and—"

"That's why we need the police," said Miss Digby slowly. "So they can help find her. If indeed she has fallen asleep, then any minute now, she's going to wake up, cold, tired, hungry, and all alone on a very dark night."

"Oh, there's a full moon," said Denis.

"And it's not too cold," said Serendipity. "It's a lovely night to sleep in a tree."

"Or a boat. What an adventure that would be!" said Denis. "Why, we might go and do that ourselves, this very night. What do you think, my love?"

"I'll get a blanket," said Serendipity.

"I'll fill a thermos," added Denis.

"Will you join us, Miss Digby?" asked Serendipity.

"I think you're both in shock," said Miss Digby. "You're neither of you making any sense. Tuesday has gone missing. She's been missing for several hours. We have to call the police!"

"Oh, it can wait until morning," said Denis. "You just wait and see. Tuesday will be jumping down the stairs, all ready for school. It's her first day back tomorrow. End of the summer holidays."

"That's what's done it!" said Serendipity. "She's

having a last night outdoors before she has to go back to school."

"Of course!" said Denis. "Why didn't we think of it before? Why, I recall now that we discussed it this morning."

"Discussed what?" asked Miss Digby impatiently.

"Well, that she might camp out tonight. She and Baxterr."

"Camp out?" asked Miss Digby.

"Yes, you know, take a sleeping bag. Find a nice spot somewhere on a hill."

"Somewhere you can see the stars," Serendipity added.

"And this sort of activity seems appropriate to you?"

"Well, we like her to be independent," said Serendipity.

"Oh, we really do!" said Denis. "It's awful these days how children are so sheltered, hardly ever given the opportunity for adventure."

"We encourage her to sleep out whenever she can," said Serendipity. "We didn't see her for days during the school holidays!"

"For days?" asked Miss Digby.

"Oh, it's normal at this age," said Denis. "They're longing to fly the coop, flee the nest, vacate the cave—"

"Of course, it's a surprise every time she does it," said Serendipity, "but we're getting used to it, aren't we, Denis?"

"Oh, we are," said Denis. "We really are. We worry at first. And then, as the hours slip by, well . . ."

"We settle into it," said Serendipity.

"Oh," said Miss Digby. "You mean it's happened before?"

"Oh, many a night. At first we thought she was sleepwalking. Then she'd be back for breakfast, telling us all about what she and Baxterr had been up to."

"And what had they been up to?"

"You know, the normal, run-of-the-mill stuff. She'd found a tunnel into a secret garden where they served one hundred different sorts of ice cream . . ."

"Or a tree that was so tall it reached all the way up to another world . . ."

"Or she'd met a girl who was looking for a flying carpet, and they tracked it down to a house a very long way out of town . . ."

"I'm sorry to have to say it, but I think you've both

gone quite mad," said Miss Digby. She sat down on the couch, shaking in her distress.

"Oh, we're so sorry, Miss Digby," said Serendipity. "We forget you're not a parent. If you were, you wouldn't be nearly so worried. Being a parent takes extraordinary fortitude. We promise that if we truly thought there was anything to worry about, we'd be the first ones to call the police."

"Of course we would," said Denis. "Parents have an uncanny knack for knowing when there's trouble. And we assure you, there's none."

"We don't want to worry the police with our young adventurer, who thinks nothing of wandering off every now and then."

"Let's get you home," said Serendipity. "You must be exhausted."

"Would you like me to call you a cab?" asked Denis.

"I'm perfectly capable of driving," said Miss Digby.

Within a few moments, Denis and Serendipity had ushered Miss Digby out the back door and through the gate into the alley where her car was parked.

"Sleep well, Miss Digby," said Denis.

"Yes, do sleep well," said Serendipity. "I will call you in the morning at nine."

"We're so sorry you've had a bit of a shock," added Denis. "Just you wait. Everything will be back to normal in the morning."

"If you say so," said Miss Digby.

"Oh, we do," said Serendipity, and waved as Miss Digby drove away.

Back in the kitchen, Denis pulled out a chair and slumped into it, burying his face in his hands. He was feeling dizzy again. He wasn't sure if it was the failure to eat anything other than pancakes since lunchtime or that he was worried about Tuesday.

"I have never told so many lies in my life," said Serendipity.

Denis raised an eyebrow. "You were very good at it."

"And you," said Serendipity, grinning. And then she began to giggle. Soon they were both gasping with laughter.

"She might have fallen asleep in a tree . . ." Denis giggled. He was feeling quite lightheaded.

"Or in a boat," giggled Serendipity. "And it's a full moon!"

"Is it?" Denis said.

"I have no idea."

This sent them both off into more fits of giggling.

"What if she's not back in the morning—what will we do?" Serendipity said, still giggling. Her stomach was beginning to hurt, but even so, she couldn't stop.

"We'll have to keep lying," said Denis, and this set them off again.

"It is deadly serious," said Denis, sobering up. A nasty pain was forming in the right side of his head. "I mean, she's gone *there,* and it's clearly dangerous."

"I know," said Serendipity, shaking her head.

"If she's not back overnight, then we'll have to convince Miss Digby that she's off at school tomorrow as usual."

"You're very good at this," said Serendipity.

"Oh, anyone who's lived with a writer as long as I have knows a thing or two about making things up. Now, what on earth are we going to do about getting Tuesday home?"

"I'll have to go after her," said Serendipity. "There's nothing for it."

"That's a terrible idea," said Denis, rubbing his eyes and trying to will away the pain in his head. "What if one of you ends up on Mount Everest and the other in Machu Picchu? I won't know who to rescue first."

"At least she has Baxterr with her."

Denis nodded uncertainly. He wondered if he was going to be sick.

"Denis, are you all right?" Serendipity asked.

Denis was staring at the tabletop.

"Denis?" said Serendipity. "Denis?"

Serendipity leapt out of her seat, but before she could reach Denis, he slipped off his chair and slid to the floor, rather like jelly wobbling off a plate.

"Denis!" cried Serendipity.

She dropped to her knees and cradled his head. "Talk to me," she said, panicking.

But Denis just closed his eyes.

Chapter Ten

The Librarian had only to turn her formidable gaze on the Library's polished timber front doors, and they opened obediently. As the doors swung noiselessly on their hinges, Tuesday felt a small rising bubble of excitement, for this was a library like no other. It was unfathomably large, and it needed to be, because it held a copy of every story ever written. Tuesday remembered, from her last visit to this place, how absolutely daunting yet utterly exhilarating it had felt to stand at the entrance to the Library's reading room and survey the vast quantity of books on shelves reaching up to the highest ceiling Tuesday had

ever seen, rows of books that disappeared into forever. She remembered, too, the tour the Librarian had
given Tuesday and Baxterr on a flying platform that
had zoomed along those long rows and up and down
the achingly tall shelves.

As she followed the Librarian into the Library's
marble foyer, Tuesday saw with a small sting of dis-
appointment that the doors that led to the reading
room were closed. She glanced toward another set of
doors that led—she knew—to another, much more
secret book room: the one that held books that were
yet to be. The shelves in that room were stacked with
stories that had been dreamed up and begun but not
yet completed, and Tuesday remembered how they
shimmered and shivered together like holograms. She
thought fondly of her own story, still to be finished,
and wondered whether it would ever make it into the
room of books with a beginning, a middle, *and* an
ending.

"Please excuse the mess," the Librarian said
crisply. "It is very difficult to maintain one's standards
in such challenging times."

Tuesday saw that one or two of the large mirrors
on the walls were hanging slightly askew and that

there were muddy footprints and puddles on the foyer's floor. The flowers in the vases were mostly dead, and up against the walls were stacks of books that were presumably awaiting their return to the Library's shelves. The far doors, the ones that led to the Library's dining room, were slightly ajar, and Tuesday could hear the loud hum of a great many people inside. There was an edge to that sound that might have been panic or even hysteria.

"What—?" she began. The Librarian cut her off.

"Come *along*, Tuesday." She was hurrying toward a door with a pane of frosted glass in a delicate shade of mauve. "We'll talk in my private study."

The Librarian's study was lovely. Its floor was covered in a plush mauve rug that gave off a slight glitter, and the walls on each side were made of floor-to-ceiling bookshelves holding thick volumes bound in matching deep purple leather. In front of one set of shelves was a long, low couch strewn with cushions in purple satin, fur, and silk. The largest thing in the room was a polished desk, and the Librarian sank down into the purple brocade chair behind it. She was framed by a colossal casement window through which Tuesday saw only thick, swirling mist.

"Have a seat," the Librarian commanded, indicating the chair on the opposite side of the desk. Tuesday sat. The Librarian pointed to a circular purple cushion on the floor, and Baxterr climbed upon it carefully, sitting to attention with his tail wrapped politely around the front of his feet.

"I'm going to ask you a question, Tuesday McGillycuddy. And I want you to think carefully about your answer." The Librarian paused. "Do you . . . *like* books?"

The intensity of the Librarian's stare made Tuesday swallow nervously.

"Yes, of course," Tuesday said.

"Would you go so far as to say that you *love* them?"

"Well, yes. I do."

"And do you feel that love, deep in your heart and right through all of your bones?"

"Yes," said Tuesday.

"So, given this fact, what would you do in the service of this place? Hmm?"

"This place? You mean the Library?"

"I mean everything that you find when you come here as a writer. The lands, the seas, the towns and cities, the people."

"Everything?"

"Yes," said the Librarian, waving a queenly hand at the swirling mists beyond the window behind her. "Everything. I wonder if you understand, Tuesday, quite what is out there. In my Library, I have every story ever written. Every story ever begun. But out there . . ." She got up from her chair to stand by the window, and for a moment was lost in thought. "Out there is every world ever created by every writer who ever lived. Every world waiting for its writer to return."

Tuesday felt her mind stretch with the effort of taking this in. The last time she had been here, she had walked through the Peppermint Forest and sailed upon the Restless Sea. Everything she had seen, touched, smelled, heard—it had all been perfectly real, not an illusion.

"You mean that for every story ever written, a whole new *world* is created?"

"Well, that would be unnecessary. The Vivienne Small stories of your mother's, for example—they all take place in the same world. The same world that you, too, seem to inhabit when you come here, rather against my best advice, as you'll recall. But let's say you, or your mother, were to come here having dreamed up a new place with new characters, new adventures. Then, yes, a brand-new world would be born and take its place among all the other, older worlds."

Tuesday thought of all the stories she'd ever read and tried to imagine the worlds they came from. There were an awful lot of them. Then she thought of all the books she hadn't read and all *their* worlds . . . and then she thought of all the books that were yet to be finished and tried to imagine all *their* worlds, all put together in one big space, jostling and bumping against one another. She remembered the words of the message. *I cannot hold the worlds apart much longer.*

"The worlds," Tuesday said. "They're running into each other, aren't they? Colliding. Doing damage—"

"Yes, Tuesday."

"And the writers?"

"Falling from one world through to the next! Being flung out of their worlds at odd angles! Managing to get back to your world, but not to their own desks or even their own countries . . ."

"What's going to happen if this doesn't stop? How do you fix it? Can *you* fix it?" Tuesday asked.

"Me? Why, no, dear. My job is to look after the books, and look after the books I do. The situation with the worlds is far beyond my control. Of course, it could be fixed—if someone were willing to fix it. I ask you again, Tuesday: what would you be prepared to do in the service of this place and all that it holds?"

"Oh, I'd do anything," said Tuesday without hesitation.

"Anything is a great deal, and not to be offered lightly, Tuesday McGillycuddy. You say it so confidently because you are young and have no idea of consequences."

"If this place didn't exist, nobody would ever be able to write another story, would they? Isn't that what you're saying?"

Tuesday tried to imagine a life in which no more books could be written. She tried to imagine a life where her mother couldn't write. Where Blake couldn't write. Where all the writers yet to come, all their stories, were lost forever.

The Librarian nodded as if she could see Tuesday's thoughts.

"That would be . . . terrible," whispered Tuesday.

"Hmm," said the Librarian. "Perhaps you *do* have some notion of consequences after all. So, Tuesday McGillycuddy, this is what I want—"

Before the Librarian could go any further, the door of her private study was flung open, and into the room staggered a man in a dirty white suit and a large white cowboy hat. In his arms was another man, who was screaming in pain, and this man wore a black tailcoat, a white shirt with a pleated front, and a high, starched collar. And although he was very dapper and well-presented, Tuesday noticed with a horrified gasp that the man was badly injured. While one foot was encased in a shiny black shoe, the other was gone. There was only a mangled stump wrapped in what might have been a large table napkin, dripping blood onto the Librarian's shimmering rug.

"Oh, heavens! It's Cordwell Jefferson!" cried the Librarian. "Put him on the chaise. Yes, that's it, on the chaise. What on earth happened?"

"Croc attack," said the man in the cowboy hat. "In nineteenth-century London, if you can credit such a thing."

"I write drawing-room comedies!" protested Cordwell Jefferson. "I was pouring a liqueur when it came out from under the chesterfield, all teeth and—arrgghh!"

He cried out in agony as the Librarian propped up his savaged leg with cushions.

"Ah, Madame Librarian," said the man in the cowboy hat, looking over to where Tuesday stood terrified.

"Oh, yes. Quite," said the Librarian. "You'll need to pop out for a minute, Tuesday, while I deal with this. Go through to the dining room and get yourself some breakfast. I don't know what you'll find, but mind you, eat something. You know how I feel about writing on an empty stomach. Writers turn out all sorts of nonsense when they're hungry, and I just won't stand for it. Off you go."

Tuesday stood, still staring at the footless man on the chaise, who was groaning terribly. "His foot *will* grow back, won't it, Madame Librarian? Once he gets back home? To our world?"

"Heavens, Tuesday McGillycuddy, he's a writer, not a *lizard*! Now, off you go. I'll be along to find you momentarily."

The man with the cowboy hat held the door open, and with that, Tuesday and Baxterr found themselves back in the Library's lobby. Tuesday shuddered at the thought of the man with the missing foot. Food was the last thing she felt like.

"*Breakfast?*" Tuesday asked Baxterr. It felt much closer to bedtime.

Tuesday recalled the Library's dining room as a place of discreet charm and elegance, furnished with curved-back chairs and round tables with white tablecloths. The last time she had been here, she had admired the silver cutlery, the fine white china, and the buffet with its platters of food covered with silver domes, just like at a fancy hotel. But now the dining room appeared more like a giant cafeteria. The cloth-covered

tables had been replaced with bare trestles and long benches, and squeezed onto those benches were people who seemed to Tuesday to have come from every corner of the globe.

On every table, dirty cups and dishes lay in untidy piles. The whole place was rather like an airport when all the flights have been canceled for several days and nobody can leave. Writers were asleep under tables and curled up against walls and pillars, and almost everybody had some injury or other. There were writers with their arms in slings, with scratches on their legs and hands, with their clothes torn, and with bruises on their faces.

Could there really be this many writers in the world working on their stories at any one time? She supposed there must be. Tuesday knew that writers

were often quiet, solitary people, but the ones gathered here were creating an absolute cacophony, ten times at least louder than a math classroom before the teacher arrived. Everyone seemed to be telling a story.

"The river was a regular size one moment, and the next, there was a great wave rushing at me out of nowhere. It picked me up and threw me onto the rocks. I thought I was going to drown in those rapids, but somehow I got hold of a branch and . . ."

"The city turned upside down. Completely upside down. I was lucky because I was inside a building. I only hit the ceiling, but out in the street there were people and bicycles and cars and buses, all of them just falling off the street into oblivion . . ."

"We were in a submarine at depth. Bottom-of-the-deepest-ocean kind of depth, but then all of a sudden, the water was gone, all of it, and we were on dry land . . ."

With Baxterr beside her, Tuesday threaded her way through the crowd to the buffet. She realized that she was actually quite hungry. Gone were all the different dishes and temptations she remembered from her last time here. Now there was only a row of huge saucepans, most of which were empty, their sides smeared with a kind of red sauce that gave off a lingering smell, both smoky and spicy. At last, she came to a pot that had a small amount of this red concoction left at the bottom.

"Chili beans," said a voice beside her, and Tuesday looked up to see the man from the Librarian's study, the one in the white cowboy hat. His face was like a mountainside that had been beaten for years by wind and rain. Every part of it was wrinkled except his warm blue eyes. "Yup. That's all there is, I'm afraid," he said. "Here, let me help you."

"Thank you," said Tuesday.

"I'm Silver Nightly. At your service."

"Oh, Tuesday McGillycuddy," said Tuesday. "And this is Baxterr."

"Mighty fine to meet you, young fella," Silver said, holding out a hand to Baxterr, who offered him a polite paw.

Behind one of the pots, Tuesday found the remains of a small loaf of brown bread and picked it up hungrily, while Silver Nightly found three rather chipped and cracked enamel bowls and two old spoons, each with a bone handle. Tuesday guessed that the very last of the Library's crockery and cutlery had been dragged out of some forgotten cupboard. Silver filled the three bowls with thick, chunky stew, and then he, Tuesday, and Baxterr looked around for somewhere in the crowded dining room to sit. All the space on every last bench was taken, and most of the wall space too.

"How's about we step outside?" Silver suggested, nodding toward the french doors that led to the balcony. "There's a thing that I think you and I should talk about."

Chapter Eleven

As Silver Nightly held the door open for Tuesday and Baxterr, a swirling breeze from outside blew the old man's big white hat clean off his head, and his white hair flew up in a crazy halo around his face. Baxterr took off across the balcony as if somebody had just thrown a Frisbee, and he managed to catch hold of the brim neatly in his teeth before the hat could whirl away and be lost forever in the mist. He trotted back to Silver, tail wagging.

"Why, thank you mightily, my friend," Silver said. "I'm indebted to you. A man without his hat is like a snake without a slither."

Juggling his bowl of chili beans, Silver wedged his hat down tight over his crinkled forehead. The breeze gusted again, this time from the opposite direction, and Tuesday felt a shiver run down the length of her spine when she saw the ruins of the once-magnificent balcony. Whole sections of the marble railings were missing, while the parts that were still standing were damaged and crumbling, as if the balcony had been chewed by giant teeth. Tuesday remembered how several sets of binoculars had been spaced out along the balcony railing. But most of them were gone, torn away with the railing itself, and the few that remained were smashed into unworkable twists of metal and glass.

"It's like there's been a . . . ," began Tuesday.

"Global emergency," Silver finished. "And you're right. That's pretty much what it is. Which is why you ought to get those chili beans on board."

They sat on a marble bench that was mostly intact. Tuesday set Baxterr's bowl on the ground at her feet. She tore the bread she'd found into pieces and shared it between them. Baxterr sniffed the food and licked at it hesitantly, but the next time Tuesday checked on him, his bowl was quite clean and the bread gone.

"Nothing like chili beans for a cold night on the prairie," said Silver Nightly when his own meal was mostly consumed. "Or sunrise on the great plains. You can have it for breakfast, lunch, or dinner, and it only gets better as the days go by. A pot of chili beans can last you a week, and you just keep adding to it. Throw in a bit of sausage, another can of beans, and another of tomatoes. I myself am rather partial to having it with a rasher of bacon and a fried egg on top, but as you can see, we're not blessed with too many luxuries today."

He winked at Tuesday.

"You might not remember me," he said, "but some time ago, I saw you right here on this very balcony. And I won't ever forget what you did. How you disregarded the Librarian's instructions and took a path not many writers would have had the courage to take."

Tuesday's mind flashed back to the time she'd come looking for her mother and the Librarian had tried to stop her from entering the world of Vivienne Small.

"It was you!" she said. "You distracted her, and I got away!"

"That's right." Silver Nightly chuckled. "I call what

you did uncommon valor. It's a rare quality to leap into the complete unknown, and you did it for someone you love. Well, what we've got ourselves here is a bit different, and some of it you're beginning to understand."

"I know the worlds are colliding," said Tuesday. "That's why writers are getting hurt."

"Is that so?" Silver mused. "Well, then, let me tell you what I know. I write Westerns. In fact, I've written one hundred and four Westerns and am right in the middle of my one hundred and fifth. I like horse country. I like canyons. I like wide blue skies and red rocks. I like sagebrush and eagles and smoke on the horizon. So all of that is exactly what I find when I step out there." He waved a hand toward the mist. "Back in the dining room, that real lovely woman with the yellow head scarf, did you see her? Well, she writes about a world that exists a thousand years from now, when the rivers have dried up and the cities have been destroyed by ice. And that poor fellow in Madame Librarian's study? He writes from a place that's a lot like the city of London more than a hundred years ago. When each of them steps off this balcony, that's where they go—into a world of their own choosing, and their own making.

"What I've thought is that there must be someone keeping an eye on how all this fits together and holding everything steady. We never run across one another. My story never runs into anyone else's. The only time us writers ever see one another is here, in the Library. Out there . . . well, it's all our own, isn't it?"

"Yes," said Tuesday, remembering vividly how very alone she had felt when she discovered this on her first visit. "So who is this *someone* who keeps the worlds apart?"

"I don't rightly know, young lady. For a long time, I figured it was Madame Librarian, but clearly that isn't so."

Tuesday nodded, thinking she was willing to bet that the person's name started with *G*.

"I've come to think," Silver said, "that it's a sort of partnership—between the worlds and the stories. Makes sense, hmm? Madame Librarian is in charge of the books and the writers. But I'd bet a whole herd of cattle that someone else takes care of the rest."

"How could they possibly manage every world that every writer creates?" Tuesday asked.

"Well, they'd need help, wouldn't they? They'd need some sort of magical powers, or a machine.

Something that could let them see into all the worlds, keep everything sorted and separate. Maybe they even have a way to move between worlds."

"Move between worlds?" Tuesday repeated. The idea was fascinating.

"Yes. There aren't many creatures that can do it," said Silver Nightly. "They have to have a little magic. Dragons, for instance. Though from my understanding, they're hard to train."

"You mean this someone might have a dragon? Maybe they *are* a dragon."

"Possibly. But I doubt it. I think they're like the Librarian. I mean human, of a sort—a very long-lived sort. My sense is that Madame Librarian has been here a good many years."

Tuesday ate the last of the chili beans and wiped out her bowl with the bread, all the time thinking as she chewed. She wanted to share the contents of the note with Silver Nightly but thought that, as it was private and addressed to the Librarian, she'd better not. Still, she wondered aloud, "What's gone wrong? Why isn't this person doing their job?"

"Perhaps they can't," Silver said. "Perhaps they're dead. Hard to do your job when you're dead. Or feeling poorly. Whichever way, you only have to look about us to see that something that was working fine is pretty much broke. Worlds have been crashing into each other, and into this here balcony too. I don't much like to think about what's going to happen if things get any worse."

"Where do you think this someone lives?" Tuesday asked.

"Ah, well, that's the great mystery. I have a feeling that our Madame Librarian is going to ask something mighty big of you, my girl."

"What?"

"Maybe she intends for you to go find this somebody."

"Why me? Why not you?"

Silver Nightly said gently, "Oh, I think this particular situation calls for a young mind of particular imaginative abilities. Someone who can think up just about anything. The thing about getting older is that your mind isn't as nimble as it once was. I love being here more than anything in the world. Since my wife died, why, I spend every moment here I can. But I tend to solve things the same way, time after time. And I don't have a dog like yours."

"Like mine?"

Although they were quite alone on the balcony, Silver dropped his voice. "I've been wondering about your dog ever since I saw him here the first time. In all my years—and one hundred and four and a half novels—I have never seen a writer able to bring a pet here. Until recently, I have always had a dog, but no matter how much they might have liked to, none of my dogs ever managed to come here with me. I have friends with dogs who never leave their sides. Lay under their desks as they write, sleep on their beds at night, and not one of them has ever accompanied them here. A lady crime writer I know has a parrot that's two hundred and seven and has belonged to four generations of writers. Even so, it has never, not once, come here with her. So what I've been thinking is, maybe your dog isn't like other dogs."

Tuesday blushed.

"Pretty rare in my experience to find a dog that can travel between worlds, yes?"

"Maybe," said Tuesday.

"I think that's why Madame Librarian might be considering sending you on this mission. You keep that in mind," said Silver Nightly. "And keep your dog close by you."

Tuesday nodded. She felt Baxterr lean briefly against her leg and sensed that he had heard and understood everything Silver Nightly had said.

Tuesday felt very grateful to Silver, but before she could say thank you, she saw something phenomenally large emerging from the mist beyond the damaged balcony. Without quite meaning to, she screamed.

The thing coming toward them was a huge globe, like a cross between a planet and the largest soap bubble you've ever seen. Its surface was transparent, glistening with a rainbow-colored sheen, but inside she glimpsed yellow fields and a farm or two and threatening storm clouds. Baxterr barked at it furiously.

"Under here! Quick!" Silver cried, and he pushed both Tuesday and Baxterr underneath the marble bench upon which they had been sitting. Then

he wedged himself in the front to protect them. "Brace!"

Then came the impact, and it felt the way Tuesday imagined an earthquake would feel. The Library shuddered and rocked. Screams and groans came from the writers inside the dining room. Saucepans hit the floor. Plates and bowls smashed. And from deeper within the Library, Tuesday heard the sound of books falling from great heights, off their shelves and onto the floor.

"Going to be a mighty effort to get them back into alphabetical order," Silver whispered to Tuesday in the sudden, eerie silence that followed.

Silver stood up, brushing dust off his arms and shoulders, and Tuesday watched as chunks of the balcony fell off into space.

"Silver! Silver!" called the Librarian, hurrying through the french doors and onto the balcony. "You're needed inside. Poor Cordwell has become utterly hysterical. Will you see to him for me? Thank you, thank you. There's a good fellow. Now, I must find Tuesday and that dog of hers. I need them right away. Right away!"

"They're just under here, Madame L," Silver said.

To Tuesday and Baxterr, still under the bench, he said, "I have to be going. You two take care, and remember all I've said."

"We will," said Tuesday. "Good-bye, Silver."

"How's about we don't say 'good-bye'? Only 'so long,'" he said with a warm twinkle in his eyes. And then he was gone.

Tuesday scrambled out from under the bench. The Librarian was more disheveled than ever.

"Oh, thank the letters of the alphabet! There you are, Tuesday McGillycuddy," said the Librarian. "And your dog?"

"Ruff," said Baxterr, appearing from behind Tuesday's legs.

"Good. Yes, very good."

The Librarian inhaled deeply. She held a small scroll of paper sealed with a blob of purple wax and imprinted with the image of a lion.

"I do not like to commission stories," she said, tapping the scroll of paper on the palm of her hand. "I have always prided myself on letting writers have their heads entirely, but in this case, Tuesday, I have no choice. No choice at all. Will you accept my commission?"

"I . . . I don't know. I'm not sure. What—"

The Librarian cleared her throat, and it came out sounding like a slightly menacing growl.

"A few moments ago, you said you would be willing to do anything—*anything!*—in the service of this place. Did you not?"

"Yes, yes, I did say that," Tuesday said in a small voice.

"Thank you. Now, what I need you to do is to write one of the most important stories of all time. Do you understand me, Tuesday McGillycuddy?"

Tuesday's heart was beating faster than she had ever known it to go. Her parents would be wild with worry as it was, and it seemed she was not going home anytime soon.

"The story I need from you is a story about a man," the Librarian continued, "who dwells in that space between worlds. He is a very, very old man. He is not known to many, but those who do know him call him the Gardener."

"He's *G*, from the note?" Tuesday said. "It was his dog?"

"Quite so," said the Librarian briskly.

"He keeps the worlds apart?" Tuesday asked.

"Up to this point, he has," the Librarian said, "and a great deal more. However, as you can see, he needs some assistance. I do not especially like to give clues. I like to let writers work things out for themselves, but time is of the essence. Are you listening? Tuesday? Baxterr?"

"Yes, I'm listening," said Tuesday.

"Ruff," agreed Baxterr, his tail wagging.

"In the world of Vivienne Small, you will find a way to him in the City of Clocks," said the Librarian.

"The Gardener?"

"Yes. Mind, you will have to keep your wits about you," said the Librarian, hurrying on with her instructions. "There will be a door."

"His door?"

"You will know it when you see it."

"Will I need a key?" Tuesday asked.

The Librarian paused. "Baxterr will be . . . essential. When you find the Gardener, you must give him this message."

She placed the scroll of paper into Tuesday's hand, which she held on to for a moment. A troubled expression passed over her face, but she shook it away.

"It will, of course, be up to you to tell the Gardener

about his dog. Naturally, it will devastate him. And then, what you must do is *help* him," the Librarian said.

"Help him? How?" Tuesday asked, wondering what on earth she could do to help someone who was either very old or very sick keep all the story worlds from crashing into one another.

The Librarian glared at her, her eyes a deep and serious shade of purple.

"How much assistance do you require with this story of yours? Hmm? For goodness' sake, girl, use your imagination! Imagine! Is that not what we do here?"

"I'm not a real . . . I mean, I'm only a beginner. I mean, what about the writers inside? There must be *hundreds* of them. Why not one of them? Why me?"

"Because this is the story that came to get you, Tuesday McGillycuddy. The dog traveled with its message through the world of Vivienne Small, and when the dog fell, a story was born, and that story came to find *you*, and no one but *you*. And that means that this story is yours to tell," the Librarian said.

Baxterr wagged his tail and barked as though in complete agreement with the Librarian.

"Hold on. You've forgotten Vivienne Small!" Tuesday protested. "We've left her out front by the lions. Vivienne has to come too."

"Yes, yes, I'm sure she has a part to play," the Librarian said. "She's exactly where you left her. Follow the balcony around to the front path. Now, go, Tuesday. And tell him . . . yes, tell him . . ." Here the Librarian hesitated for a long moment, and then she said, "Oh, never mind. Give him my note. When he reads it, he will know what to do."

The Librarian's face was both fierce and gentle at once.

"Make your story strong, make your story true," she said. "And please, *please*, Tuesday dear, give careful thought to how it ends. Or yours could be the very last story . . . ever."

Chapter Twelve

As the Librarian had promised, Vivienne Small stood quite unhurt and unchanged, as if frozen in time. Tuesday's head ached slightly from all the new information that had been shoved into it. The Gardener, a door, the City of Clocks, Silver Nightly's advice, the Librarian's message, Cordwell Jefferson's missing foot . . . How would she explain it all to Vivienne? Baxterr bounded ahead to sniff at Vivienne. Tuesday took a deep breath and reached out to touch Vivienne's cheek. Instantly Vivienne said, "—seeing things? I can't see any lions."

It was strange to see her friend suddenly spring

back to life, and for a moment, Tuesday stared at Vivienne, startled.

"What?" said Vivienne indignantly. "So show me them. Your lions."

It appeared that, although Tuesday had been gone for an hour or more, not a single moment had passed for Vivienne.

"We can forget the lions," said Tuesday with as much confidence as she could muster. "I think we'll find what we're looking for in the City of Clocks. Do you know it?"

"Of course," said Vivienne. "It's one of the most beautiful cities in the world."

"Well, that's where we have to go. The Winged Dog belonged to a man called the Gardener—the *G* in the letter. He lives, I think, in the City of Clocks."

Vivienne was perplexed. "You think?"

"Yes," she said. "Is it far?"

"Five days on foot, at least, from the Peppermint Forest," said Vivienne. "We could shorten the journey by crossing the hills to the Mabanquo River. It's a long day's walk, but we could camp out and start early tomorrow."

Vivienne took out her compass, but the hands only

whirred around and wouldn't settle on any direction. Baxterr whined and gave a little shrug with the folded edge of his furred wings.

"No, doggo, we can't fly," said Vivienne. "We do *not* want you up in the sky with those vercaka about."

"How would we get down the river?" Tuesday asked. "Is there a ferry?"

"There is on the Rythwyck, but not on the Mabanquo," Vivienne said, frowning. "With a bit of luck, though . . ."

She threw her satchel to the ground and began searching through its many buckled pockets. She tossed out packages of food, and then, more gently, she removed several leather pouches.

"I never leave home without it," she muttered. "Shouldn't pack in a rush . . . but surely I wouldn't have . . ."

At last, from a pouch of faded red leather, she pulled out a small glass bottle containing a miniature red-hulled sailing boat.

Tuesday grinned. "*Vivacious!*"

"Where there's a river, there's a way," crowed Vivienne. "But first a camping spot before it gets dark."

"Where did you have in mind?" Tuesday asked.

"I won't know until we get out of this mist and I can tell exactly where we are," Vivienne said.

"Well, then," said Tuesday, "Doggo, lead the way."

Baxterr barked happily and bounded away, the mist parting as he went. Tuesday and Vivienne followed in his wake, Vivienne telling Tuesday in more detail about the strange people from another world who had come into the forest on things that were like large dragonflies, hunting the vercaka. In almost no time, the sky had cleared and the sun was shining low on the horizon, turning the hills to silver.

"Which way?" asked Tuesday as they reached a path that forked to the left.

"Actually," said Vivienne, "straight ahead."

Tuesday looked down into a deep gully thick with ferns and flowering vines that climbed all over curious, spiky trees. "Really?"

Vivienne grinned. "Of course."

The two girls and Baxterr clambered down into the gully as the sun set behind them and evening laid its cloak across the land. In the gully the gloom was deep. From time to time there were spiderwebs, and Vivienne was careful not to disturb them as she squeezed past.

"Do you have any idea how much work it is for a spider to build one of those?" Vivienne said.

At last they pushed their way into a clearing, and Tuesday stared. The dim glade was circled by towering ferns. The fronds almost touched in the middle, making a bower high above the girls' heads. In the middle of this was a pool, and the surface of it was steaming. Around it were mossy rocks and a huge tree, covered in yellow flowers, that bent almost to the water's surface.

"Wow!" said Tuesday.

"Last one in's a rotten egg." Vivienne laughed, and in a moment she had stripped off her clothes and thrown herself into the water.

Tuesday hurriedly followed her, tossing her shoes and clothes in all directions and then gingerly feeling her way into the water. It was deliciously warm and smelled slightly of vanilla. Baxterr hesitated, sniffing the water.

"It's the flowers, Baxterr," said Vivienne. "It's the best smell in the world."

Baxterr had a modest dip and then shook himself and lay down on the mossy area beside the pool and proceeded to sleep after his long walk. The girls floated

and chatted until Tuesday's fingers had gone wrinkly, and Vivienne at last said, "I'm starving."

They dried themselves as best they could, and Vivienne led them away from the pool and behind the great tree.

"This is the not the best equipped of my homes," Vivienne said as she drew back a curtain of foliage. "I don't often come here."

It was entirely dark. After a moment, Vivienne located a tinderbox, struck a match, and lit the lantern that hung from a hook above. Now Tuesday could see that they were in a circular dwelling made of giant living ferns, their fronds arching to make a roof. The floor was dried moss. The trunk of one giant fern was covered in hooks, and from them hung a spare bow, a quiver of Vivienne's turquoise-feathered arrows, and leather pouches, pods, and gourds of all shapes and sizes. Outside, the night birds had started to call to one another and rustle around in the fern foliage, making Baxterr prick up his ears, peer about vigilantly, and give the occasional growl.

Vivienne brushed back a pile of dead fronds and pulled out a battered wooden chest with a large rusted padlock that she unlocked with a key that hung on a length of leather about her neck.

"Here we go." She opened the chest and passed Tuesday a jar of pickled fish, a jar of jam, a tin of dried biscuits, and some twists of pepper-sprinkled jerky. To this she added food parcels from her satchel containing two sorts of cheese, a bag of nuts, and slivers of dried pikwan. She divided all this up, setting aside enough for the following day. Then from deeper inside the trunk, Vivienne drew out two thick brown blankets and a pair of pillows that felt as if they were stuffed with down.

"No fire, unfortunately," Vivienne said. "It's not safe for the ferns. But we can still have a picnic. And if we get cold, we can jump back into the pool again."

And so, with their blankets about them and the dappling light of the lantern playing over the inside of Vivienne's bower, the two girls ate slippery bits of fish, put jam onto dry biscuits with cheese, chewed on dried fruit, and gnawed on the spicy, peppery jerky, sharing it all with Baxterr. He turned his nose up at the fish, and the pepper on the jerky made him sneeze, which reminded the girls of the day they'd all met. They talked of that adventure, and Vivienne told stories from the time when the Winged Dogs flew in the skies above the Peppermint Forest, and Tuesday told Vivienne about the amazing fish she'd seen when she'd been snorkeling on her holiday in the Pacific Ocean. Baxterr listened and lay on his back and allowed both girls to scratch him on the tummy.

"We should sleep," Vivienne said. "Tomorrow we have a long and difficult journey."

She yawned, found her pillow, and lay down, and Tuesday did the same. Baxterr crawled in beside Tuesday, his yawn accompanied by a faint whine. Vivienne jumped up and blew out the lantern flame, plunging the whole bower into blackness. Tuesday's thoughts turned to all that lay before them.

"When we get to the City of Clocks, we'll be searching for a door," she said to Vivienne in the darkness. "I think it could be any door. And Baxterr will help. That's all I know."

"That's not very useful," said Vivienne.

"I know," said Tuesday.

"Still, it wouldn't be an adventure if we knew what was going to happen," Vivienne said.

Tuesday pulled the brown blanket up to her chin and thought. It seemed she had always known about Vivienne's tree house, and she had actually *been* to her cave near the Cliffs of Cartavia. From reading her mother's books, Tuesday also knew about Vivienne's hammock house in a giant sky flower in the Oasis of Evermore, and about her bolt-hole in the trunk of a heartwood tree in the Eldritch Forest. But Tuesday had never read about this bower. She wondered if her mother even knew it was here.

"Vivienne, exactly how many homes do you have?" Tuesday asked.

"Seven," said Vivienne matter-of-factly. And then, thinking of the damage to her new tree house, corrected herself. "No, wait, six. Why is it always my favorite homes that get ruined?"

"Will you build another tree house?" Tuesday asked.

"Definitely," said Vivienne. "And my next one will be so strong that absolutely nothing will break it apart. Not pirates, not falling dogs, nothing! It will be the strongest and most beautiful tree house in the world. So there."

Tuesday laughed and held her dog close to her in the dark, enjoying the warmth and the slightly damp doggy smell of his fur. She felt very happy. She loved being here—here in this world, here with Vivienne Small again—but she also felt guilty for enjoying herself quite this much when she knew that Denis and

Serendipity were at home waiting for her to return. Probably they were frantic with worry. Even if they had guessed that a story had come to get her, they would still be concerned, thinking that she could end up in Malta or somewhere south of Cape Town. Just before she fell into sleep, Tuesday imagined her parents sitting up together at the kitchen table at Brown Street.

"I'm all right, and I'll be home as soon as I can," she thought, and she tried to send that thought all the way home to Brown Street like a falling star.

But Denis McGillycuddy and Serendipity Smith were not sitting at the kitchen table at Brown Street. They were not at home. Instead, they were at the City Hospital, Denis looking nothing like himself. Serendipity sat with her elbows on the white sheet of the bed, holding one of his hands and willing him to be okay.

Denis had come to the hospital by ambulance, and Serendipity had followed in a yellow taxi, urging the driver to go faster and faster through the quiet

Sunday-night streets of the city. Denis had been rushed into various rooms with large machines that photographed his brain, tested all sorts of levels, and provided every kind of measurement. He did not wake. Serendipity had filled in forms, given a medical history, then another one, told of everything that had happened, then told it again, until she wished she had written it down in the first place and could hand a copy to each new doctor, rather than having to tell it over and over. In the early hours of the morning, Denis's head had been shaved, and he had been taken into surgery and returned with a very large bandage on his head. There were tubes coming out from under those bandages. He was connected to screens that beeped, bags of fluid that dripped, and a machine that breathed for him at regular intervals. Serendipity was told he would not wake until his brain was feeling better.

Before leaving Brown Street, she had scrawled two hurried notes—one for the kitchen table and the other for Tuesday's bed. They each gave a phone number and said: *Call me immediately. Daddy in City Hospital.* So every few minutes she went to the nurses' desk. But no call had come from Tuesday.

"You really should go home, Mrs. McGillycuddy," a kind nurse said to her.

Serendipity noticed that he was wearing rather worn tennis shoes threaded with purple laces. "He won't wake before morning."

"I can't leave him," said Serendipity.

"I understand," said the nurse. "That chair reclines if you want to try to get some sleep. If you need anything, buzz me right away."

At some point, Serendipity was aware of the same nurse tucking a blanket about her as she curled up in the recliner chair. She dozed, half conscious of staff coming and going, checking the monitors, replacing the drips, and checking Denis's temperature. Denis slept on through all this and did not stir.

At nine in the morning, Serendipity made a call from the public phone in the hallway of the hospital.

"Hello?" said Miss Digby crisply.

"I'm at the hospital—" Serendipity began.

A note of panic came immediately into Miss Digby's voice. "Why didn't you call sooner? Is Tuesday all right?"

"No. Yes, but—" Serendipity began.

"What *happened* to her?"

"Not Tuesday. Denis," said Serendipity, and her voice wavered. "You see, after you left us . . ."

Serendipity proceeded to relate to Miss Digby the series of events that had led to Denis being in the hospital and Serendipity spending the night beside him.

"But, if you're at the hospital, where on earth *is* Tuesday?" Miss Digby asked.

This was, Serendipity had to admit, a very good question.

"Tuesday . . . is . . ." Serendipity faltered.

"At school?"

"Of course," said Serendipity.

"Well," said Miss Digby, "shall I meet her at the end of the day and bring her to you at the hospital?"

Miss Digby could be a little frosty with children. So Serendipity was quite touched to find her so concerned for Tuesday. But then, Miss Digby had always been good in an emergency. There had been many of them over the years, most of them involving canceled or delayed flights and the subsequent rescheduling of television shows, interviews, visits to schools, and book launches. There had been mix-ups with luggage or hotels, cars and trains, the odd flu, and a rare bout of food poisoning. In every instance, Miss Digby had been unflappable and efficient. So perhaps it wasn't such a surprise that she was taking this particular emergency in her stride.

But if Miss Digby found that Tuesday was still missing . . . what then? Serendipity hadn't the least idea what she would tell Miss Digby about where Tuesday had gone. Would Serendipity finally have to let Miss Digby in on what writers really did? She needed to buy Tuesday some time.

"No, no," Serendipity said hastily. "No need for that. She's very independent. Prefers to be alone. Especially after school. She often slips straight off into her room, and we don't hear a peep out of her until dinnertime. You know how girls are at that age. And I'll be home, anyway, by then."

"I'll come over," said Miss Digby. "I'll use the spare key. I'll bring something to eat. That way you don't have to worry about anything. You can spend the day with Denis, and we'll see you when you get there."

"Of course," said Serendipity. "If she's late, don't worry about her. I mean, Tuesday may go to a friend's—"

"On the first night of school?"

"Of course," said Serendipity.

At last Serendipity managed to dismiss Miss Digby and hang up the phone.

"Lying's not nearly so much fun without you," she said to Denis.

She leaned over and kissed his cool, pale forehead beneath the bandages and murmured that she loved him. For a moment she half expected him to say, *The Leith Police dismisseth us; the Leith police are thorough,* which was one of his favorite tongue twisters, but he did nothing. Denis simply lay there quietly. Much too quietly.

"Please be all right," Serendipity whispered to him. "I couldn't bear anything to happen to you."

Serendipity thought of Tuesday too. "And please come home soon," she said silently to her daughter.

But of the two of them, Denis was the one she was more worried about.

Chapter Thirteen

Baxterr and the two girls journeyed through patches of forest and around the edges of small, deep-green lakes. For a time, they climbed along the side of a series of steep valleys, following what appeared to be sheep trails. Or maybe they were goat trails. In the fields they passed, Tuesday saw both sheep and goats grazing peacefully, the bells of the goats making a tinny sound as they moved about. Baxterr showed remarkable restraint in not chasing them, although he did chase quite a few rabbits.

When Vivienne glanced up at the sun and announced it was lunchtime, the three travelers sat down on a pair of rotting, mossy logs in a boggy stretch of open forest. No sooner had they sat down, drunk from their flasks (Baxterr from a nearby stream), and bolted some food than Vivienne Small was back on her feet and ready to continue.

"Can't we have a bit more of a rest?" Tuesday begged.

"You don't want to rest here," Vivienne said.

"Why not?"

"Leeches," said Vivienne.

"I don't care about the leeches," said Tuesday, lying back on one of the soft, mossy logs and feeling the midday sunshine warming her face.

"You will care in a moment," said Vivienne. "See?"

Tuesday followed Vivienne's pointing finger to a horribly oversized, bulbous black leech—about the same width as her own forearm—inching toward her. Tuesday wasn't at all the kind of girl to squeal at a spider, or a scorpion, or even a normal leech, but this was something quite different. So she squealed, and Vivienne chuckled, and Baxterr barked as Tuesday hefted up her pack and they set off once again, Tuesday looking behind her to make sure the leeches weren't following.

Sometime after lunch, Tuesday's feet went beyond being hot and sore and entered a state of numbness. Her legs ached. The path took them through a broad plain of short, wheat-colored grass that rippled in the breeze. Tuesday made Baxterr walk very close to her, convinced that she had heard slithery sounds nearby.

By late afternoon, Vivienne was slightly ahead, tramping along with even, measured steps. The terrain rose to a crest ahead of them, and Tuesday watched as Vivienne lifted her wings and fluttered up to the top, then stood still with her hand shading her eyes.

"Yes!" she said. "Come on! Come on up."

Tuesday and Baxterr scrambled wearily up the rise, and there in the distance was a broad, tranquil river carving its serpentine way through green hills and tawny valleys. Along the river's edge were small villages with low buildings of timber and stone.

"The Mabanquo River," Vivienne announced.

"Why is it called that?" Tuesday asked as she set off after Vivienne once more, this time with a fresh spring in her step.

"It was named after a famous explorer," Vivienne

said. "Letitia Mabanquo. There's a statue of her in the City of Clocks."

Vivienne struck a pose of a person pointing upward. "That's what the statue does," she explained. "You'll see it when we get there."

They reached the riverside at twilight. On the grassy bank, the two girls pooled their supplies and made a meal for Baxterr. Although they had intended to ration their food for tomorrow, they were so hungry after their long walk that they ate most of it. Tuesday, with a full stomach and no farther to walk, felt the delicious feeling you get after being outdoors for an entire day.

"Shall we get going, then?" said Vivienne.

"We'll sail at night?" asked Tuesday, a little surprised.

"I'm game if you are."

"Hurrrrrr," said Baxterr, who was not especially pleased to see Vivienne unwrap the miniature red boat in the glass vial. Tuesday could understand why.

"It's all right, doggo," she said. "There won't be any falling in this time . . . I hope."

Some of you may be wondering how one small girl and one regular girl, along with a small-to-medium dog, were going to sail a swift, deep river in a tiny boat in a glass bottle. Well, it was entirely possible, but it involved a little bit of magic.

Vivienne placed the bottle on the grass, as close as she could to the river's edge. From her pocket she took a silver-and-gold marble, which she unscrewed into two parts. The silver half fitted neatly into the neck of the bottle; the gold half fitted into a groove in the bottle's base. Then they waited and watched as the bottle wriggled itself into two glassy halves, and the little red dinghy began to grow.

It was not the first time Tuesday had seen this happen, and she had read about it happening a hundred times or more. That didn't make it any less strange or magical. Tuesday remembered the last time she had seen *Vivacious* grow. She was glad that this time Vivienne was here and she wouldn't have to manage alone.

In a matter of seconds, *Vivacious* was the size of a normal sailing dinghy. She had a varnished interior with a centerboard, a single mast, and two sails fully rigged—a smaller one at the front and a larger one in the middle. Ropes were beautifully coiled on her decks.

Vivienne unlaced her long boots and threw them into the dinghy, and Tuesday tossed her sneakers in after them. She could hardly wait to feel the cool of the river water on her tired feet.

"Come on, then, in you get," Vivienne said to Baxterr.

Baxterr gave a reluctant whine.

"Oh, doggo," Vivienne scolded. "It's a lovely evening for a sail. Go on, you can jump in now, and you won't even get your feet wet."

Baxterr hesitated only a little, then seemed to decide that Vivienne was offering a good deal. Once he was safely aboard, the two girls slid the boat into the river, pushed off from the shore, and jumped in too. A gentle breeze filled *Vivacious*'s white sail, and Vivienne expertly steered the small craft into the middle of the broad river. Soon the twilight became darkness, and Tuesday could only wonder at the billions of stars above.

"It's hard to imagine there's anything wrong in the world when the stars are so perfect," she said, pulling her blanket out of her pack and wrapping it around her. "Maybe things will settle down tomorrow. Maybe everything will go back to normal."

Vivienne gave her a puzzled look. "You do know that's not the way things usually happen in an adventure, don't you?"

"Yes. I know," Tuesday said, and giggled.

And so Tuesday, Vivienne, and Baxterr were carried downstream toward the City of Clocks, *Vivacious* a silhouette on the thoroughfare of the Mabanquo River. Although neither of the girls said anything about it to each other, both of them had the strange sensation that something was about to happen. It reminded Tuesday of the sound in a concert hall right before an orchestra begins to play. The whole audience has settled, and it's very quiet, and everyone is waiting for the first note, and no one knows quite how it's going to sound.

After a time, Tuesday fell into the kind of dreamless sleep that often comes at the end of an exhausting day.

"Sleep is a wonderful thing," Denis had said to her on many occasions. "Enjoy it while you're young, because you get precious little of it when you get older."

Denis and Serendipity never minded if Tuesday wanted to spend the day in bed reading, as long as, at some point, she took Baxterr for his walk and got the regulation amount of fresh air, which Denis insisted was at least eighty-seven minutes for someone Tuesday's age.

"Rain, hail, or shine," Denis said. He did not order; he compelled.

So, in the hallway at Brown Street there were always numerous raincoats on pegs and umbrellas in the hallstand.

But there was not an umbrella in the world that would have withstood the sudden downpour into which *Vivacious* sailed sometime in the early hours of the morning. Tuesday woke from the depths of her sleep with a gasp, thinking that someone had thrown a bucket of freezing water over her. As she scrambled to sit up, she realized the cold, cold water was coming from the sky in a deluge that threatened to swamp *Vivacious* entirely. Baxterr barked ferociously; Vivienne struggled to control the helm.

"What is *happening*?" Tuesday yelled over the thunderous sound of the water hitting the deck. "Is this rain, or have we sailed under a waterfall?"

"Not a waterfall! We're in the middle of the river. I wish I had a boat with a cabin!" Vivienne called back.

Baxterr continued barking at the rain as if he thought this might make it stop. Tuesday put her arms around him to soothe him. She would have put her blanket around him to shelter him, but it was completely drenched and useless.

"Ruff, ruff, ruff," Baxterr told the rain crossly.

"Hush, doggo. That's not helping," Tuesday said.

Tuesday wondered how so much rain could fall so quickly and make so much noise.

"What *is* this?" Tuesday yelled.

"I have no idea," Vivienne yelled back. "One minute there were stars, and the next they were gone. All the lights from the houses along the shore went dark. I can't see a thing!"

The deluge went on and on and on. Tuesday found the bucket that Vivienne kept for bailing and began scooping water out of the hull of the little dinghy. As fast as Tuesday bailed, or perhaps even faster, the water plummeted down.

Tuesday called to Vivienne, "We're wetter out of the water than in it!"

Vivienne nodded. "I'm hoping we don't run into a cliff or a jetty or a rock. We're picking up speed, which means it's flooding. Watch out for debris in the water."

They rushed faster and faster down the river.

"At the rate we're going," called Vivienne, "we'll miss the City of Clocks and get dragged out to sea!"

"Isn't there anything we can do?"

"Keep bailing!"

So Tuesday kept bailing, Vivienne kept helming, and from time to time Baxterr barked at something that only he could see out in the darkness. Quite where they were, or where they would be by daylight, was a mystery. Tuesday thought that she had never been so wet in her life, not even in the bath or a swimming pool.

And then, as suddenly as it had started, the deluge stopped. Bright stars reappeared in the sky, and the sparkling lights of the eastern and western shores of the river were once again visible. Still, Tuesday and Vivienne could hear the water behind them pouring down in a torrent from the sky into the river.

"What *was* that?" Tuesday asked.

"I have no idea," Vivienne said. "But I'm glad we're on the other side of it."

At length, some light began to leak into the sky, but it was a strange light that came from high above. It was clearly not dawn, because the light did not emerge from behind hills or gradually appear on the horizon. This pale light appeared as if someone far away was shining a torch through the top of the sky. Tuesday and Vivienne stared. Baxterr whined. All three of them gaped.

A sun was coming up in a completely different world: a world that appeared to have run into theirs. Their own sky was like the bottom of a fishbowl, curved inward as if it had been dented by the weight of the other world above it. As the sun rose in that world above, the girls could see the other world's ocean tilted strangely toward them. Water from the ocean above was pouring like a waterfall through the sky and down into the Mabanquo River.

"Are you seeing what I'm seeing?" Tuesday whispered loudly to Vivienne.

"I am," said Vivienne. "If what you're seeing is completely crazy and unbelievable."

Tuesday nodded. Neither of the girls, nor Baxterr, could take their eyes off this extraordinary sight. It was both beautiful and terrifying at the same time. Tuesday thought of the Gardener's message to the Librarian. *I cannot hold the worlds apart much longer. Have you found our answer?*

Who *was* this Gardener? Tuesday wondered. And what amazing powers must he have? *Help him*, the Librarian had said. But how? Tuesday wondered. If he was in charge of something as monumentally important as keeping the worlds apart, he must be a genius, or perhaps a creature of supernatural power. So what could she, Tuesday, possibly do to help him? Vivienne remained perched on her seat at the helm, marveling at the scene in the sky, but Tuesday, with her feet deep in the water sloshing in the dinghy, felt overwhelmed. Baxterr, sensing her mood, licked her gently on the face.

"Look," said Vivienne, pointing to the horizon. "Dawn!"

And indeed, morning was breaking in Vivienne's world too. The Mabanquo River was suffused in pale pink light that gradually shaded to orange and gold, and the world became incredibly beautiful in a water-color sort of way.

The day's light revealed how much the river had flooded. In every direction were boats: sailing boats of every size and color and rigging, but also a great many houseboats, brightly painted in blue, green, yellow, and red. And rushing past *Vivacious* in the current were all manner of things. Three goats and four chickens passed them on the roof of a barn. Along came a bicycle, a bed, and a chair, and a damp cat on an upside-down wheelbarrow.

"Oh!" said Tuesday as she saw a tall, conical hillside rising high above the floodwaters. It was glimmering with soaring, elegant golden spires.

"The City of Clocks," Vivienne said, her voice hushed in awe. "Didn't I tell you it was beautiful?"

Tuesday had traveled a great deal with Denis and Serendipity. She had seen wonderful places. But this was, without a doubt, the most mesmerizing city Tuesday had ever seen in her life.

"Oh no," said Vivienne, pointing. "Trouble."

From beyond the city's spires there came a flock of birds. At first, to Tuesday's eyes, they were only specks, but as the birds made their way toward the river, it became clear that they were larger than any bird Tuesday could think of. Even an ostrich on the wing would have been a quarter the size of these creatures.

"What *are* they?" Tuesday said.

"Vercaka!" Vivienne said, readying her bow and arrows. She was absolutely certain that these were the birds from the world of Tarquin and Harlequin. With their pear-shaped bodies, they flew like long-necked sheep.

The birds began to dive, spearing downward toward sailing boats and houseboats. Suddenly the air was full of screaming and panic. One of the hideous birds came to rest on the roof of a nearby houseboat and deposited a deluge of oily, smelly bird-poo slime down its windows. Its beak was cruel-looking—metallic in color and serrated like a bread knife along its edges—but the bird's dull eyes gave it a dimwitted look. Its feathers were dirty white and shabby, and its wing-span was enormous.

A shadow crossed over *Vivacious*. Vivienne swiftly loosed an arrow that glanced off the bird's scaly belly and fell back into the water. The bird swooped down and lunged at the boat.

"I think you made it angry!" said Tuesday.

"Get down," yelled Vivienne.

Tuesday flung herself into the bottom of *Vivacious* with Baxterr underneath her body. She was terrified. But it wasn't the speed of the bird's flight, nor the breadth of its wings that most frightened her. It was what she heard the bird say as it swooped over the top of them.

"Your father is dead," it shrieked in a ghastly, wheezy voice that Tuesday heard both through her ears and inside of herself.

Was Denis dead? How could the bird know?

"Dead, dead. Completely dead," the bird repeated, its voice echoing through the chambers of Tuesday's skull and inside her ribs. "All your fault too."

"Vivienne," Tuesday gasped, "did you hear that?"

"Ignore them!" she called back to Tuesday. "It's how they hurt you. You have to ignore them."

The bird turned its attention to Vivienne. "You've got spiders on your back. They're crawling toward your neck."

"Won't work on me," Vivienne cried, firing off another arrow. Tuesday was certain this bolt would strike the bird in the face, but the vercaka swiftly jerked its ugly head back into its woolly-feathered shoulders and was unharmed.

"And you," the bird said, stretching its naked neck out long again and aiming its words at Tuesday. "You've gone blind."

The words penetrated deep into her head. Tuesday's eyes felt gluey, and the world buckled and blurred.

"Vivienne!" gulped Tuesday. "Am I okay?"

"You are fine. Nothing they are saying is true. You have to ignore them. They're just stupid, ugly, hateful birds."

"She doesn't want you," the vercaka shrieked, zooming in close. "Never did."

Beneath Tuesday, Baxterr whimpered and shook.

"No, doggo, it's not true," Tuesday cried.

Hearing her words, Baxterr found some courage and dived out from beneath Tuesday to snap at the vercaka passing overhead.

Vivienne's next arrow skewered the vercaka right through the grayish skin of its wrinkled neck. The bird, choking, flapped helplessly and plunged into the river, its wings beating the water into a froth.

"Yeah!" cheered Tuesday, leaping to the deck and throwing her arms in the air.

Then the shadow of a second bird fell across them. Tuesday didn't even have time to look up before she felt its claws dig into her shoulders. It had hold of her, and she was being lifted up and away. Baxterr barked and tried to lunge at the bird, but Vivienne grabbed him and pulled him back. Tuesday screamed as she was torn up into the sky.

"Vivienne!" she cried. "Vivienne!"

Chapter Fourteen

V ivienne's arrow whistled past Tuesday's ear. She couldn't see where it struck, but she knew it changed nothing because the bird still had her firmly in its grasp. Vivienne was swift on the reload, and Tuesday watched as another arrow, and another, and another, came flying at the bird. With every one, Tuesday grimaced, hoping it wouldn't strike her, but each hit the bird and had no effect at all. In fact, it appeared to delight in teasing Vivienne. It swooped back over *Vivacious*.

Pulling against the talons that had closed, viselike, around her shoulders, Tuesday wriggled and kicked in an attempt to get free. It was no use. The vercaka had her in its clutches. Its skin was leathery and tough, and no arrow was going to pierce it. Beneath her, Tuesday could hear Baxterr barking. She watched, helpless, as Baxterr, on the deck of *Vivacious,* flared his golden-brown wings and prepared to take flight. She knew that he wanted to protect her, but she could also see that his movements had attracted the attention of at least three vercaka nearby. They wheeled on their tatty wings and headed straight for him, their serrated beaks opening in anticipation.

"Your little pet is dead meat," wheezed the vercaka that had hold of her, and Tuesday felt her blood turn icy.

"No, doggo, no! You mustn't!" Tuesday yelled. "Vivienne, stop him!"

Down below, Vivienne hurled herself on top of Baxterr, pinning his wings with her arms.

"Stay . . . with . . . Vivienne!" Tuesday called to Baxterr. "Be a good dog. Stay. Stay!"

And Baxterr, hearing Tuesday even across the distance that separated them, retracted his wings, though he continued to bark and snarl, his lips drawn back angrily over his teeth.

"We'll get him anyway," said the vercaka, its voice echoing inside her head as well as grating on her ears.

Tuesday winced with the pain of the talons in her shoulders and watched in terror as a vercaka shredded *Vivacious*'s sails with a single swipe of its talons.

On board, Vivienne reached for her Lucretian blowpipe with its poisoned darts that would instantly put to sleep any foe. With luck, she thought, the birds would fall in the river and drown. One, two, three vercaka screeched as Vivienne's needle-sharp darts struck them—up the nostril, in the gullet, in the softer skin beneath the wing—but the poison had no effect. The birds kept flying.

"She's lost," one cried to Baxterr.

"Never coming back," said another.

"You're a coward," said another, and it took all Vivienne's strength to stop Baxterr from taking to the air.

With its sail in ribbons, *Vivacious* was caught in the swirling floodwaters and heading for the open sea. From high in the sky, Tuesday had a view of the ocean beyond, spotted here and there with sand-rimmed islands, but there was nothing she could do to help Vivienne and Baxterr, and nothing they could do to help her. To make matters worse, a pack of ver-caka had spied her dangling in the vercaka's claws.

"Meat!" screamed the vercaka as they came for her.

To them, she realized, she was nothing more than a morsel. She might easily have been a crust of white bread thrown by a small child to ducks on the lake at City Park. The vercaka that held her, sensing the threat from its companions, flapped its wings with all the energy it could muster. It rose up and up, higher and higher. Tuesday shivered in a gust of freezing wind that was coming through the rip in the surface of the other world. The vercaka was making for the place where the ocean of that world continued to pour through into the Mabanquo River, and for a moment, Tuesday's feet were dragging in the torrent of water.

In the other world she glimpsed a large, pale sun riding high in the sky and another smaller sun beyond it. She saw the strange angle of the watery horizon and the twin arcs of the two skies colliding. She real-ized that she was going to be dragged into another world entirely, one in which there were aqua-blue icebergs floating in a milky sea. *No*, thought Tuesday. Her heart hammered in her chest. *I can't go there. I'll never get back. I can't. It's not where I'm meant to be.*

"Let me go!" she screamed at the bird. Then, realizing how high up she was, she decided this wasn't such a clever thing to suggest.

"Take me back!" she cried. "You have to take me back."

"You'll be dead in a minute," hissed the bird, and its claws clenched her shoulders even harder.

At the sound of a sharp beak snapping right beneath her, Tuesday screamed. The other vercaka were upon them. The vercaka that held her in its grip barrel-rolled in an effort to lose its competitors, but it was outnumbered. Whichever way the bird turned, the would-be thieves were there, jostling, squawking, and hassling, coming at her with their terrible beaks. Tuesday's bird, under immense pressure, could no longer keep hold of her. It loosened its grip ever so slightly, and as it did so, Tuesday felt herself slip. The vercaka had hold of her only by her jacket. She heard the sound of fabric tearing and saw her precious ball of silver thread, her only way of getting home, the one thing that a writer should never lose, fall.

"No!" she screamed. Then she was falling. Too fast. It was as if she were being sucked downward.

"No!" she screamed again, though nobody was

listening. Not even the vercaka. She was outpacing them. Somehow she was falling even faster than they were flying.

It was then that Tuesday realized she was falling not toward the thousand spires of the City of Clocks that glinted in the morning sun, nor toward the slanted icy ocean, although she could see into both worlds. She was falling into a wedge of a dark, starry sky in between them. She couldn't hear anything but the strange effect of her falling, which sounded a little like the empty sound in an elevator going down.

Everything slowed. She was falling past a world of pink sand and towering pyramids. And then past another world of amber deserts and herds of painted horses. There was a world of gloomy streets and people scurrying away in cloaks. There was a world of high, icy mountains and a cliff path, goats, and girls with head scarves. There was a world where people dressed in red and white were playing a game of croquet. There was a man in a boat with a school of flying fish fluttering past. She saw a cat walking on the sky-line of a city, and a giant accompanied by a girl, and two children in a beautiful walled garden, and a wizard with a fire-breathing dragon. She saw a world like a jewelry box and another like a windmill.

Still Tuesday fell, and the worlds about her grew very big and very small all at once, so that she couldn't tell if she was enormous or actually quite tiny. She thought that she hadn't breathed in a long time, which was absolutely true and always led to trouble. Dots formed in front of her eyes, so she closed them. She wondered if she would ever land anywhere or if she would keep falling forever. She thought maybe she'd sleep, because this falling might take a very long time. She was, she thought, immensely tired.

Worlds continued to slide past her, and Tuesday past them, and she would have been fascinated by how familiar some of them were, but by then she had closed her eyes and fallen into a deep, quiet place that wasn't sleeping nor was it dreaming, and from that place she saw nothing, heard nothing, and felt nothing, as she continued to fall.

Chapter Fifteen

"Mrs. McGillycuddy," whispered the nurse with the purple-laced tennis shoes.

The nurse was standing beside the recliner chair in which Serendipity had spent a second fitful, uncomfortable night at Denis's bedside. He put a gentle hand on Serendipity's shoulder and whispered again.

"Mrs. McGillycuddy . . . it's Tuesday."

Serendipity sat bolt upright.

"What? Where? Is she back? Is she all right?"

Serendipity's eyes adjusted to the light in the hospital room, and she remembered where she was.

Denis was unchanged. Her eyes scanned the room, but there was no sign of Tuesday.

"Where is she?" Serendipity asked the nurse. "Is she here?"

"I meant it's Tuesday morning, and you've been here—" explained the nurse.

"Oh, I thought you meant my daughter," said Serendipity, sinking back into the chair. "I thought . . ."

"Your girl is called Tuesday?" the nurse asked. "Not the one that's gone missing?"

Serendipity stared at him. "What do you know?"

"I heard it on the news at midnight. There's been a huge search going on through City Park all night. I didn't realize . . . I thought 'McGillycuddy' was a coincidence. I mean, you didn't seem like a mother whose daughter was missing."

With a groan, Serendipity realized she hadn't returned to Brown Street as she'd arranged with Miss Digby. She'd been so overwhelmed by all that had happened to Denis, she'd completely forgotten. She'd eaten a rather grim hospital meal and fallen asleep in the recliner chair, exhausted from the events of the previous night. Miss Digby must have been alone at Brown Street for hours. Miss Digby would have seen the notes Serendipity had left and Tuesday's bed clearly not slept in.

"I have to get home," said Serendipity, scrambling up and collecting her things.

"Of course," the nurse was saying. "I promise the hospital will call the moment there is any change in Mr. McGillycuddy's condition. Any change at all. And I'm so sorry about your daughter . . . I had no idea . . ."

In the taxi that took her home, the radio repeated the overnight news of a girl called Tuesday McGillycuddy, who had been missing since Sunday afternoon. Serendipity recognized the voice of her next-door neighbor, old Mr. Garfunkle.

"They're a very quiet family. Tuesday is a lovely girl, and her dog never digs up my garden like some of the dogs in the street do. I want whoever has taken her to bring her back immediately. It's outrageous to think that a child can't take her dog for a walk in the park on a Sunday afternoon without something going wrong."

Serendipity had never realized how much she liked Mr. Garfunkle until then.

"The police search began in earnest at midnight last night and will continue today," the newsreader said, and gave a description of Tuesday and a number to call if anyone had information. After the report, the taxi driver turned down the volume, and Serendipity could barely hear the rest of the news, which was about the latest writers to have been discovered in Mongolia and Beirut and the remote island of Tristan da Cunha in the southern Atlantic Ocean.

"Terrible about that young girl, isn't it?" the driver said as he turned the corner onto Brown Street.

Before Serendipity could answer, she saw something that filled her with horror. Outside her home was a flotilla of journalists and camera people, their tripods set up on the footpath, their lenses trained on her curtained windows. Serendipity handed a bunch of bills to the driver and scrambled out of the cab and up her front steps. As she fumbled with her key in the lock, she was assailed by the clicking of cameras, the sudden flares of flashes, and the hubbub of twenty or more people asking questions all at once. She was quite accustomed to media attention, but she was usually dressed for it as Serendipity Smith in a long red wig and high-heeled boots and a glamorous velvet coat. She was not used to facing this sort of thing with a bare face and in her crumpled black Sarah McGillycuddy clothes that she had been wearing since Sunday.

"Where is your daughter, Mrs. McGillycuddy?" someone shouted.

"Did you have anything to do with her disappearance?" another journalist asked.

"Have you got any clues at all? Mrs. McGillycuddy? Mrs. McGillycuddy? Mrs. McGillycuddy?"

Serendipity offered no comment and at last made it through the front door to stand, panting, on the other side of it. And there in the hallway, twisting her hands together nervously, was her assistant.

"Miss Digby, what have you done?"

Miss Digby, it turned out, had done quite a few things. Miss Digby had called the City Police and set off a citywide search for Tuesday. Through the night, no park bench or paddle boat had been left uninspected. Every pathway, tree, rocky outcrop, cave, and underpass was scoured for signs, then scoured again. Several people, Miss Digby reported, hearing the overnight news, had come forward to inform the police that they had seen Tuesday and Baxterr walking through the park on Sunday afternoon. Someone even remembered seeing her at the phone booth. But no one could say where she had gone after that.

"I came here, as planned, to make dinner," Miss Digby explained. "I waited and waited. I called the school principal and was told Tuesday had not attended classes yesterday. I called you at the hospital, but you were asleep, and there had been no other visitors, so clearly Tuesday was not with you, nor was she here, nor had she been here, it appeared, for two nights."

"You called the school?" Serendipity confirmed.

"Absolutely. She is missing, Serendipity. You do know that, don't you? I can only assume that Denis's condition is causing you to behave in this most unorthodox way. I'm sorry—I could no longer stand back. I had to take action. So a police search is under way. And they are on their way here. They will want to question you, and they will want to search the house."

Miss Digby went on to say she had also put out a press release to advise that Serendipity Smith, the world's most famous author, had been delayed from returning to the Mirage Hotel, but that she was perfectly well and exactly where she was meant to be. *Serendipity Smith is not missing. She is currently engaged in fruitful research toward her new series of adventure novels*, the release had said.

"I have a small problem," said Miss Digby. "You see, I can't leave the house. Not with all these reporters here! Of course, I've been most careful to have all the curtains drawn, so none of them could know that I'm here or make a connection between me and the very famous you. But I can't go anywhere at all."

Serendipity led the way to the kitchen, where she saw that Miss Digby had done a truly incredible job of cleaning up. There was a pie on the bench. Serendipity thought it may be chicken. She realized she was famished. Serendipity lifted back one corner of the kitchen blind to discover that Miss Digby was absolutely correct. There was no way out of the house that wouldn't take her past curious reporters and very long, probing camera lenses.

"So what do you suggest that we do next?" she asked Miss Digby.

Before Miss Digby could reply, Serendipity plopped into a chair at the kitchen table and began to cry.

After Miss Digby had fed Serendipity pie (it *was* chicken, and very good, and despite being breakfast time, it was the perfect thing to eat), and made cups of tea, and issued several handfuls of tissues, and sent her upstairs for a shower, the police arrived. Serendipity came out of the bathroom to find four police officers in Tuesday's bedroom, going through every drawer and cupboard. After their search, the police interviewed Serendipity and Miss Digby, separately and together.

"We'll need to go to the hospital, to interview Mr. McGillycuddy," said an officer.

"I'm afraid that won't be possible," said Serendipity.

"We'll be the judge of that," the officer said.

Serendipity began to protest, but the officer interrupted.

"You know it doesn't look good for you," he said. "Your daughter goes missing, and you don't even report it. It takes your friend here to raise the alarm. I think you'd better come back to the hospital with us, in case we have more questions. Please get your things."

The sight of Serendipity being marched from the front door of her house to a waiting police car was enough to draw all the journalists from the back of the house around to the front. And this gave Miss Digby time to dash across a temporarily empty backyard and let herself out the gate.

It wasn't until the police officers were standing right at the door to Denis's hospital room—thankfully, the nurse with the tennis shoes wouldn't let them go any farther—that they believed what Serendipity had been telling them: Denis was unable to be questioned.

The officers went away, but two others came to the hospital later that afternoon to see if Denis had woken. Finding that he hadn't, they interviewed Serendipity all over again, this time in a small office down the corridor from Denis's room that was used to store towels, boxes of plastic gloves, and large containers of pink handwash. Serendipity said, as she had said before, that she didn't know where Tuesday was, that Tuesday had gone for a walk on Sunday afternoon, with her dog, and hadn't come back.

"So why didn't you call us on Sunday night?"

"Well . . . um . . . ," Serendipity said, knowing how hopeless she sounded. "I can't really answer that."

Serendipity wondered if she would eventually have to tell the truth. But each time she imagined how that would go, she bit her tongue and kept quiet.

"So, you're telling us that your daughter has gone to a mysterious, otherworldly place that writers go to write stories?"

"Yes."

"And how exactly do you know this?"

"Oh, because I'm actually Serendipity Smith, the most famous writer in the world, and I've spent a great deal of my life there."

"I see. So why don't you go and find her and bring her home?"

"Well, it's very dangerous out there at the moment, and since Tuesday has a Winged Dog with her, she's actually much safer . . ."

She would sound like a complete lunatic.

Serendipity longed for Denis to wake up. She longed for him to open his eyes and say, "Hello, my love." She longed for him to ask for tea and toast. She also worried about what the police would do when Denis did wake up. Would they charge him with some crime in relation to Tuesday going missing?

That evening, Serendipity sat watching Denis

sleep, the bandage around his head, the tubes and drips, and the machine breathing for him with its rhythmic rush of air in and out.

"You know she's *there*, Denis, don't you?" Serendipity whispered when there were no doctors or nurses around to hear. "She's not really missing. She's probably having the time of her life. But I need you to come back. Please, please come back. Please be Denis again. Please come back from wherever you've gone."

Chapter Sixteen

The City of Clocks had one thousand and one spires with nine hundred and one clocks. There was debate about this figure, some people insisting the precise number of clocks was exactly nine hundred, and others insisting it was nine hundred and two. There were some who believed there were actually nine hundred and twenty-three clocks, but they were considered mad radicals, and very few people paid them any attention.

What everyone agreed was that it was impossible to know the number of cats in the City of Clocks. In fact, many a visitor said the city had been misnamed.

Never had there been a place so congenial for cats. The Mabanquo River fed the city by a series of pumps and tanks, bringing not only water but fish up into the town. Residents thought it good luck if a fish came out of their tap. So wide-mouthed taps were an enduring fashion, and no effort was ever made to change the plumbing. There was plenty for everyone to eat—and lots of bones.

Cats had come from far and wide to live in the City of Clocks. And as you know, where there are two cats, soon enough there are seven, then forty-seven, then one hundred and seven. Stalking along every roofline. Stretched out upon every sunny doorstep, sitting on every sunny corner, by every fireside, on every fence post. But these were not just any old cats. The cats of the City of Clocks were the most beautiful cats in the world. In any world. They were sleek and shiny, with beautiful eyes and perfectly shaped ears. They had deep, rumbling purrs, and if they had white patches, these were always perfectly placed: on their paws or under their chins or angled exquisitely across one eye. The cats were smoky gray, polished brown, dappled tortoiseshell, rippling orange, pristine white, and midnight black: every one of them as beautiful as a drawing.

You can probably imagine that these superb cats were not pleased when they spied a dog entering their city. Some of the most well-traveled cats remembered wilder lands where Winged Dogs had once flown. But the existence of dogs lurks in the knowing of all cats, as does the existence of mice.

Some of the cats raised their hackles at the sad brown dog trudging beside the small, wild-haired girl. The day had already brought them so many surprises and terrors. At dawn that very morning, it had become obvious to everyone in the City of Clocks—human and feline alike—that another world had collided with theirs and was spilling its freezing ocean into the Mabanquo River. Then the City of Clocks had been attacked by giant birds who had perched on some of the city's very finest spires and screamed such terrible things to everyone below that many people had taken to their beds and were yet to rise again. Not only that, but the birds had done untold damage when they did what birds do on many significant clock faces, leading to a rush of concerned citizens carrying ladders, buckets, and cloths up all those stairs.

When Baxterr saw the first cat, his whiskers prickled. He did not as a rule like cats, but he was a dog of manners. He had learned that cats, being creatures of overwhelming self-importance, were best ignored. When he saw the second, third, fifth, and fifteenth cats, a shiver ran down his spine. Something twitched in his brain. Then one of the cats on a nearby wall arched its back and hissed at him.

Maybe if the day had not gone from bad to worse. Maybe if he hadn't nearly drowned in a freezing rush of water from above, then been attacked by vercaka. Maybe if his beloved Tuesday hadn't been snatched from him, without his being able to do a single thing about it, things might have gone differently. But to have one of these cats hiss at him after all that! Baxterr took a flying leap at the cat on the wall.

Startled, the cat attacked, jumping onto Baxterr's shoulders and digging in its claws. Baxterr howled with pain and took off down the street, attempting to shake the cat from his back. He spun about corners and rolled into walls, but the cat held on, and every cat Baxterr passed was excited into pursuit. Soon there were cats leaping across fences, bounding along awnings and gutters, scampering down laneways, and racing down roads. Despite his best efforts, Baxterr could not unsettle the feline on his back.

Faces were appearing at every window; people were stepping out of their doorways, all of them wondering what on earth was causing this hullabaloo.

Vivienne had been hoping to make a very discreet entrance to the City of Clocks, to locate this door that supposedly led to a gardener—who could apparently solve the whole mess with the vercaka and the mountains and the colliding worlds. She hadn't wanted anybody in the City of Clocks to even know that she was here. Instead she was sprinting through the streets and winging her way around lampposts, down alleys, past people selling fabrics and fruit, herbs and hanging lamps, paintings and potted plants, bottles and bath salts. Most people were cheering for the cats, but some were rooting for the dog. At last Baxterr ran out into a huge square, in the center of which was a towering statue of Letitia Mabanquo. Her long hair flowed like sculpted liquid around her shoulders. One massive, stony arm was pointing to the sky, and a mighty jet of water arced high above her from one side of the fountain to the other, creating a permanent rainbow. Vivienne knew, almost before Baxterr did, what he was about to do.

"No, doggo!" she shouted.

Baxterr ran toward the fountain, the cat still cling-ing on for all it was worth, and a thousand cats behind giving chase. Vivienne saw Baxterr leap into the air, she saw his wings spread out, she saw him fly straight for that huge arc of water above the statue. She saw the whole square come to a grinding halt: men, women, children, and a thousand cats all screeched to a stop to watch the dog soar through the pluming rainbow. As they hit the jet of water, the cat gave a tremendous howl and tumbled off the dog's back into the pool below.

If it had ended there, Vivienne felt sure that every-one would have remembered the wings Baxterr dis-creetly tucked back into his sides as he landed deftly on four paws, his tongue hanging out of his mouth and a satisfied expression on his face as he turned to see the waterlogged cat clambering from the foun-tain, looking not the least bit elegant, superb, or dig-nified. Baxterr might have become the subject of extraordinary scrutiny if something had not hap-pened at that moment to eclipse even the image of a flying dog.

Two of the strangest creatures anyone had ever seen were descending from the sky on what appeared

to be very large dragonflies. Both of the riders were dressed in white, with shell-like helmets upon their heads, and everything about them shimmered even more brightly than the rainbow over the Letitia Mabanquo fountain. It was the second time that day that the residents of the City of Clocks had been confronted with unusual creatures in their skies. Nervously they shied away from the winged creatures, the crowd pushing out to the edges of the square.

Vivienne Small stepped forward and waved. Even while the creatures still hovered above the statue, Vivienne heard a musical voice chiming inside her mind.

"We are pleased to see you again, Vivienne Small," said Harlequin from afar.

The flying steeds came in to land, and the crowd watched in amazement as the two riders alighted from their farouche and stepped across the square to shake hands with a small, blue-winged girl who was known to none of them.

"Harlequin, Tarquin," Vivienne said.

"Our enemy plagues your skies," Tarquin said, and Vivienne heard his eerie doubled voice from his mouth and in her head.

"They are even more horrible than I imagined," Vivienne said. "They took my friend." Her shoulders sagged. "I think she's dead."

"We are here to help, Vivienne Small," said Harlequin.

Vivienne, sensing the tension in the crowd, fluttered up onto the stone rim of the fountain and called out in the loudest voice she could manage.

"People! Cats! Please don't be afraid. This is Harlequin, and this is Tarquin. They come to us from another world, where they are the sworn enemies of the vercaka, the terrible birds that attacked your city. These two . . . they have come to help you rid your city of these birds forever."

As the people of the city stirred and murmured uncertainly, Miranda Templeton, the mayor of the City of Clocks, swept in from the Town Hall at the edge of the square, wearing a magenta-feathered hat of surpassing elevation. Baxterr emerged from among the legs of astonished onlookers and sat quietly beside Vivienne, while the cats of the city resumed their daily rituals of grooming and yoga and pretended that the dog did not exist.

"Clockians, one and all," Miranda Templeton said

in her compelling yet mellifluous voice. "Let us welcome these newcomers with our usual grace and generosity." She tipped her spectacular hat to each one of the visitors in turn and invited them to follow her in the direction of the Town Hall.

"I propose that we convene the council at noon precisely," she said. She turned to Harlequin and Tarquin and added, "And when *I* say noon, I—as the mayor—take my time from the Town Hall clock, which, as you can see, is mounted on the highest and most elaborate of our dreaming spires and is also the largest and loudest of any clock in the city."

"I'm sorry," Vivienne said, craning to look up at Miranda, who would have been tall even without her very tall hat. "Could we have a word in private?"

Miranda leaned down to the small girl with the fierce green eyes and blue wings.

"What is it?" she murmured.

"My name is Vivienne Small," said Vivienne quietly. "This dog and I, we have our own quest. We have come to the city to find a door that leads to a gardener who is able to stop the worlds from colliding." She indicated the world above, still pouring its icy waters into the Mabanquo River, although the flow had slowed to a large trickle.

"I do not know this gardener, Vivienne Small," said the mayor. "But your name is well known to me, and I am sure if anyone can find such a person to aid our world in this time of peril, it will be you. Meanwhile I offer my home to you and your dog, for as long as you remain in the City of Clocks."

Vivienne blushed a little and thanked the mayor. She said farewell to Harlequin and Tarquin, promising to meet with them later to discuss their plans. Then, with Baxterr at her side, she set off for the largest of the streets leading away from the city square, her gaze already assessing every door they passed.

"Nice job on the cat, doggo," she said.

"Ruff," said Baxterr.

Chapter Seventeen

On Thursday morning in the hospital cafeteria, Serendipity caught sight of a news bulletin that caused her to splutter into her coffee. Filling the television screen were pictures of her own home on Brown Street—but who was *that* standing in the front doorway? It was a woman Serendipity didn't recognize—a woman with short pink hair, a rather hideous pale blue velour jumpsuit, and a vacuum cleaner.

"How long have you worked for the McGillycuddys?" yelled one journalist. "What do you know about Tuesday and her dad?" called another.

"Where do you think Tuesday is?" said one,

running up to her and flashing a camera in her face. "Have the police got any leads?"

"Why don't you lot get on your bikes and get out of here?" said the woman.

And although she spoke in a very un-Miss-Digby-like accent, Serendipity realized with awe that it was, nonetheless, Miss Digby in that extraordinary garb.

"Go on. Off you go, the lot of you."

On the hospital telephone, Serendipity rang the house at Brown Street.

"McGillycuddy residence, and you'd better not be a journalist," said Miss Digby in that extremely un-Miss-Digby-like accent.

"I seem to have acquired a new staff member. With pink hair. And an interesting taste in velour jumpsuits," Serendipity said.

Miss Digby chuckled.

"It was rather fun," she said. "But you need to come home. There is someone here that I think you should see."

"Not a journalist?" said Serendipity with a grimace.

"No, of course not," said Miss Digby.

"The police again?"

"Actually, no."

Serendipity sighed. She wanted Tuesday to come home, she wanted Denis to wake up, she wanted a long hot bath, and she wanted to sleep. She did not want to talk to anyone. Then she wondered. Surely not . . .

"It isn't Tuesday, is it?" she asked cautiously, hopefully.

"No, I'm sorry," said Miss Digby. "It isn't."

"Then how important can it be?"

"I believe it may be vital," Miss Digby said.

And so, after speaking to her favorite nurse and making him promise to call her if Denis so much as wiggled the tip of his little finger, Serendipity stepped out of City Hospital and hailed a cab in the pouring rain. A few times on the drive home, her eyes closed and her head fell heavily to her chest. Each time she woke with a start and jerked her head back up again, only to look out the windows at the wet, dismal city streets. She tried to hold on to the distant hope that, by some wonderful chance, Miss Digby was trying to surprise her and it *was* Tuesday waiting at Brown Street to see her.

The rain appeared to have frightened most of the

journalists away, and only two of them remained in a huddle beneath the trees on the street. They called to her, asking if she had news. Serendipity shook her head and continued up the steps to the front door.

Once inside, she called out, "Hello?"

Miss Digby emerged from the living room, and Serendipity saw that the pink wig and the blue jump-suit were even more dreadful in real life than they were on television.

"He's in here," she said.

In Serendipity's living room, getting up off the couch, was a tall young man. No, thought Serendipity, he was still mostly a boy. And he was very familiar.

"Hello, Mrs. McGillycuddy," he said, flicking his bangs out of his face. "My name is Blake Luckhurst. I'm a writer, and I know where Tuesday is."

"He seemed very genuine when he came to the door," Miss Digby said. "And very insistent. So I let him in. If I have made an error, I can easily call the police. What do you think, *Sarah*?"

Serendipity regarded Blake. Then she eyed Miss Digby. Blake had met the famous Serendipity Smith on two occasions. The first time was on a television show about books, and the second was at a writers' festival where Serendipity had given Blake an award. But right now, Serendipity was not looking the least bit Serendipity-ish. She was in a particularly disheveled version of her Sarah McGillycuddy clothes: black pants, a black shirt, and flat black shoes. Her brown hair was its usual short cut and rather unkempt. Miss Digby, who had also met the very famous Blake Luckhurst on the same two occasions, was in disguise as well. Serendipity, despite her tiredness, could not help but smile at this turn of events.

"No, no. Thank you, Miss Digby," said Serendipity. "Could you please bring some tea?" And then she realized her mistake. She had referred to Miss Digby as "Miss Digby." She hadn't thought to ask the pink-wigged Miss Digby her new name. On television she had simply been described as the housekeeper. In her state of utter fatigue, in front of a person who might be able to put two and two together, Serendipity had slipped up. She saw Miss Digby give a tiny frown before disappearing down the hallway toward the kitchen, closing the door behind her and leaving Serendipity with her unexpected guest.

"Your housekeeper is really familiar," said Blake. "I mean, that wig is a bit distracting but—"

"Oh?" said Serendipity innocently.

Blake leaned forward on the couch and put his hands together. He took a deep breath. "Mrs. McGillycuddy, I understand you may not know who I am, but I'm an author. I've sold millions of books, and I'm probably, apart from a few exceptions, the most famous writer in the world."

Serendipity's eyes widened.

Blake shrugged. "A film of one of my books is about to come out? *Jack Bonner*?"

Serendipity gave him a small nod.

"What I have to tell you, I know, is going to sound very strange."

"About Tuesday?"

"Yes, about Tuesday. I only come here to tell you this because I know you must be out of your mind with worry."

Serendipity bit her lip.

"You're going to think I'm mad, but the main thing is that Tuesday is fine. Really."

Serendipity waited.

"What you may not know is that Tuesday and I have been corresponding for months. She's a . . ." Blake dropped his head and stared at his hands. There was a long pause. At last he continued. "She's a fan of mine . . . and she called me on Sunday afternoon to tell me that she was . . . coming to visit."

"Really," said Serendipity mildly, raising an eyebrow.

"I didn't come to you sooner," Blake continued, beginning to squirm, "because, well, she's come to my place to . . . write her first novel! I know it was reckless of her. I told her not to. But she was determined. So, in fact, she's at home with my parents, in a room of her own, typing away at a desk we set up for her . . . and she's perfectly safe and happy. She said she needs . . . maybe another week, and then she'll be home."

"So, if I wanted to, I could ring her at your home?" Serendipity asked.

"Well, no, she's not taking calls. But she does want you to know that she and Baxterr are fine."

"She *and* Baxterr."

"Yes," said Blake.

"And you know Baxterr?"

"I do," said Blake.

Serendipity nodded.

"And she wants you to know she really is all right.

Both of them are all right. And to say sorry for all the worry and fuss she's caused," Blake continued.

"And that's what you wanted to tell me?"

"Yes."

"Our daughter has run away to write a book?"

"Yes!" said Blake. "That's exactly it! And Tuesday doesn't want you to be worried."

"She said that?"

"Exactly those words."

Serendipity nodded again. Miss Digby came in with the tea. She settled the tray on the table and poured two cups and offered Blake a ginger nut cookie. Blake refused the cookie and slurped the tea.

"I know where we've met!" he said suddenly, staring at Miss Digby as she was exiting the room. "It was at the TV station, wasn't it?"

Miss Digby smiled her enigmatic smile. "I have a common face. I'm always being mistaken for someone."

"I swear it was you," Blake said. "I mean, without the wig. It was that interview I did with Serendipity Smith. You were doing a crossword puzzle in the green room!"

"I don't do puzzles," said Miss Digby with admirable restraint.

"Then was it the awards thing? When I won Best Young Adult Author? You helped me get my cufflinks on."

"I don't think so," said Miss Digby. She nodded to Serendipity and Blake, then departed swiftly.

"Blake, I do appreciate you coming to see me," said Serendipity, trying to distract Blake from his thoughts about Miss Digby. "I know Tuesday's father will be so relieved to hear that she has simply run away. To write a book! Of all things! I'm enormously relieved myself. It's been such a stressful time. So thank you! We are very grateful."

Blake nodded.

"Blake," Serendipity continued gently, "consider the police. I would have to tell them all you've told me, and they would want to interview you. Then they would want to come and see that Tuesday is, as you say, at home with your parents."

"You don't think you could put them off?" said Blake, frowning. "The police? Until she's ready to come home?"

"I could try. But they're bound to be suspicious. I mean, I know you have a very high profile. And no doubt when this comes out, there will be young writers everywhere arriving on your doorstep, hoping that you might offer them the same support and hospitality."

"Oh, that can't happen," said Blake.

"So are you really sure, I mean one hundred percent sure, that you want the police to know all of this?"

Blake blinked. Tuesday's mother didn't look cross. She looked tired. But was there the faintest gleam in her eyes? Was she laughing at him?

"Can I use your bathroom?" asked Blake.

"Of course," said Serendipity. "It's down the hall after the kitchen."

As Blake passed the kitchen door, he spied Miss Digby wiping the table. He would have to go past her if he wanted to escape via the back door. Maybe he should turn around and make a run for the front door. But what about the media? He'd worn his hooded jacket. He was sure no one had recognized him when he'd arrived and pleaded with Miss Digby to let him in. But if he came flying out the door and ran off down the street, there were sure to be photographers and journalists in pursuit within moments. There was nothing for him to do but go into the bathroom and lock the door.

He studied himself in the mirror.

"You have to get out of here," he said to himself. "She thinks you've abducted her daughter, you idiot. Possibly murdered her. The police are probably on their way right now. That's why she's being so nice to you. It's all to keep you here so the police can arrive and arrest you."

The bathroom had one small, high window. There was no way he was getting out of there. He listened at the door. Were Mrs. McGillycuddy and Miss Digby waiting outside, ready to throw themselves down upon him and hold him captive until the police arrived? He could hear nothing.

"Why didn't you tell her the truth, loser?" he berated himself. "Because then she'd be calling a psychiatrist instead of the police. Either I'm a kidnapper or a nutcase. Perfect."

What had he been thinking? he wondered. He hadn't been able to bear the publicity about Tuesday splattered all over the TV and newspapers. He had felt so awful for her parents, and he alone knew where she was. He'd only wanted to help.

"So," he said to his reflection, "what would Jack Bonner do?"

He thought for a moment, then nodded wisely to himself in the mirror. He slipped the lock of the bathroom door very quietly. The hallway was empty. He could hear the sink running in the kitchen; Miss Digby was washing dishes. There was only one option.

Blake ducked across the hallway and started up the stairs. These old townhouses usually had a way to get out onto the roof. If he could find the way, he could escape across to the next house, and the next, until he found a way down. He would claim complete ignorance if anyone asked him anything.

Officer, I was never there. I never professed to have Tuesday McGillycuddy at my house. I do not know her!

I'm going to go to jail, Blake thought. *I'm going to get caught, and they'll find out she did call me and, after that, she disappeared. I'm sunk. My fingerprints are on the teacup. They'll be able to prove I was here.*

But Jack *wouldn't get caught,* his thoughts continued. *Jack would run. He'd say he'd gone to the house as a sympathy visit. He could produce letters Tuesday had written him. She was a fan. A fan!*

By now he was on the third floor. He glimpsed a bedroom and kept climbing. Next he came across another bedroom; it was clearly Tuesday's. He paused to see if she'd hung up the signed *Jack Bonner* movie poster he'd sent her. She had. He nodded. She *was* a fan!

He reached the top floor and searched about for a skylight or a way of getting out onto the roof. He opened the door into a large office with a huge window. He crossed to it and checked for access to the roof above. The window clearly opened, but there was no visible access to anywhere other than five floors down. Two photojournalists across the road had tripods set up with their cameras trained on the front of the house.

Blake surveyed the room again. It had a very beautiful old desk and chair. There was a lounge chair, too, that was the ideal thing to read a book in. And there were bookshelves crammed with thousands of books all higgledy-piggledy. For a moment Blake forgot the urgency of his mission and walked toward the shelves. His fingers traced along the spines of the books. There were volumes of poetry, old and new. There were books on history and geography. There were biographies and autobiographies. There were novels for children and adults all in alphabetical order, and every bit of available bookshelf space was crammed full. Blake inspected the *L* section. Sure enough, there was every one of the Jack Bonner books. He nodded, impressed. Was this Mr. McGillycuddy's room? Was this why Tuesday wanted to be a writer, because her house had all these books? Her parents were obviously readers.

Blake walked all the way to the far end of the shelves, taking in the titles and authors. He gazed down at the collection of books by Serendipity Smith. There was the complete Vivienne Small series in hardback and paperback, plus all the other novels Serendipity Smith had written before.

Blake ran his fingers across the spines of the Vivienne Small books. Tuesday had run into Vivienne Small, he remembered, on her first trip to the world of stories, when he'd first met her. She'd even come across Carsten Mothwood, the villain of the whole series. He noticed that there were Vivienne Small books in other languages. *Vivienne Small und die Berge des Margolov*, *Vivienne Small et la lutte finale*, *Yo sé de Vivienne Small*. There must have been twenty different editions of each book. Or maybe thirty. Blake slid one of the books from the shelf and opened it at the author picture on the inside back cover. There was Serendipity Smith with her red hair and glasses. All of a sudden, a fact came to him. It crystallized, perfectly clearly, in his mind.

A voice from the doorway said, "So you've worked it out?"

It was Tuesday's mother. Blake went pale. Was it possible? Could this petite person really be that towering redheaded woman with the long velvet coats and the fabulous boots?

He looked back at the photograph. "It can't be. *Can* it?"

"It is." She smiled. "My grand disguise to keep a little privacy in our lives."

"You are actually Serendipity Smith," he grinned. "Wow!" Then he frowned. "I'm sorry. I didn't come here to pry."

"It's all right, Blake. I'm not at all cross. In fact, I'm deeply touched that you would come all this way to try to reassure us that Tuesday is safe."

"It wasn't a very good story," he said. "I intended to tell you the truth, and then at the last minute, I lost my nerve. I thought you would think me a complete nutcase if I told you there was a place writers go to. I'm sorry. I thought you must think I'd abducted her, so I was going to . . ."

"Escape across the roof?" she said with a smile. "Very Jack Bonner."

Blake looked sheepish. Serendipity took the book from him and glanced at the photograph. "It's worked quite well until now."

"Until now?" Blake repeated.

"Well, I think if Tuesday doesn't come home soon, I'm going to have to tell the police the truth. Tell them who I am, and that there is a place that writers go to, and worlds beyond this one, and at the moment there's something very wrong, and the return journey is anything but safe."

"You can't," said Blake. "Nobody will believe you."

"Well, they might if Blake Luckhurst was standing beside me," she said. "The most famous writer in the world, give or take a few exceptions?"

He grimaced and said, "I would never have

said that if I'd known it was you I was talking to, Serendipity. I was—"

"Establishing credibility. I know. It's very useful, fame, for that."

"You can't go telling people the truth," said Blake. "What if that somehow ruined it for every writer? Somebody might muscle in and make us all get travel permits, or licenses? We've all kept it secret for so long. For thousands of years . . ."

"Have you heard from anyone who's come home? I mean, recently?" Serendipity asked.

"Not a word. The writers I know aren't writing. Or else they're missing." Blake sat down in the big red chair and clasped his hands together. "I could go. I really could go. I mean, Tuesday might need help."

"No, Blake, it's too risky."

"If I don't, and she doesn't come back, you might go to jail."

"I might," said Serendipity. "But that would all take months, and she's sure to be home by then."

"How are you going to explain it when she does come back?"

"Well, I could tell them that she ran away to work on a novel at the home of her friend, Blake Luckhurst?"

Blake grinned a little ruefully. "Okay . . . then why didn't I alert the police?"

"Because she was hiding in your attic and stealing food from the kitchen by night, obviously."

"And Baxterr?"

"Same."

"Agog," he said.

"What?" asked Serendipity.

"I remembered it before you came into the room. It was the word Miss Digby was looking for in the crossword at the television station that night. I asked her what the clue was, and she said 'highly excited, in a state of anticipation.' "

"And you said 'agog'?" asked Serendipity.

"Yes," said Blake. "So *she* knows—Miss Digby, I mean? Where Tuesday is."

"No. I think she would be agog if we were to tell her."

"You know, I always wondered," said Blake, nodding, "how Tuesday got to be with the characters in your world."

"Oh yes," said Serendipity. "That was unexpected, wasn't it? Of course, she helped me make so much of it up. She was always telling me what Vivienne would say and do. I'm very fond of both my capable girls."

"Yeah," said Blake. "They're all right."

"Blake," said Serendipity, trying not to smile, "right now, I have simply got to get some sleep. Let's go find something for you to eat, and then you can decide if you're going to go home or if you'd like to stay here until Tuesday gets back."

"I think I'd like to stay, if it's okay with you," said Blake.

"Of course," said Serendipity. "I'll have Miss Digby make up a bed."

They descended the stairs together.

Miss Digby came out of the kitchen to meet them.

"Miss Digby," said Serendipity, "Blake understands everything. He'll be staying with us for a few days. Perhaps until Tuesday gets home."

"What does he understand exactly?" Miss Digby asked, giving them both a piercing glance. "Am I right in assuming that you two know where Tuesday is?"

"I'm so sorry, Miss Digby," said Serendipity helplessly. "I wanted to—"

"Some kind of writer's code, between the two of you?" asked Miss Digby.

"Kind of," said Blake.

"Well, it's complicated. You see—" said Serendipity.

"No, no. You need neither explain nor apologize. I appreciate a good secret." She sighed. "If you had told me there was nothing to worry about, we might have saved ourselves a lot of trouble with the police. So when *is* she coming home?"

"We don't know. When she's ready," said Serendipity.

"Well, we're stuck with all this now. Best make the most of it. Maybe one of you can use it in a story one day."

"Agog," said Blake. "I am agog, Miss Digby."

Miss Digby smiled. "Ah, yes. That's very good, Blake. You have quite a memory. But once Tuesday is home again, there are some things that you will have to forget."

"I'm not sure what you mean," said Blake politely.

"If you ever, I mean *ever*, give any indication that Serendipity Smith is anyone other than Serendipity Smith, or that any member of this family is anything other than exactly who the world currently believes them to be, then I will personally ensure you die a long and painful death."

"Miss Digby! I think that's going a bit far," said Serendipity.

"On the contrary," said Miss Digby in her sternest tone. "I think that's exactly the sort of language Blake Luckhurst understands. Am I right?"

"Yes, Miss Digby," mumbled Blake.

"What did you say?" barked Miss Digby.

"I swear I will faithfully keep the secrets of this family forever and never reveal them to anyone, even under pain of death," said Blake.

Miss Digby smiled. She offered her hand to Blake, who also shook hands with Serendipity.

"You are an incredible woman, Miss Digby," said Serendipity.

"It takes one to know one," said Miss Digby mildly.

Chapter Eighteen

Every day for three weeks, vercaka came to the City of Clocks at sunrise, perching on the city's spires and crying out in their ugly voices to the people below.

"Your wife doesn't love you."

"Your neighbor is going to burn your house down."

"Your parents are not your parents."

"Your daughter is stealing your money."

"Everybody knows how ugly you really are."

Their words unleashed chaos. Secrets that had long been buried were unearthed. Husbands confronted wives, neighbors feuded, children cried, cats fought, and the dreadful birds watched on, enjoying it all.

Each day there were more vercaka, and every day the people of the city became more terrified. Most people kept to their houses until noon, when the birds rose suddenly from the spires in a great mass of tattered white and flew south to terrorize other townships up the Mabanquo River.

The smell the vercaka left behind was appalling, as was the green-and-mustard-colored poo all over the clock faces and spires. The vercaka took things too. Every morning they snatched away humans and cats alike, carrying them off into the sky, the sounds of screaming and howling lingering long after they were out of sight. Those who were taken did not come back.

For three weeks, Vivienne and Baxterr searched the city for a door that would lead to the Gardener, leaving no park or garden unexplored. Vivienne questioned everyone she found with a lawn, or a fence lined with roses, or fruit trees bending their boughs to the street. She interrogated every city official responsible for the extensive parks and gardens across the city. Baxterr sniffed at window boxes, at potted plants, and even the grassy strips between footpaths and roads. Vivienne must have asked a thousand people if they knew the Gardener, or if they had seen someone called the Gardener, or perhaps noticed a door that had something strange about it.

"In what way, *strange*?" the people would ask. Vivienne couldn't tell them. *We'll know it when we see it*, Tuesday had said, and that was all Vivienne knew.

By the third week of searching, Vivienne was losing hope. And although Baxterr followed her wherever she went, loyally searching beside her, it was clear that his heart was as heavy as his paws. The city, too, was thick with sadness and fear. This most beautiful of cities, home to long boulevards of towering trees, wide streetscapes with flower beds and fountains, was under attack. And for the first time in history, some of the city's clocks stopped, their workings seized up and ruined by sludgy vercaka droppings.

Vivienne had begun searching beyond the boundaries of the city. On this particular afternoon, she had made her way down to the Mabanquo River, checking every door in every house along the way. By the long pier, she came across a small crowd examining a dead vercaka. Its feet were turned up, and it resembled a giant, ugly chicken. One woman, a fish merchant, was loudly describing the vercaka attack.

"I swear I thought I was dead," she was saying. "I mean, it came at me, snapping its jaws, waving its wings."

"So what did you do?" someone in the crowd asked.

"Well, it was the darndest thing. It started scooping up all my fish. Guzzling them off my table. And I was so cross, I threw my coin box at it. And blimey, if the bird didn't fall down dead."

"You mean you killed it with a lump of wood?"

"I know it's strange," the woman said, "but that's what happened. The box burst right open when it hit the bird, coins flying everywhere, and I was thinking how stupid I'd been, that not only was I going to lose all my fish, but I'd thrown away all my money as well. Then it keeled over."

Once the crowd had dispersed, Vivienne spoke to the woman, asking her to tell the story one more time. She asked several more questions and then she turned back toward the city, Baxterr at her heels. At the mayor's house, she came across Harlequin, newly returned from her latest expedition far to the north, or south, or east, or west, seeking the rivers that might contain the poison they needed to kill the vercaka. And there Vivienne related all she had heard from the fisherwoman.

The following morning, very early, Harlequin and Vivienne did something very dangerous. They set about trying to catch a vercaka.

Some people, when they are frightened, get very vague and forget what they are doing. Other people get very cold and require blankets and cups of tea. But the most useful of people, when faced with extreme fear, become very focused. And this is what happened to Miranda Templeton, the mayor of the City of Clocks. For three weeks she had been meeting daily with the Council of Wisdom in an attempt to agree on a battle strategy to fight the vercaka and rid the town of their ugly and terrifying presence.

The meetings had faced problems since the first day, for on the Council of Wisdom was a man called Nigel Finkwatter. Some years earlier, Finkwatter had wanted to be mayor but had not received sufficient votes, and he had therefore devoted his energies to making Miranda Templeton's life as difficult as possible. As a sign of dissent, he stopped wearing hats and instead went about with his mane of long, white hair curled and coiffed into towering arrangements.

On this day, Finkwatter was again objecting to Tarquin's presence at the meeting.

"He talks with his mouth *and* inside one's head," Finkwatter had said, "which, as everyone knows, is not normal but a trick of mind! He, and that other one who came with him, should not be welcomed here. How do we know that they did not bring the vercaka here deliberately? You tell us they are seeking a poison to kill these birds, but how can we be sure they are not planning to invade our world? How do we know they didn't bring these birds here to do this? To distract us? Terrify us! Maybe it's these two who are causing more birds to come every day!"

Nigel Finkwatter was very rich, and he had become so by being very persuasive. He had a handsome face with a rather large nose, and his voice was smooth and slippery. Like the vercaka, he knew exactly how to play on each person's worst fears. So, as he spoke, several people on the council nodded.

"As I have said before, if we are to fight these birds," said Miranda Templeton with her usual dignity, "then we must have the help of people who have fought them all their lives."

"I am sorry we have been unable to find a suitable poison," said Tarquin, speaking as he did with his mouth but also into the minds of the councillors. "At this moment, my sister is attempting a new course of action with Vivienne Small. We will know soon if they have been successful."

Finkwatter shook his head as if trying to dislodge Tarquin's voice.

"I will not tolerate these mind games!" he fumed.

"We are sorry if this unsettles you," Tarquin said. "Imagine how very strange it is for us that you cannot communicate with your minds."

"Insults!" Nigel Finkwatter roared, then thumped the great council table. "I demand your removal from this meeting! You have nothing to give us. We will kill these vercaka ourselves."

Miranda Templeton insisted that Tarquin stay. Tarquin sat patiently and silently, listening as councillors put forward new ideas and strategies, all of which he knew would be unsuccessful.

In the middle of Finkwatter's next tantrum, Tarquin spoke directly into the mayor's mind.

"Excuse me, Mayor Templeton, but my sister approaches the door," he said. "And with good news."

To the puzzlement of the councillors, Miranda Templeton strode to the doors and threw them open. There stood Harlequin and Vivienne, trailing behind them a large cage containing a vercaka. There was a stunned silence as everyone in the room took in the sight of the enormous bird.

"How on earth—" began Miranda Templeton.

"You can't bring that bird in here," exploded Finkwatter.

"Your children would be happier without you," it screeched.

"Quiet, you vile bird," said Harlequin, and everyone heard her words in their heads. The bird shut its mouth and glared at her with its huge, dull eyes.

"We wish to offer the council a demonstration," said Vivienne Small, holding out a large fish. Into the fish's mouth she slipped a gold coin.

"We have been searching for the poison in the wrong places," said Harlequin.

The bird was already salivating at the sight of the

fish in Vivienne's hands. Vivienne tossed it through the bars, and the bird snapped it up and gulped the fish down. Within seconds, the bird slumped to the floor of the cage.

"Is it dead?" asked Miranda Templeton.

"What? The fish is poison?" asked another councillor.

"No," said Harlequin. "In our world, the poison that kills these birds, as we have told you, is a liquid that runs in small rivers across the ground. But here, thanks to Vivienne Small, we have discovered it is a solid. We believe you call it gold."

"That's money!" exclaimed Nigel Finkwatter.

"And it kills them," said Vivienne.

"We can't fight with money. It would be unthinkably expensive . . . ," spluttered Finkwatter.

"You are quite sure?" asked the mayor, looking from Harlequin to Vivienne.

Harlequin nodded and smiled. "We will need a great deal."

"How much?" the mayor asked.

"All that can be acquired," said Harlequin.

"This is preposterous!" cried Nigel Finkwatter, and the council erupted.

There are no fights worse than the ones people have over money. And in the City of Clocks, there were no fights nastier than those that involved Nigel Finkwatter. For Nigel Finkwatter was stingy. He wouldn't lend you enough money to buy a toothpick. If one of his children broke a shoelace, he made them knot it rather than buy a new one. His family lived on fish soup, dry cheese, and biscuits. And even if ver-caka were destroying the City of Clocks and preying on its residents, Nigel Finkwatter was not going to throw *gold* at the problem.

And so three days passed. While most of the city prepared for battle, Nigel Finkwatter refused to help.

"I have said it before, and I will say it again," said Miranda Templeton late on the third day. "The city will find a way of repaying you, Nigel, but we must act *immediately*, before it is too late."

"Your plan will never work," he insisted.

Miranda's hat had fallen sideways, her clothing was disheveled, and her eyes were red with fatigue. Other than to go home and sleep for a few hours, she had worked tirelessly for the past three days in prepa-ration. When word got out that gold was needed, the city folk had come forth with coins in bags and purses, boxes and suitcases. Miranda Templeton had ensured a list was kept of every cent loaned to the city, and had posted guards to the room where the money was to be kept under lock and key. She noticed that many of the poorest people had given the most, and she herself had emptied all of her savings.

"If that is your final word, Nigel, then we will manage without you—and your gold," said Miranda Templeton.

"And you will fail," said Finkwatter.

"And you sound more like a vercaka every day," she retorted. To the council, she said, "We will begin at dawn. Make the necessary arrangements."

The councillors dispersed, and word went out across the city.

As Miranda Templeton wearily made her way home, she did not look up. If she had, she might have seen hundreds of cats making their way along the city rooftops, and if she had watched for long enough, she might have seen them all come to sit on a single rooftop and gather for a great meeting while a full moon rose into the sky. If the city was extra quiet that night, people put it down to the coming battle. They kissed their children more than usual, went to bed early, and slept fitfully. Quite a few people noticed that their cats had not returned home.

Chapter Nineteen

But where, for all of that time, was Tuesday?

She was in a room that was large and circular, with curved glass walls that opened up into a boundless night sky like a planetarium. But instead of being dotted with a billion stars, this sky was filled with worlds. There were so many you could never have counted them all, just as you couldn't hope to count the stars in the night sky above you. Many worlds were old, some were still expanding, and some were being born.

One half of the room Tuesday was in was a like a workshop, with a long bench that was piled with books and notes. Farther along it were all manner of implements and tools in disarray. There were magnifying glasses and microscopes. There were tweezers, miniature secateurs, and tiny hammers, as well as scissors of every size and sort. There were tiny paintbrushes and trays that held stacks of miniature bricks. There were jars of sand in many different colors, toothpicks, tiny spray bottles, and watering cans. There were also a number of round things on stands, each one covered by a green cloth.

At either side of the round room was a jetty leading out into the darkness. One was as wide as a street but narrowed as it neared the room. The other was the width of a footpath. The narrow jetty had a door leading to it; the other, no door at all, only a round glass chute in the wall. Of course, there was no water beneath them—only that world-filled sky all around.

The other half of the room was set out like a home. There were clearly spaces for eating and reading and sleeping, with couches and tables, rugs and chairs. However, there was hardly anything in the way of walls—only the occasional painted screen. And it was in this half of the room that Tuesday slept. She lay on a primrose-yellow velvet couch, and although she was

pale, her breathing was even and a soft primrose comforter was keeping her warm.

In the center of this room, standing on a large blue rug, a man was at work, reaching up with a boathook into the infinite galaxy of worlds above him. He was an old man, with gray hair and a weary face. He wore a primrose suit with a slightly creased white shirt and a mauve tie with purple roses upon it. The boathook he was wielding was impossibly long, and he was attempting to reach out into space and swipe at a large globe that had smashed into the surface of another. Again and again he swooped at it, trying to snag the golden loop attached to its underside, and at last he caught it. He heaved and strained to pull the colliding worlds apart, but his arms were shaking. He pulled harder, almost upsetting a table that stood behind him laden with teapots and a large cake under a glass dome.

"Clear the mind, clear the mind," he reminded himself. Despite his best efforts, the worlds continued to crumple together. At last he gave up and dropped the boathook to the floor.

"Well, a fine kettle of fish," he said. "A fine nest of nettles."

He slumped into a chair at the workbench and, resting his head on a large pile of books, closed his eyes.

"If a tree falls in a world, and nobody hears it, does it make any sound?" he murmured.

At that moment, Tuesday opened her eyes. She tried to remember what she had been dreaming, but when she took in the sight of the worlds above her, she gasped. She tried to stand and found that she had to sit down again. Her jacket was badly torn, and her head was spinning. The man turned and stared at her, bewildered. He searched through the notes in front of him. With great delight, he found one and read aloud, "*Girl. Fell from the sky.* Ah, yes. That's right."

He said to Tuesday, "You fell from the sky. You'll be feeling rather strange."

"Where am I?" Tuesday asked. "Are Vivienne and Baxterr here?"

Above them, quite close, an orange world and a green world collided. They did it slowly, squeezing together until white lightning forked across the sky.

"I don't think they should be doing that," Tuesday said, her eyes wide in horror.

"No, you're quite right," said the man. "Fall seven times, stand up eight."

To Tuesday's amazement, the man picked up a boathook and reached up into the vast sky. Impossibly, the boathook stretched all the way to the two worlds, and the man grabbed onto one of the worlds and tried to pry it away. As he was doing so, a world spun in very close to the room and landed gently on the wider of the two jetties attached to the building. It began rolling ominously toward them. Its exterior was made of glass, and inside it was a sky filled with sunset clouds and a wintry city.

"Excuse me, but something seems to be happening," Tuesday said, her heart racing.

The man glanced across and observed the incoming world.

"Oh, it's only routine maintenance," he said. "Hope for the best, prepare for the worst."

As it got closer, the world became smaller, so that by the time it reached the end of the jetty, it was only the size of a large fishbowl. An automatic arm then swept up the world and deposited it into the clear glass chute. The world rolled down this chute around the perimeter of the room until it popped out onto a cushioned stand on the workbench. A metal arm whizzed out and unscrewed the top of the world, as if it were made of glass. It set the lid down gently on the bench and returned to its place. A bright beam of light came on and shone directly into the world.

"Ready for inspection?" the old man called, still grappling with his boathook.

"I'm guessing . . . yes," Tuesday said.

To Tuesday's dismay, the man put down the boathook, forgetting all about the colliding worlds. He hurried to his workbench and put on a peculiar pair of spectacles that were like two microscopes. He peered down into the newly arrived world.

"Oh dear," he said. "Oh dear, oh dear, oh dear."

"What's the matter?" Tuesday asked, peering over his shoulder. The city's buildings appeared old, and the skyline they formed was familiar.

"Is that *London*?" Tuesday asked, incredulous.

"Hmph," said the man. "In one way, yes absolutely. In another way, no, not remotely. You know how it is between writers and reality. Oh dear. Dear, oh dear, oh my."

"What? What is it?"

"Crocodiles," said the man. He turned away from

the miniature London and examined the sky. "I can't imagine where they've fallen from. It could be anywhere. Oh, it's all going so badly."

Tuesday thought about Cordwell Jefferson on the Librarian's couch with his missing foot. Then she noticed a large word written on the back of the man's hand. It said POCKET. The man raced over to his desk and again began searching through his pile of notes.

"Crocodiles . . . crocodiles," he said. "Nothing. Nothing. Perhaps I didn't . . . oh, I'll have to put them somewhere."

The man fossicked around his bench and found a small jar and a pair of tiny tweezers. He reached inside the world and began picking out very tiny things that wriggled and . . . were they *squeaking*? Tuesday picked up a magnifying glass from the implements arranged untidily on the table and squinted to see what these squirming creatures were. She gasped. They were very, very small crocodiles gnashing their long, toothy jaws at her.

"Oh, they're even in the houses," the man was saying. "It's very serious. They've been causing chaos. And, if I remember rightly, we need to take a peek farther north. Ah, yes. Glacier, glacier, glacier. There it is. The blighter. Moving far too fast. Icepick, please!"

Tuesday rummaged until she found what must surely be the smallest icepick ever made.

"Most helpful," he said, shaving off slivers of ice and tossing them over his shoulder onto the floor.

"Pins, please! Glue! Hammer!"

Tuesday found each of these and passed them to the man, whose hands moved in a flurry of activity over the miniature icefloes, trees, and rocks of the world before them.

"Much better," said the man, taking off the glasses. His gray eyes sparkled. "I think that glacier will be fine for a while yet. Unlikely to budge more than an inch or two for several hundred years."

Tuesday observed the tiny implements in his hands. Then it dawned on her.

"You're the Gardener!"

"Of course," he said. The automatic arm swept in, placed the lid back on the world, and lifted it up to another glass chute, which took it straight back out into the sky above. It shot into the darkness between the other worlds, and within seconds, it resumed its normal size.

"Age does not grant wisdom—it only makes one go more slowly," the man murmured.

"Pardon?" Tuesday said.

His eyes clouded. "I'm not keeping up."

The man lifted several green cloths over stands to reveal more worlds. "Bad week, last week. It was last week, wasn't it? So tired. So terribly, terribly tired. Worries wash away better with soup."

He went to the table with its array of afternoon tea. She watched as the man cut himself a huge slice of carrot cake with cream cheese filling. Her mouth watered. She realized she was starving.

"How long have I been asleep?" Tuesday asked.

The old man spun about and stared at her as if seeing her for the first time. "What are you doing here? Nobody can be here! Get out! Get out!"

Tuesday ran to the desk and searched through the pile of notes as the man tried to shoo her away with his hands. There it was!

Girl. Fell from the sky. Asleep on the couch.

"This is me," she said, waving his note at him. "The girl on the couch. My name is Tuesday. I woke up."

The Gardener blinked and shook his head.

"Ah, yes, you're quite right. You've been asleep for

days. Or not. Time can be pressed, borrowed, or ripe. You only have to look out there. Some worlds go fast and some slower. Years are days, and days are minutes. It's an impossible calculation," he said, forking a piece of cake into his mouth. He ate slowly and thoughtfully before glancing again at Tuesday and saying, "You cannot be here. I have no idea how you fell, but fall you did, now that I recall it. This cake is delicious. Would you like some? And tea?"

"Yes, please," said Tuesday.

"You fell right onto my couch. I have never seen anything like it," the Gardener continued, extending a laden plate and a steaming cup to Tuesday.

"Thank you," she said. Gratefully she bit into the cake and found it delicious. The tea had an almost instantly recuperative effect, and Tuesday's thoughts cleared.

"I'm sorry to have arrived in a strange way," she said. "I didn't mean to. At least, I think I didn't. I was on my way to the City of Clocks, to look for a door. But, in truth, I was searching for you. The Librarian sent me."

The Gardener looked stunned.

"Lucille? Lucille sent you?"

"Madame Librarian sent me."

"She never did like her name," the man said with a mischievous smile. "Don't tell her I told you, will you?"

Tuesday took first the scroll with its purple seal from the pocket of her shorts. It was flattened and tattered. It had, after all, been on a long walk, camped overnight, been completely soaked, and survived a flock of vercaka. The man shook his head and refused to take it.

"This can't be right." He appeared suddenly very upset, as if Tuesday had told him to eat peas with his ice cream. He started wringing his hands and then noticed the word written there: POCKET.

He patted his various pockets and pulled out a piece of paper from inside his yellow jacket. He read it carefully to himself and then read it aloud to Tuesday, rather formally.

"Hello. I am the Gardener, and this is the Conservatory. I am losing my memory. I am behind in my work. I have sent my dog for help. The worlds are colliding, and this may have something to do with the fact that my faculties are fading. I'm waiting for help to arrive. I am certain help will come."

Tuesday nodded. "I think that's me," she said. "I am here to help. Please read this note."

The Gardener shoved his own note back into his pocket, took the Librarian's, and broke the seal. When he had finished reading it, he crumpled it up as if he were angry.

"You're much too young," he told Tuesday. "You can't."

"I have to," said Tuesday. "I promised Madame Librarian."

"Yes, yes. We all did at some point," he said harshly, and then all the fight went out of him and he slumped into silence.

"Being young is a fault that improves daily," he murmured. "No snowflake ever falls in the wrong place."

Another bolt of lightning flashed loudly between the colliding green and orange planets.

"Don't you think we should get to work?" said Tuesday. "People, animals, creatures of all kinds . . . well, they're getting hurt up there."

"I sent for help," said the Gardener, as if suddenly remembering. "My dog will be back soon."

"No, she won't," said Tuesday, pulling the dog's

collar from her shorts pocket and holding it out to the Gardener. "I'm so sorry . . . so very sorry to have to tell you this, but she was attacked by vercaka over the Peppermint Forest."

The Gardener's eyes filled with tears.

"Vercaka? There are no vercaka in that world. It's a safe route. She loved that world. It was once her home, of course."

"I don't think that anywhere is safe. Not the way things are."

"My dear old girl," he said, perching the cake plate precariously on his cup on the table and taking the collar outstretched in Tuesday's hand. "Is she all right? Is someone with her?"

"She's dead," said Tuesday, almost whispering these terrible words. "I'm so sorry."

"She . . . we . . . no . . . ," the Gardener said, gripping the collar and bringing it to his nose, where he smelled it. "Oh no! Then it's over. All good things must come to an end. All good things . . ."

His tears ran down his cheeks.

Tuesday, her own eyes blurry with tears, said, "I'm so sorry. I have a dog too. I understand. I really do. But it's not over. I truly am here to help."

"You have a dog . . . ," whispered the old man. "A Winged Dog?"

"Yes." Tuesday nodded.

"No snowflake ever falls in the wrong place," he said again. Then he began looking about. "Where is she? Your dog?"

"It's a he, and he's up there, out there, with Vivienne Small, I hope."

"You'll need him," said the Gardener.

"I know," said Tuesday. "I've never been anywhere without him. Only school."

"Oh dear. You are definitely too young for this. I was too young," the Gardener was saying. He had closed his eyes. "I should never have left her. I didn't realize. I didn't know how long forever would be. Forever is much longer when you're alone."

Great shards of blue fell off the green world. Lightning and fire were flaring and sizzling from the orange one.

"I loved her," the Gardener said. "I didn't understand how far we would be from each other."

Tuesday didn't think he was talking about his dog anymore. She thought he might have been talking about the Librarian. *My great love . . .*

"I don't know if this is the time to talk about all that," said Tuesday. "Please, you need to use your boathook."

"If you pick up the hook . . . ," the Gardener murmured.

Tuesday crossed the room and hesitated a moment, then bent down and grasped the handle of the boathook. "Tell me what to do!"

"If you pick up the hook . . . ," the Gardener repeated, and shook his head. He continued to grasp his dog's collar close and did not open his eyes.

"I got that bit," Tuesday called back.

"I mustn't let you. It would be a mistake."

The worlds above were sparking and crumpling together.

"Tell me what to do," Tuesday cried.

"But if you pick up the hook, then . . . ," said the Gardener, and slumped onto the yellow couch. "A clever person turns great troubles into little ones and little ones into none at all."

Tuesday levered the hook up into the sky, and it shot out toward the green and orange planets that were intent on destroying each other. Even though the worlds were so far away, Tuesday spotted a loop on the outer side of the orange one. She slid the hook through the loop and pulled with all her might. It felt heavy, but not impossible to move. As she held it fast, she watched the green world free itself and spin clear.

"I did it!" she called.

The Gardener opened his eyes and turned to her, staring.

He stood and walked toward her. "If you pick up the boathook, then it's forever."

"What's forever?" asked Tuesday, watching the sky to see if any other worlds were getting dangerously close to one another.

"The journey of forever starts with a single step," he said.

"I don't understand," said Tuesday.

"You, my dear, have just become the Gardener."

"That's not possible," Tuesday said. "You're the Gardener."

"No, I'm not. Not anymore." He sighed. "You should never have come. Never have picked up the boathook. I might have stopped you, but I . . ."

He looked perplexed, confused. Tuesday thought he might once again have forgotten who she was and how she'd arrived.

"I'm Tuesday. I fell from the sky," she said.

"You are the Gardener," he said, his face breaking suddenly into a radiant smile. "Congratulations! My, you're in for a wonderful time! I'm not sure it should be, but it must be. She sent help after all. It's a weak man who doubts the strength of a woman."

And then, as if he had remembered his age, he said, "I'm so terribly tired. I think if you'll excuse me, I'll sit down and have a rest."

"You can't . . . I mean, I'm not . . . I haven't the least idea what I'm doing!"

Tuesday stood holding the boathook, her mind a whirl of confusion. Some kind of terrible mistake was being made, but there wasn't anything she could do to stop it.

The old man regarded the sky.

"Is it night? Oh, yes, yes. How stupid of me. It's always night here. You'll get used to it."

He limped a little as he crossed the room, then turned back.

"A new Gardener. Ha! Good, good. What did you say your name was? And did you say you had a dog? Best call him. He's going to be essential." Glancing at his hand, he added, "Who the blazes is *Pocket*?"

Chapter Twenty

Even before the old man had fallen asleep in his chair, another world had trundled down the wider walkway, shrinking as it came. It shot through the glass chute and arrived in the inspection area in front of Tuesday, and the mechanical arm swung out and opened the world's glass lid. Bright lights went on.

"What?" Tuesday said to the world that waited there, open and ready for inspection. "I'm not the Gardener, you know. Anyone can see that he's confused. I'm only here to help. Just to help . . ."

Tentatively, Tuesday picked up the glasses the Gardener had been wearing, adjusted them to her eyes, and peered down into the world. Inside the world, time stood still. She saw people paused in the midst of mending nets on a sandy shore and palm trees leaning as though they were stopped in the middle of a brisk breeze. On the beach were several fishing boats and some fisher folk pulling in a net, but Tuesday hadn't the least idea what she was meant to do. There was a small town behind the beach. Nothing was tall, not the buildings nor the trees.

She looked deeper into the world and found at the outskirts of the town some very poor houses. Gently she lifted a roof of palm fronds and squinted down into the rooms. There was a chair and a bed. On the bed was a faded blanket and beside it a well-read newspaper. Tuesday noticed that some coals had spilled and the grass mat on the floor was smoldering and smoking. Nobody appeared to be home. She carefully removed the burning coals with the smallest tweezers and replaced the damaged mat with another that was hanging over a fence on the far side of the village. Then she replaced the roof and made it secure with a hammer and the tiniest nails she had ever seen. It wasn't a great job, but it was an improvement.

She was about to press the button that would replace

the world's lid when she noticed a fisherman far out at sea being circled by a school of sharks. His boat was only a skiff, and his sail was a patchwork of sacks. The man was very old. Should she remove the sharks? Or bring the fisherman back close to shore? She didn't know, and before she could decide, two worlds above her head smashed into each other at high speed and a searing flash lit up the dark sky. She tore off the glasses and ran to the boathook and attempted to pull one of the worlds away from the other, but they were crushed together, stuck. She heaved and heaved on the boathook until at last there was a shift. With all her strength, she levered the worlds apart, and they spun away, wobbling in a way that she thought looked extremely unsafe.

Tuesday was shaking with the effort and with worry. What was she even doing here? Was she really helping or simply making more of a mess of things? She thought of Baxterr, and tears sprang to her eyes. Where was he? And what was he going through? What kind of damage had the world of Vivienne Small suffered? Could whole worlds be destroyed, along with everyone inside them? Tears began to prick at her eyes. She realized that all the worlds in the sky were quivering.

"Stop that!" she shouted up to them. "You're not allowed to do that!"

Then she heard the sound of yet another world landing on the jetty. She watched a great orb of sand and swirling wind coming toward her, but it didn't reduce in size. The automatic arm attempted to pick it up and squeeze it into the tube. Tuesday winced as she heard the world creak and the automatic arm groan.

"Stop, stop!" she cried. She raced to the long bench and tried to find a control panel, but there was none. The storm world crashed into the side of the Conservatory, making everything shake.

"This is bad," said Tuesday. She rushed to the Gardener and knelt beside his chair.

"Mr. Gardener, Mr. Gardener. You have to wake up!" she cried. "Things are going wrong."

The Gardener stirred and opened his eyes. The small rest appeared to have done him good.

"Garnet. Did I tell you that? That's my name. I haven't thought of it in years. And you're the new Gardener, eh? Congratulations! Wonderful life it is, wonderful!"

He closed his eyes again.

"Garnet!" Tuesday said, shaking his shoulder. "You have to wake up!"

"Oh! The work of the Gardener is to garden," he said. "To garden is a game of division and multiplication. Of fractal geometry and organic geology."

"You're not making any sense," Tuesday said. "A world is stuck out there. It won't fit in the chute."

"Ah, so the task is too big, is it, Ms. Gardener?" he asked, swinging his legs around and sitting up.

"Tuesday," she said. "My name's Tuesday."

"Time to leave all that behind, I'm afraid. Life is not meant to be traveled backward."

"The world is too big," Tuesday said, rather impatiently.

"All things that happen out there are also happening in here," he said, patting his chest.

"You're still not making any sense," said Tuesday. "You have to come see."

"That I can do," said the Gardener, getting up out of his chair. "In fact, I feel better than I've felt in weeks. Months even."

And though he looked older, Tuesday noticed that he was more lucid. At the entrance to the Conservatory, he gazed at the storm world banging against the chute and gave her a sage smile.

"You must understand that you are not too small," he said. "Nor is the challenge too big."

"The world won't fit," said Tuesday. "You have to make it smaller."

"*You* have to make it smaller," he said.

"That's impossible," said Tuesday.

"You'd be surprised how many times I said those words myself when I first arrived here," he said.

"I'm only here to help you," said Tuesday. "I'm not here to take over. You know that, right? I mean, I'm not even a grown-up. I shouldn't be doing this. I don't know how."

"Doubt is always a bad idea," said Garnet. "It makes everything a bit . . ."

Above them, worlds were spinning away.

"Where are they going?" Tuesday asked.

"Who can say?" he said. "But until you become more certain, they won't come back. Which will cause all sorts of problems. Is your dog here yet?"

"Of course not," said Tuesday. "He doesn't even know I'm alive. How would he ever find me here?"

"I understand everything is uncertain. But you will learn certainty," he said. "Did you ever notice that the Librarian and the Library are connected? She knows every book that is being written at any moment. Every book that has ever been written. There is nothing she does not know about books. Writers are simply the sunshine and the rain that make books grow. In the same way, the Gardener must know every world. You aren't expected to know it all straightaway. Yet you will be surprised how soon you become acquainted. There's a pattern to it all. Some days are maintenance days. Some days are for visiting other worlds. Some days are for finding a favorite lake and fishing. This whole universe is yours. Can you imagine the wonder of what you will see? Of whom you will meet?"

Tuesday shook her head miserably. The storm world was banging against the side of the building again, and this time several items fell from a nearby shelf with the impact.

"In the meantime, Ms. Gardener," Garnet said, "you need to focus."

"I can't focus. There's a world right there currently experiencing . . . what? A sandstorm?"

"And possibly a black blizzard, a khamsin, a sirocco," he said.

"I can't do this. I ought to be home with my parents. I ought to—" Tuesday took a deep breath and determined not to cry. "I need my dog."

"Of course. Where did you say you left him?"

"In the City of Clocks."

"Ah, in the world of Vivienne Small. Excellent world. Truly elegant mountains. And those dogs! If that awful fellow Mothwood had had his way, they would have become slaves. But I have protected them."

"The Winged Dogs? Where?"

"Oh, I hid them. Such beautiful creatures. My, how they've flourished too. Nothing so loyal as a Winged Dog. Of course, you know that. We'll find your dog later, will we? When you've calmed down. Mustn't go hauling in worlds when you're in a state."

"I don't understand. Hauling in worlds? What do you mean?"

"Ah! You've been at work, I see," Garnet said, observing the world with the palm trees and the fisherman inside which Tuesday had been gardening. "Excellent, excellent."

He picked up a large magnifying glass and peered about.

"Nicely done, nicely done. What did you think about the sharks?"

"I didn't know," she said. "I thought about picking up the boat and bringing it in closer to the shore."

"That could have ruined a wonderful story," he said. "The writer wouldn't thank you."

"I did save that house from a fire," Tuesday offered, pointing.

"So you did." Garnet nodded. "Santiago—he's the fisherman—would thank you if he knew. But he never will. Righto, I think that one can go out again. Push that button there."

Tuesday touched the button Garnet indicated, and the mechanical arm replaced the world's lid and carried the globe to the exit chute, where it shot up and out and was soon back among the constellation of worlds above.

Garnet said, "Do you think you might be ready for that world out there?"

Tuesday thought the waiting storm looked a little smaller and more manageable.

"You might even like to leave a little message."

"A message?" Tuesday asked.

"Yes," he said. "Sometimes I leave a rainbow when I'm finished. Nobody but me knows what it's about, but still, it's my small way of letting everyone know that everything is all right. You can never feel too worried when you see a rainbow, no matter what is happening."

"Happening?" said Tuesday.

"Well, you might see battles happening. You might see terrible tragedies that will touch your heart, or love stories. You might see vicious creatures and valiant heroines. These are worlds where the magnificence of imagination is alive and at work every day."

"They never see you?"

"Not during routine maintenance. No, no. Everything stops. For everyone down there, time stands still. Ready?"

Tuesday nodded, and the world of roiling wind and sand outside was suddenly in the chute and rolling around the room above them until it popped out onto a stand on the worktable.

Garnet handed her a very small vacuum cleaner and the special microscope glasses. Tuesday adjusted them, turned on the vacuum cleaner, and, at a nod from Garnet, sucked up the dust storm to reveal fields of bright yellow grass. To one side was a great city made of tents. Flags were flying. There were hundreds of horses. Beyond the city lay a desert of iridescent sand.

"I always find, in this world, the grass needs trimming," Garnet said, handing Tuesday a tiny electric razor. She turned it on and proceeded to mow the yellow grass.

"Then remove those reeds that always try to clog up that river."

Tuesday did as he suggested.

All this time, Garnet had not once looked into the world. He was standing leaning against the table, tiny and wizened, but his eyes were bright.

"Next," he said, "you'll need to replace a bit of sand. I like to add a few ripples and patterns." He handed Tuesday a vial of sand and a pin that she used to create waves across the desert.

"A little rain will help the wildflowers bloom," said Garnet, handing Tuesday a miniature watering can.

He then handed her a final spray can. "Try that," he said. "Up in the sky."

Tuesday sprayed, and the most beautiful rainbow appeared. It gave her such a surprise that she stopped halfway.

"Oh, don't worry about that," said Garnet. "It's always difficult to get a perfect arc."

"This is fun, but you will be taking your job back soon, won't you?" asked Tuesday. "After all, you're the one who knows everything."

Garnet smiled and carefully took the microscope glasses off Tuesday's face. "Ms. Gardener," he said.

"Tuesday," she reminded him.

"I was so worried when you arrived. I thought the

Librarian had made a terrible mistake. I would never have allowed you to become the Gardener. You're so young. I suspect you have books you want to write yourself. You haven't yet fallen in love. I'm sure you have a family waiting for you. But you picked up the boathook before I had even a moment to warn you. And you pulled those worlds apart as if you knew exactly what to do. The way you tidied up that world, and the one before it, it's as if you've been doing it forever, and I think Lucille was right."

"Really?"

"She was the love of my life, you know."

Tuesday blushed.

"She will always be the love of my life. She and North Wind, my dog."

Tuesday again thought of Baxterr. Looking up into the sky, she wondered how—even if she knew which world was Vivienne's—she would bring him here.

"Good point, good point," Garnet said, as if he had read her mind. "I'm beginning to run out of steam again, so I'd best show you the doors right away."

As they crossed the room, Tuesday noticed that the table, which had not so long ago been laid out with cake and teapots, was set for dinner. Tuesday smelled mushroom soup and possibly a lasagna.

"Does it just arrive?" Tuesday asked.

"Three meals a day, plus morning and afternoon tea. You'll never starve."

"Who made this place?" Tuesday said, suddenly in awe at everything she was discovering.

"Well, a writer, I imagine," said the old Gardener, and he chuckled. "Whoever it was, they were thorough. There's always hot water, good towels, clean linen. I do so like fresh sheets—don't you? Take your hook."

Tuesday lifted the boathook.

"And let's grab that world . . . there. Yes, that nice small one. Can you see the loop?"

Tuesday could. Effortlessly, she slid the hook into the loop on the side of a small world in which she could glimpse green and gold fields, the occasional farmhouse and barn.

"Tow it down to the end," Garnet said, nodding to the opposite jetty.

All of this was surprisingly easy, and the world latched on to the end of the jetty as if by magnetism.

"Ready?" Garnet said, his eyes twinkling. "This

is my favorite part of gardening. You must never neglect this part of the work. Walk in the worlds, learn their geography, their atmosphere, their essence. Learn how things should be, speak to people on your travels. I never tire of this. Never."

The glass door onto the jetty opened automatically, and Tuesday followed Garnet to the waiting world. To her surprise, the world had a timber door. It appeared quite unremarkable but for a small brass plaque etched with a picture of a cobweb that had the word TERRIFIC woven into it. Tuesday's eyes lit up.

"We won't stay long. Only a glimpse today," Garnet said. "Once I'm gone, you'll have all the time in the world."

Tuesday hardly heard what he said, so eager was she to open the door. She blinked in wonder as she found herself in a barn. There was the smell of manure and the sound of a horse whinnying. There was a clean, chubby pig in a stall, and Tuesday thought she saw a rat's tail flicker beneath the feed trough. Garnet pointed to one corner of a large open doorway, where a spider rested in the middle of a beautiful web.

"Is it . . . really?" said Tuesday, amazed.

"It is." Garnet nodded. "Never forget to close the door behind you, will you?"

Tuesday glanced back at the door they had come through, and it appeared a very ordinary barn door.

"What would happen if someone from this world went through that door?" she asked.

"Oh, they'd end up out in the pen with the geese," Garnet said.

Tuesday breathed it all in.

"I feel as if I already know this world," Tuesday sighed. "It's one of my favorites."

"This is a key world, Ms. Gardener. The first time a writer creates a whole new idea, a key world is made. And it becomes like a sun in a solar system. When writers come along and are inspired by that world, their worlds are then like planets circling the sun. No less important, but related."

"Is Vivienne Small's world a key world?" Tuesday asked.

"Of course," he said. "Come, come. Let's be getting home."

"My home is a long, long way from here," said Tuesday with a pang.

"Nonsense," Garnet said. "It's through here." And he led Tuesday back out of the barn and onto the jetty. At the glass door, he pulled a lever, and she watched the world spin away and fly back up into the constellations above. Returning to the open-roofed Conservatory, she noticed that Garnet had lost the spring in his step and begun once again to stoop.

"Keep on, won't you? While I sleep," Garnet said.

He settled onto the couch, closed his eyes, and then half opened them. His body was so fragile that Tuesday worried he might never get up again.

"The last thing you need to know," he said, "is that you must not be distracted or diverted. No matter who you meet or what you do out there, you hold all this together until such time as a new Gardener comes. The boathook is yours, and yours alone, until someone comes with a willingness to wield it in your stead. Until then, you must keep on. Or all of this will end."

He put his feet up very slowly and closed his eyes. Without opening them again, he said, "Why don't you have a little rest too? Hmm? Because it's always night doesn't mean it isn't night."

Sleep. Tuesday felt as if she'd already slept for days. So she sprawled instead on the blue rug in the center of the room and stared up into the dazzling, swirling firmament above the Conservatory.

So many worlds, so many lives. Watching the worlds spiral and spin, Tuesday realized that any book she could think of would have a world, and any world she could think of, she could visit. The thought of it made her mind stretch with possibility. Then she began to think of all the things that she would never do if she stayed to be the Gardener.

She would no longer go to school, or sleep in her bed at Brown Street. She would no longer make up stories on her baby blue typewriter, nor fly out windows on silvery thread. Worse than that, she would no longer curl up in bed reading books with Serendipity, and she would never again eat one of Denis's blueberry pancakes. And how would anyone ever find her here? Who else might ever come to take this job from her? She understood it was a vital job. A job that meant books stayed alive forever. She too might live here forever. In the midst of all these story worlds. And never go home. The thought of that made her heart ache so badly that she cried.

Chapter Twenty-One

"Doggo," she whispered, "I would feel so much better if you were here."

Above her, two large worlds passed right over her head, grinding and grumbling as they scraped at each other's sides. From farther away, there were the sounds of collisions and explosions. Flashes of yellow, green, and red burst like fireworks inside distant worlds. The sudden brightness speared into the Conservatory, where the lights that illuminated the workbenches and jetties had dimmed down, as if they knew Garnet wanted to sleep.

Tuesday looked up at the sky and worried. It was

supposed to be the Gardener's job to tend to the worlds, to keep them calm and separate. But things were still going wrong, and the task of making everything go right felt immense and impossible. She thought of the world of Vivienne Small and hoped with all her heart that Baxterr and Vivienne were all right.

Tuesday closed her eyes and breathed as evenly as she could. At last, the worlds in the sky had settled a little, and Tuesday drifted into a sleep full of dreams about Serendipity and Denis and blueberry pancakes. She had no way of knowing how much time had passed when she woke again, this time to a small, curious sound that was coming not from the sky above but from inside the room. *Tap, tap . . . tap, tap, tappety, tap . . .*

In the darkness, Tuesday pricked up her ears. It sounded like someone was walking about the Conservatory, but they were moving too fast for it to be Garnet. And a snore from the yellow couch confirmed that it wasn't him.

Tuesday stood up, and the lights in the room began to brighten.

"Gracious!" cried somebody in surprise.

And there, over by the workbench and staring around in a rather alarmed fashion, was a small person. From the waist down, he was covered in gleaming black fur, while from the waist up, he wore nothing except a fluffy red scarf that was knotted tightly around his neck. His curling hair was as dark as the fur on his legs, and out of it poked two small, knobbly horns like a goat's. He had a lively face with a pointy beard. His umbrella was in ribbons.

"Hello?" said Tuesday, blinking in disbelief.

The small, goatlike person stared, then took one or two steps toward her. His dainty hoof steps rang out, *tap-tap*, on the polished timber floor. It really was—*he* really was—a faun, Tuesday realized. A very particular faun.

"Oh . . . ah . . . ," he said, nervously. "Greetings, young lady. I wonder if you might, perchance, be able to tell me . . . ah . . . whereabouts it is exactly that I find myself?"

"Mr. *Tumnus*?" Tuesday stammered. She glanced up at the sky in amazement, then looked back at the faun. "Are you really Mr. Tumnus?"

The faun smiled in a polite yet mystified way.

"As it happens, I am. Have we met before?"

Tuesday barely managed to keep herself from hugging him. Instead, she held out her hand and shook his, smiling with delight.

"I'm so sorry, but I don't recall—" he said.

"I can't tell you how lovely it is to finally meet you," Tuesday said.

The faun frowned.

"So, we've not met before. Am I dead, then? I think I must be. There was an appalling crash and then one side of my home was ripped away, and the next thing you know, I was flying clean out into the snow. I tried to catch hold of the lamppost as I fell, but they're wretchedly slippery things, you know, and I couldn't hold on. I appear, though, still to be breathing. Is that natural, when one is dead?"

"You're not dead," Tuesday reassured him. "You're in the Conservatory. You've . . . well, it's hard to explain. You've fallen out of your world. I wonder if it's a key world. Of course it is. It would have to be. Oh, I'm sorry, I'm talking to myself. You see, I'm the new Gardener, and unless something truly terrible has happened to your world, we can probably get you back to it. I might be able fix it. Your world, I mean. If I really try."

Mr. Tumnus looked utterly perplexed.

"All those up there," said Tuesday pointing, "each one of them is a world. Yours is there somewhere."

Mr. Tumnus stood, dumbstruck, peering upward. After a while he held a hand to his head and said, "I think I need to sit down."

"It is rather a lot to take in," Tuesday agreed, and she ushered Mr. Tumnus to one of the seats beside the dining table.

Since she had only just woken up, Tuesday expected the food under the glass dome would be something breakfasty, like a bowl of porridge or bananas with yogurt. Instead, what she found when she lifted the dome were some lightly boiled eggs, sardines on toast, a teacake beautifully dusted with sugar, and a pot of tea.

"Are you hungry, Mr. Tumnus?" Tuesday asked.

The faun took in the spread, and the sight of it brightened him up. "In fact, I believe I am a little peckish. Despite my fall. Or perhaps because of it. I'm not dead, you say? Well, that is something. I'm sorry . . . what did you say your name was?"

"Tuesday," said Tuesday.

"Oh, Tuesday," said Mr. Tumnus. "That is my

favorite day of the week! Excellent for beginning things. Much better than Mondays, I always say. Mondays are good for warming up to what needs to be done on Tuesday, don't you find?"

Tuesday smiled and poured the tea, and the two began to talk as if they had been friends for years. Which, of course, in a way, they had. Before long, there was nothing left on the table but eggshells and crumbs and empty plates and teacups, and Tuesday and the faun—their stomachs quite content—were standing in the center of the Conservatory staring up into the mass of worlds above their heads, searching for the one that belonged to Mr. Tumnus.

"How do we know which one is mine?" Mr. Tumnus asked.

"I wish I knew," Tuesday said. "I've only recently taken over the job, you see, and I still have an awful lot to learn. That's the old Gardener, over there."

She pointed to where Garnet was still peacefully sleeping on his yellow couch.

"I don't want to wake him, if I can help it," Tuesday said, again searching the sky. "Where would it be? Where?"

Mr. Tumnus gave a little laugh.

"You know, I once met a little girl. Younger than you, but not entirely unlike you, I must say. And she used to say that my world was in a cupboard. Isn't that funny? I always told her that it must have been a rather large cupboard." He gave a small, goatish laugh.

"That's it," Tuesday said. She felt as if a lightbulb had switched on inside her head. "That is precisely it. Mr. Tumnus, you're a genius."

And almost straightaway then, she saw it—a huge, mahogany-colored world limping around on its orbit. As Tuesday peered more closely at it, she saw that its surface was decorated with detailed carvings of oak leaves and acorns and animals of all shapes and sizes. Part of its curving side had been smashed open, leaving edges of splintered timber. She would be getting that one in for routine maintenance, Tuesday thought, as soon as she had got Mr. Tumnus back home. She hoisted her boathook and slid its far end into the world's golden loop.

"Extraordinary," breathed Mr. Tumnus, as he watched Tuesday tow the world down to the far end of the walkway. "And that is my world? That is how it appears, on the outside?"

"I guess it is," Tuesday said.

"Oh, well done, Miss Tuesday. Well done, indeed. Wonderful job! Remarkable," Mr. Tumnus said, giving a small leap and landing neatly on his shiny cloven hoofs.

The damaged world clicked into place. Tuesday set down her boathook and slid her arm through the crook of the faun's elbow.

"Shall we?" she said.

"We shall," he agreed.

I think you can probably guess the first thing Tuesday and Mr. Tumnus encountered when they passed through the door at the end of the walkway. I expect you know that it was a row of thick fur coats. What you might not guess is that when Tuesday rather breathlessly took one of the coats down from its hanger, put it on, and slid her hands into its pockets, she found there two squares of chocolate wrapped in a piece of tattered silver foil. She thought the chocolate must be very, very old—much too old to eat—but precious in any case.

Tuesday and Mr. Tumnus pushed through until

fur turned to fir, and Tuesday smelled the Christmas-like smell of pine needles and felt the scrunch of snow under her feet. The weather was calm, but ahead of them, Tuesday saw evidence that a vicious wind had blown through the place, presumably when the side of the world had torn open. Trees had been uprooted, and a lamppost a short way ahead of them had been twisted and bent over on a strange angle. She made a mental note to fix these things as soon as she could.

"Oh, dear," Mr. Tumnus said, pointing. On the other side of a stand of damaged trees was a gaping hole in the side of the world. Beyond that was a wedge of dark sky with other worlds drifting by.

"Tsk, tsk," tutted Mr. Tumnus.

"Don't worry," said Tuesday. "I'll put it at the top of my list. For now, though, is there somewhere else you can go? Until I've had a chance to mend your house?"

"Yes, yes. Don't bother about me. I'll be right as rain," he said. "My sister will take me in. And when my house is repaired, you will come for tea, won't you? I'll toast crumpets."

Tuesday smiled, then she and the faun said a fond farewell. Mr. Tumnus tucked his useless umbrella under one arm, and Tuesday watched as he trotted off through the snow, the ends of his red scarf flapping in the wind.

Returning the fur coat to its hanger, Tuesday sighed. Although she hadn't exactly meant to become the Gardener, she had to admit that the job had some spectacular perks. She stepped back inside the walkway and released the mahogany world into the sky. The gash in the side of that world was horrible, and Tuesday determined to fix it as soon as she could. But there was one thing she had to do first. Something that couldn't wait any longer.

The lights in the Conservatory had dimmed while she had been away, but as soon as she stepped back inside, the room grew steadily lighter. Beneath the glass dome on the table was a steaming cup of hot chocolate and two plump marshmallows on a saucer. She drank, and ate, and grew warm again. Over on the yellow couch, Garnet slept on.

Tuesday set down her empty cup and took a deep, determined breath.

"You can do this," she whispered to herself.

She picked up her boathook and stood on the rug in the center of the Conservatory, staring up into the sky that teemed with worlds. She had found Mr. Tumnus's world, and she would find Vivienne's. She thought of Vivienne and Baxterr, of the Peppermint Forest, of the Mabanquo River and the Mountains of Margolov. She sent her thoughts out to them. And then she saw it. Far, far away was a world of blue skies that was spinning about with another world squashed hard into it. The far side of the world appeared to have mountains breaking through it. It had to be the world of Vivienne Small. She was certain of it.

"I'm coming to get you, doggo," she whispered.

Tuesday gripped the boathook with sweating palms and felt it lurch out into the sky in the direction of the conjoined worlds. If only she could catch the loop on the side of Vivienne's world, she would be able to tow it in to the walkway.

Well, Madame Librarian, thought Tuesday, *I might find that doorway after all. From the other side!*

Tuesday's heart was beating fast, and the faster it went, the more rapidly the other worlds in the sky began to whoosh and whirl around the ones she sought. She must remain calm. She must not lose sight of the world of Vivienne Small.

Taking long, deep breaths, Tuesday levered the boathook out into space. And then, with a flick and a flourish, she snared the golden loop on the underside of that dented blue-sky world. She mustered all her strength and gave the boathook one almighty heave.

Chapter Twenty-Two

In the City of Clocks the day of battle had arrived.

Four colossal catapults had been wheeled, under cover of night, into Letitia Mabanquo Square. There came a breeze, as if in warning. It scurried about, whispering in door locks, rattling windows, twisting leaves, and turning weather vanes. Then it settled, and the vercaka came.

Horns sounded from each of the city's four gates, and every face, young and old, turned to the sky. No one who stood in the shadow of the swirling flock massing above the beautiful spires, could fail to realize that they were hideously outnumbered. Despite the days of preparation, despite the contributions of every child, woman, and man (except Nigel Finkwatter), there were so many more birds than they were prepared for.

There was no time to admire the sunrise, or lament the lack of sleep, or feel how fast the heart beats at such moments, because the vercaka were coming in the hundreds, screeching and diving. The mayor gave the signal. The first of the catapults launched its load high above the square. There was a great flurry as fish, each with a piece of gold in its belly, shot high into the air. They were like silver fireworks, and the townspeople gasped. The birds dived and swooped and scooped up the fish, gobbling them down, squawking with rage when another vercaka stole their catch. And then the birds who had eaten the poisoned fish began, one by one, to fall from the sky.

The mayor's heart leapt into her mouth. The plan was working!

The next catapult launched, and more of the fish flew up into the sky, again catching the early sun, dancing on the morning light. For three days, the residents had captured every fish that had flopped out of any tap. For three days, every sink and bath and bucket had been filled with fish. Many, many fish had given their lives to save the city. And then adults and children alike had used their fingers to stuff coins into the mouths of those fish.

At vantage points across the city, guards had been stationed. They shot at the birds, their arrows searching for the softest places behind the birds' eyes, under their chins, in their bottoms. This infuriated the vercaka, but before they could attack the guards, another catapult was released, and again the birds swarmed. They massed on the flying fish, savaging one another in an attempt to feed. More of the vile birds swallowed the gold in each fish and then, only seconds later, plummeted from the sky. Poisoned vercaka rolled off rooftops and crashed onto cobblestones; they fell into lanes and backyards, splashed into ponds and fountains, their legs turned up, their eyes open and empty.

The toll was not only on their side. On the streets lay injured guards, bleeding from wounds from the terrible beaks of the vercaka. Many people had been snatched up and carried away, while others had been released high over the city and had fallen to terrible, bone-crunching deaths.

Have you ever thrown a chip to a seagull? One minute there's one bird; the next, there are one hundred cawing and screeching. The vercaka were exactly the same. It was as if the City of Clocks had sounded a bell for feeding time. Wheeling and circling, the vercaka hunted more fish, and when they couldn't find fish, they snatched up any person or cat and gulped them down. Children who had snuck out ran terrified back to their homes, pursued by snapping jaws and vicious claws.

Dead vercaka fell from the sky, landing with thumps and thuds all over the city, but their fellow vercaka took no notice of these deaths, nor what might be causing them. They appeared to have forgotten their nasty words. Instead of curses and insults, they only said, "Want more, eat more, more, more, more."

Foul-smelling poo dropped from their bodies in great gushes, splashing onto spires and rooftops and streets, turning them slippery and green.

"More fish," they shrieked. "More, more, more."

Vivienne and Baxterr saw all this from their vantage point on a low balcony above the doors of the

council chambers. Vivienne fired arrow after arrow while, beside her, the mayor raised a trumpet-shaped tube to her lips. Her voice echoed out to the people in the square and atop the buildings, as well as to those hiding with their children in their homes.

Let not your courage fail you,
Be valiant, stout, and bold,
And it will soon avail you,
My loyal hearts of gold.
Huzzah, my valiant citizens, again I say huzzah!
'Tis nobly done—the day's our own—huzzah, huzzah!

"Huzzah! Huzzah!" called back the guards and residents.

Even as the mayor rallied her troops, there remained enough vercaka to darken the sky. Then came the cats.

A tidal wave of tabby, tortoiseshell, white, black, gray, blue, and brown swept through the city streets, and within moments the rooftops were alive. The cats leapt onto the backs of the swarming birds: one, two, three, five, seven on every vercaka. They dug their claws in hard and bit into wings, necks, and legs.

A thousand vercaka screamed and shot upward,

trying to dislodge their biting, clawing passengers. But the cats persisted, and the vercaka flew higher, farther, up through the sky and into the world above. Once they had breached that world, the vercaka kept flying, the cats riding them like demons into the distance and far out of sight. Neither those cats nor those vercaka ever returned.

Within minutes, a fresh flock of vercaka was circling the city. Once more, they began tormenting the town with their words.

"You have bad breath."

"Your hair is falling out."

"You are a liar, and everyone knows it."

"Your children hate you."

"Your mother never wanted you."

"You will never succeed."

"Your town is lost."

"You will be dead and forgotten."

Tarquin and Harlequin flew their farouche up to the mayor on the balcony.

"The time has come," said Harlequin.

"We have this last chance," said Vivienne.

"We must not delay," said Tarquin.

The mayor nodded. And then a most extraordinary

thing was wheeled into the square. It was a single enormous fish, poised upright on a launching platform. At least it resembled a fish, but it was actually, upon close inspection, fashioned from silver paper, and made strong and sturdy for the purpose. Vivienne watched as guards ran in to light the base. To begin with, there was only the fizzling of fuses and a little smoke wafting from the huge fish. Then it took off with a deafening *whoosh*.

The giant fish flew straight up into the air, and the last of the vercaka lifted their dull eyes and stared, mesmerized. Their hunger still keen, every one of them took flight after it. But the fish was too fast. It was going too high. They couldn't possibly reach it. Still they climbed after it, and the fish went faster. A hush fell over the city. Faces leaned out of windows. Archers put down their bows to gaze up into the sky. The mayor held her breath, and Vivienne and Baxterr stood with heads back and mouths open. Waiting. Waiting . . .

The giant fish exploded, and out flew the last of the gold coins of every citizen in the City of Clocks and every donation that had come to them from beyond. The sky was filled with a shower of gold coins falling down, down, down onto the swarm of vercaka below.

The vercaka swooped and ate, gobbling down the coins, their only thought being *food, food, food.* Even the breeze rose to the occasion, tossing the falling coins about, which only tantalized the vercaka even more.

Nigel Finkwatter, who had been watching the battle from the turret of his home, saw the falling gold and scrambled out onto his roof to gather it up. Then he saw it had also fallen onto the roofs of his neighbors. They were all much too busy watching the battle to notice him. So Finkwatter stuffed coins into every pocket. He took off his jacket and used it as a sack into which he could scoop yet more coins. Then he took off his socks and shoes and crammed them with coins. He sang as he went, surprised that he had not anticipated the profit that could be made from a battle.

About him vercaka were dropping like flies.

"I think we're going to be all right," Vivienne said to the mayor.

She spoke too soon. For at that very moment, two vercaka, bigger and possibly wiser than the rest, swooped in over the town. They were not distracted by silver fish and golden coins. One of them saw a man on a roof with no shoes or socks and scooped him up, flipped him about, and swallowed him feet first.

Before he disappeared down its gullet, he was heard to call out, "Don't you know who I am? I am Nigel Finkwatter, I am—" And then he was gone. The bird flew on only for a moment, before it was poisoned by the gold in Finkwatter's jacket and socks and pockets. The vercaka fell like a boulder into the Mabanquo River and was eaten by fish, which was entirely appropriate.

The very last of the birds soared over the Letitia Mabanquo statue and the piles of dead vercaka that lay all around it. On the balcony above the council chambers, Miranda Templeton was putting to her lips a horn with which she intended to announce the city's victory. Perhaps it was her pink jacket, or perhaps it was the height of the mayor's fascinating hat, but whatever it was, something about Miranda Templeton caught the interest of the last vercaka. With deadly intent, it swooped in and plucked her up as if she were a cherry on a tree.

Vivienne leapt onto Baxterr's shoulders. "Come on, doggo!" she cried.

Baxterr spread his wings and sped through the air like a missile. Vivienne could see the mayor screaming and kicking in an attempt to get free. Vivienne's first arrow struck the vercaka's head, her second glanced off one of its grubby wings, but still the bird refused to let go its catch. It banked and then soared toward the other world in the dented sky. It flew faster, wings beating furiously, but Baxterr caught up with it. Growling and snarling, the great dog ripped at the bird's wing with his teeth, and for a moment, it appeared that the vercaka would let the mayor go. But it did not. It circled about and mounted a counterattack, hurtling toward Baxterr and Vivienne.

Vivienne screamed, "I think it's changed its mind about what it wants for dinner."

As the bird flew at Baxterr, its beak opened and Miranda fell. Baxterr changed course, plunging down toward the falling figure of the mayor.

"Food, food, food," squawked the maddened vercaka.

Baxterr swooped underneath Miranda, who fell onto his wide back, her hat all askew but, amazingly, still firmly pinned to her hair.

"Hold on!" Vivienne cried.

Then the vercaka was upon them. Vivienne and Miranda braced for the impact of the bird's outstretched talons.

But then the world jolted. Everything moved, though not in any way anyone had ever experienced before. Seventeen faces fell from seventeen clocks. Twelve spires crumbled. The Mabanquo River lurched and slopped and, in one movement, washed away jetties and docks and nests of ducks. There was a most peculiar grinding noise, and then, as people watched—wide-eyed and with mouths agape—the huge world that had crashed into theirs slid away. Shards of ice fell from the sky, and one pierced the very last ver-caka, stabbing it right through its head. The creature dropped onto the upward-pointing finger of Letitia Mabanquo in her shimmering fountain.

And at that moment, Baxterr, with Vivienne and the mayor upon his back, pricked up his ears and gave a whimper.

"What is it, doggo?" Vivienne asked. "Are you hurt? No?"

"Did you hear something?" asked Miranda anxiously. "Is it more birds?"

It was not more birds, and Baxterr had not heard anything, precisely. What he had felt was not a sound, nor a smell, but a *feeling*, as if Tuesday were close by. Baxterr peered down into the city, where the residents were beginning to venture out from their homes and turn their faces upward to gaze at the strange and beautiful sight of the other world disappearing into the sky, but Tuesday was not among them. He sniffed deeply. He could detect nothing of Tuesday's scent. Yet she had been close. He was certain. But where?

Down in Mabanquo Square, people watched as the blue sphere they had always thought of as their sky sealed itself once more. Into the awed silence that followed, a horn sounded. And then an enormous, magnificent, golden Winged Dog soared to the square. The people of the City of Clocks clapped and cheered and broke into song. It was a truly magnificent sight, and nobody who saw Baxterr come in to land beside the fountain could possibly have guessed how heavy was his heart in that moment. For although he had helped to save the City of Clocks from the vercaka, all Baxterr could think of was that he had failed to rescue the person he loved the most.

High above the Conservatory, the world of Vivienne Small swayed against the far end of Tuesday's boathook. It felt like having Jupiter on the end of a string. Already the icy ocean world had drifted away and out of sight in the swirling mass of globes. Tuesday watched in wonder as the glassy edge of Vivienne's sky righted itself to an almost perfect curve. Still piercing the sky on one side were the jagged peaks of the Mountains of Margolov. She would need to fix this the next time the world came in for maintenance.

Still holding the loop of the world fast with her boathook, Tuesday wondered where Baxterr and Vivienne were and what they had been doing at the moment the worlds came apart. As she tried to pull the world down, a multitude of other worlds got in the way, each one of them moving at its own speed. Some of the smaller ones orbited around like racing cars on a track, while some of the larger ones drifted by in lazy figure eights. It was like a huge three-dimensional puzzle.

On the couch, Garnet stirred a little in his sleep.

"You are the sky," he muttered. "Everything else is just weather."

And while this made little sense to Tuesday, it nevertheless soothed her nerves. She pulled on the boathook, causing Vivienne's world to inch down through the sky. She only narrowly missed a tiny world full of bright red flames, then had to rapidly swerve sideways to avoid a very large, dark world that sparkled with galaxies of stars.

"The obstacle is the path," Garnet muttered in his sleep.

Tuesday turned back to her task, concentrating as hard as she could.

"The obstacle is the path," she repeated, trying to keep her breathing even and her gaze focused.

And then something surprising was happening. The other worlds were shifting about, seeming to make a pathway. Tuesday drew the world down, nearer and nearer, and soon it was so close, looming above the Conservatory, that it obscured the view of almost all the other worlds. Hauling on the boathook, Tuesday towed it to the end of the narrow jetty, where she felt it click into place. She let the boathook fall to the floor and took off at a run.

"I'm coming, doggo," she said.

Chapter Twenty-Three

The City of Clocks lost many people, many cats, and even more fish on the day the vercaka were defeated. All were mourned, and all were honored. In time, some new features were added to Letitia Mabanquo's fountain. Standing on her shoulder was a cat, and at her feet were two gleaming silver fish.

For days after the battle, the City of Clocks was alight with fires burning the dead vercaka. ("If only they tasted delicious," so many people commented, but those who had tried vercaka assured their friends that they were tough old birds with a nasty bitter taste to their flesh.) There was bird slime to clean up and many buildings and clocks to repair; there were ponds and fountains to scrub clean.

Also, there was a lot of celebrating and feasting to be done. The mayor put on a great banquet in the square and invited every resident, cat and human alike. They ate and played music and read poetry, told stories, and danced as if every one of them were young, until morning.

Every coin that could be collected from the insides of vercaka or the few fish that had fallen into gutters and had gone uneaten, and the coins that had fallen from the fish rocket, were gathered up and redistributed. It was a thing of wonder for years to come, and caused many songs to be sung and legends to be born, that the gold that was returned to each resident was far more than any of them had contributed in the first place. And if, in the years to come, Mrs. Finkwatter was happier and her children better fed, it was certainly not because she kept all the gold in her husband's den to herself. Where it went, only she and the mayor would ever know.

By the time the official histories of the great battle of the City of Clocks were written, most of the historians had decided that the great Winged Dog that had soared through the skies and alighted in the square at the moment of victory had been a vision, a magnificent illusion shared by the overjoyed citizens. After all, said the historians, the dog had never again been seen in the skies above the City of Clocks, nor even in its streets. There were people who said they had seen the dog shrink to the size of a large tomcat, but the historians argued that even if this had been so, no such animal had ever again been seen in the city streets. Some recalled that at the height of the victory celebrations they had seen Vivienne Small, battle weary and bleeding, walking out of the square in the direction of the home of the mayor. And ever after, when anybody asked Vivienne about the great Winged Dog, she only shrugged her shoulders and said, "What dog?"

For the record, what happened was this. As Vivienne and Baxterr trod the road between the square and the mayor's house, Baxterr caught a scent that caused him to lift his dejected head.

You may not ever have thought of this, but one of the reasons blind dogs, and deaf dogs, get around so well is that what dogs see and hear isn't even the half of it. It's what they can smell that really matters. Dogs' sense of smell is so good that they can even smell if you're happy or sad, anxious or angry. A dog will never be fooled by one identical twin pretending to be the other, because to a dog, every single person in the world has a smell as unique as a fingerprint. And all dogs can smell out their special person, even if they are underwater, or quite deep underground.

"Ruff, ruff, ruff, ruff!" barked Baxterr, dashing ahead of Vivienne and then stopping abruptly at a door.

"What is it, doggo?" Vivienne asked.

The door was quite ordinary. Painted green, it was set into the garden wall of the mayor's house. Being a garden door, it had no number, nor—Vivienne noticed—a handle. She stared at it and then at Baxterr, who was shivering with excitement. She remembered this door. She had climbed the wall, but the door led only into the mayor's garden.

"Doggo? What is it?" Vivienne asked.

Baxterr was worrying his nose into the gap under the door, as if he could smell rabbit or blueberry pancakes.

"What is it, doggo?" Vivienne laughed. "What are you trying to tell me?"

As you know, Baxterr was a dog of exceedingly good manners. But he forgot every single one of those manners when the green door to the mayor's garden swung open and out stepped Tuesday. He hurled himself into her arms with the energy of a puppy, licking her all over her face, and she held him so tight she almost squeezed the breath out of him.

"I know, I know," Tuesday cried.

Baxterr kept on licking her cheek, but if he could have spoken, he would have told her how small were her chances that she would ever be allowed out of his sight again.

"You know," said Tuesday, after a moment, holding her dog close, "you really smell."

And he did. His golden-brown fur smelled disgustingly of fish, and gold and vercaka. Tuesday didn't care one bit.

"Ahem," someone coughed.

It was Vivienne Small, leaning against the stone wall of the mayor's garden. Tuesday noticed that her knee was bleeding, her clothes were torn, and there was a savage graze across one cheek. Tuesday would have liked to hug her, but instead she reached out and gently pulled a tangled lock of Vivienne's dark hair.

"We looked, and we looked, and we looked for you," Vivienne said with a scowl. "You can't have been in the mayor's garden for all of this time. We would have found you."

Vivienne tried to sustain the cross expression on her face, but a smile was twiddling around at the corners of her mouth.

"Thanks for taking care of my dog," Tuesday said with a grin, and Vivienne couldn't contain herself any longer. She threw herself at Tuesday and Baxterr and enclosed them both in a swift, bony embrace.

"Actually, I think he took care of me," Vivienne said. "So where *have* you been?"

"I don't know how to answer that," said Tuesday truthfully.

And Vivienne, who in her heart of hearts knew that Tuesday was in some important respect not at all like anyone else in her world, realized that she didn't need to know. What mattered was that Tuesday had reappeared.

"We took care of those stupid vercaka," Vivienne said, changing the subject.

"Tell me," said Tuesday.

And so the girls sat, with their backs against the sun-warmed stone, with Baxterr panting happily between them, and talked. Tuesday ruffled Baxterr's fur when Vivienne described how he had torn through the streets of the City of Clocks with almost every single one of its cats in pursuit of him. She shook her head at the stupidity of Nigel Finkwatter and was stirred by the bravery of Miranda Templeton. She had her heart in her mouth as Vivienne related how close Vivienne and Baxterr had come to being captured in the vicious beak of a vercaka, and she laughed at the tale of the great silver fish launching its deadly cargo into the sky.

"You were amazing," she said to Vivienne.

"Well, if the worlds hadn't come apart at precisely the moment they did, then Baxterr and I would have been amazingly dead," Vivienne said. "*That* was a piece of luck."

"Yes, I guess it was," agreed Tuesday.

A small silence settled between them, for both of them knew what came next.

"I have to go, Vivienne," Tuesday said.

"Through there?" Vivienne indicated the door.

"Yes. Through there."

Vivienne nodded.

"I'll see you again, won't I?" Vivienne asked.

"Every chance," said Tuesday, wondering how soon she and Baxterr might be able to take a walk in the world of Vivienne Small. She wondered how long it would be before this world came in for routine maintenance. How much, she pondered, should a Gardener help with the clean-up in the City of Clocks, and how much ought she leave for the people of the city to do for themselves?

Tuesday scrambled to her feet, and it was only then that she observed something rather troubling about the green door. It had no handle. Nor any keyhole. She bit her bottom lip in concern. And that was when Baxterr stood back and barked, very precisely, three times. At his command, the door swung open. Through it, Tuesday could see the jetty stretching up toward the glass door that led into the Conservatory. Vivienne, however, saw nothing but a corridor of pale mist.

"You will be all right, won't you?" Vivienne asked.

"You bet," Tuesday said. "Good-bye, Vivienne. Don't stop having adventures."

"Never," said Vivienne, with a small salute. "Not ever."

It seemed to Vivienne, then, that Tuesday and Baxterr simply disappeared into the whiteness of the mist. And almost the instant that the green garden door swung closed, Vivienne began to forget.

It wasn't a bad sort of forgetting. Not like somebody having a car accident and waking up with amnesia. Or like pushing a bad experience deep inside yourself and hoping it will never surface again. Rather, it was like Vivienne's mind gently moved Tuesday and Baxterr from the very front and center of things to a drawer at the back—one that she wouldn't be opening for some time.

This is how it is in the place that stories come from. For it is the job of characters to forget about us, their writers, and to get on with their lives and adventures as if we had never visited them at all. But perhaps, sometimes, we leave traces of ourselves in their hearts and minds, a bit like the way a dream leaves a feeling behind, even if we can't remember what it was about.

And so it was that a few minutes after the garden door swung shut, Vivienne Small was a little perplexed to find herself standing alone in the sun outside the mayor's garden. There was a green door in the wall. It had no handle and no keyhole. When she scrambled up the wall and looked over, there was nothing unusual to see, only the mayor's neat and tidy garden, with beds for flowers and beds for vegetables, fruit trees, nut trees, and a swing seat. She sat on the wall, puzzled. She felt as if she had forgotten something important.

Overhanging the wall was the branch of a lemon tree. It was weighed down by ripe, yellow fruits, and Vivienne had a sudden desire to eat one. She reached out for the one she liked best, and as she did so, she saw something moving in among the tree's glossy green leaves. It was a rat, and a very young one too, small and sleekly black.

Vivienne saw the rat, and the rat saw Vivienne, and for a moment the pair sat, quite still, regarding one another. Then the rat nosed forward, sniffing in the small girl's direction. Vivienne held out her hand by way of invitation, and the rat stepped onto it.

"Well, you're a brave one," Vivienne said, then laughed. "I suppose you have to be, living in a city once full of cats."

The rat ran up her arm and perched on her shoulder. Vivienne patted it.

"I think your name is . . . Ermengarde," said Vivienne Small.

The rat sneezed a tiny sneeze.

Vivienne giggled as its long whiskers tickled her neck.

"Ermengarde, would you like to come on an adventure or two?" Vivienne asked.

Chapter Twenty-Four

Tuesday set Baxterr down on the walkway and spun around happily.

"Race you," she said to him, and he didn't need to be asked twice.

Tuesday sprinted up the walkway with Baxterr right beside her, his short legs a blur of golden-brown fur. They reached the glass door at precisely the same moment.

"You wait until you see all this, doggo," Tuesday told him. "You won't believe where we're going to live."

Baxterr tilted his head, perplexed.

"Ruff?"

"Yes, here," Tuesday said. "You see, I have to be the Gardener. Someone has to take care of the worlds, doggo."

The glass door opened, and Baxterr, taking in the extraordinary sky above him, gave a little growl.

"Ruff, ruff, ruff," he said quickly, as a bright yellow-and-green world swooped low over their heads.

"North?" came Garnet's voice from the primrose-colored couch.

He sat upright, and it seemed to Tuesday that he had grown even older while he slept. His gray hair had transformed to a snowy white, and his eyes had clouded over.

He struggled to his feet.

"Where is she?" he cried. "I heard her! I heard her barking. She's come back! North Wind! Where are you, my girl?"

The Gardener, looking wildly about him, caught sight of Tuesday and Baxterr and took a few staggering steps toward them. Tuesday, seeing that he was about to fall, rushed to catch him. The moment she reached him, he collapsed—almost weightless—against her. She steadied him with an arm about his waist.

"North? Is that you?"

"It isn't her," Tuesday said as gently as she could. "It's my dog. He's come."

"It isn't? It's not? I'm sure I heard . . . ," he said.

Tuesday felt his knees buckle again.

"I think you should lie down," Tuesday said, and with Baxterr following closely at her feet, she helped the Gardener back to his couch. She straightened the pillows all about him and pulled the comforter up to his chest.

"It really wasn't her?" he asked sadly.

"I'm sorry," Tuesday said.

Baxterr put his paws up, ever so gently, on the couch beside the old man, who peered back at him critically.

"This is your dog, Ms. Gardener?" he asked. "I must say, you keep him very *small*. He's almost a bonsai, isn't he? I always kept North Wind bigger than that. About the size of a decent wolfhound. That was more my style. But you know, whatever suits."

"Garnet. This is . . ." She paused for a moment. She almost said "doggo," but then decided to risk it. "This is Baxterr."

Garnet reached out a gnarled hand to pat Baxterr on the head.

"Baxterr, eh?"

"With a double *r*," Tuesday added. "It's for his growl, you know."

"Growl," the old man sighed. "Yes, a growl can be a useful thing."

Garnet closed his eyes, and Tuesday worried that he would never open them again. But after a moment, he did.

"I'm glad you're here," he said, addressing Baxterr. "And now that you are, I think I'll be off. Remember, it's a fine and noble thing to be the Gardener's dog. Like the Gardener's life, the life of the Gardener's dog can be difficult at times, and lonely. But friends are never so very far away. Not if one uses one's nose . . . hmm?"

He slowly tapped the side of his nose with a wizened finger, then took a breath that Tuesday heard as a rattle in his chest.

"It has been an extraordinary life," he said in barely a whisper. "We were far apart, my love and me, and yet we were together in purpose every day."

Garnet stared up at the sky swimming with worlds.

"Look at that, will you, Ms. Gardener. Just look up at that! Do you see? Over there, a new one."

High in the sky, something flashed, platinum white against the indigo. It was small, but growing.

"What is it?" Tuesday asked.

"It's a world, being born," Garnet said. "You know what that means, don't you?"

Tuesday did. It meant that someone, somewhere, had put pen to paper. Or fingertips to keyboard, or chalk to a blackboard, or sharpened stick to a sandy beach. And they had done it in a way that had made magic.

"You know, I only ever made one world that I was truly happy with. A very special bit of gardening that. I hid it. So precious."

"Which one is it?" Tuesday said. "Can't you tell me?"

Garnet gave a barely perceptible chuckle. "Goodbye, Ms. Gardener. Thank you for coming in my hour of need. Take care of the worlds for me, won't you? And, Baxterr, remember the nose."

With that, the old man closed his eyes and sighed the longest of sighs. When at last it stopped, he did not take another breath. He began to shimmer and then to vanish. A moment later, the comforter collapsed onto the couch, suddenly empty of his form.

"Good-bye, Garnet," Tuesday said.

Shimmering in the air before her, Tuesday saw a pale golden dust. Mesmerized, she reached out. At her touch, it vanished altogether. As Tuesday drew her hand back, she saw something strange. Baxterr gave a little whine of concern. Tuesday got up and went over to the workbench to examine her hand in a better light. It wasn't her imagination. Her fingernails *had* changed. Where there would normally be a curve of paler pink, they had changed to faint shade of green. Tuesday glanced back to the vacant couch, and then again at her fingers.

"I really have become the Gardener," Tuesday whispered. "Is that all right?"

Baxterr licked her hand as if to say that everything was all right, so long as the two of them were together.

"I don't even know if it's good or bad, if it's wrong or right, but this is the story I've written."

They sat together, then, on the blue rug, Tuesday with her knees drawn up to her chin, and Baxterr with his small body leaned up against her legs. Together, girl and dog peered up into the sky full of worlds. There were so many of them.

Chapter Twenty-Five

In the hospital corridor, through a window on the third floor, Serendipity Smith gazed out over the glittering lights of the city. It had been a good day, medically speaking. In the morning, Denis had been unhooked from his breathing machine, and much to everyone's relief, he had—after a short heart-stopping moment—breathed on his own. But still he had not woken up.

It was late Friday night, and the city pulsed ever so slightly to a beat that Serendipity could not hear. Out there, she knew, there were couples sitting down to dinner in restaurants, families filing out of cinemas with new stories still big in their minds, and people dancing to music so loud that they forgot all their cares. Across town, at Brown Street, she could imagine Miss Digby and Blake at the kitchen table, playing their hundredth game of Scrabble in order to pass the time.

"It's been too long," she whispered to Tuesday.

"Too long," she whispered to Denis as she returned to his room.

She closed her eyes and wished, but when she opened them again, nothing had changed. Perhaps, she thought, it was time to do more than simply wish. There was a pen dangling from the clipboard at the foot of Denis's bed. There wasn't much paper about, but Serendipity supposed she could use the backs of the medical charts for her purposes. Once more she glanced out the window. Someone had to go. No matter how risky or dangerous it was. Someone had to go *there* and bring Tuesday home. She bit the end of the ballpoint pen and thought. Then, using the bed as a desk, she touched the nib down on the page. Without warning, without opening his eyes, Denis reached out and grabbed her hand.

"She's lost to us," he said in a hoarse voice. "She's never coming home."

Serendipity stared at him, her heart racing.

"Denis?" she said. "Denis, speak to me!"

But Denis did not speak again.

Serendipity ran out into the corridor and called to a passing nurse.

"He spoke!" she said. "He spoke!"

The nurse hurried in and checked the monitors, and then shook her head.

"They do that sometimes. It's random brain activity. It doesn't mean much. He is still in a coma."

"He could wake up at any time, though."

"Yes, he could," the nurse said. "Sometimes they do."

When the nurse returned two hours later to check Denis's blood pressure and temperature, she found Serendipity curled up on the bed beside him, her head on his shoulder, her arm across his body.

"Mrs. McGillycuddy, you'll have to move," the nurse said.

"I can't," Serendipity said, stirring groggily. "I could never leave him."

"Into the chair with you," said the nurse. "Here's your blanket."

In the bathroom at Brown Street early on Saturday morning, Blake Luckhurst ran his fingers through his hair and eyed himself in the mirror. He squared his shoulders, angled his jaw, and gave his reflection a steely glance.

"*Serendipity,*" he said to his reflection. "*Somebody has to go, and that someone needs to be me.*"

"*But, Blake,*" he replied in a parody of Serendipity's voice, "*you can't. You mustn't. It's too dangerous.*"

Blake rehearsed the conversation again as he sat down and rather awkwardly tied the laces of his boots.

"*Serendipity, you must remember I am not simply Blake Luckhurst, author. I am, in this instance, Blake Luckhurst, action hero.*"

He wondered briefly what sort of action he would face, then he strode from the bathroom down the stairs and said good-bye to Miss Digby, who was sorting paperwork in the kitchen.

"Blake, I think I should mention that your T-shirt is not only the wrong way around, but inside out," said Miss Digby, following him along the hallway.

"Thank you, Miss Digby, but none of that matters,"

Blake replied, waving his hands in a theatrical gesture and closing the door behind him.

The gray-faced and disheveled woman in the chair was the antithesis of the very tall, glamorous, and colorful Serendipity Smith the public knew. Blake was still a little discomfited to remember she really was *the* Serendipity Smith, world's most famous author. Tired as she was, Serendipity managed a smile when Blake arrived. She introduced him to Denis, who was, Blake observed, showing no sign of waking from his coma.

Serendipity related what had happened in the night.

"I was thinking that I have to go, I have to go and bring Tuesday home, but I can't leave him, Blake. I can't."

"Serendipity, I have come to an important decision," Blake began. "And these recent developments assure me that it is time for action. So I propose—and please, do not try to stop me—that I begin a story and transport myself *there* to do whatever it takes to ensure Tuesday does actually return home safely."

Serendipity blinked. "Blake. That's all very noble, but what if something happens to you?"

"Please do not try to stop me, Serendipity. My mind is made up. What matters most is that you are here for Mr. McGillycuddy—and that Tuesday comes home."

Serendipity put her arms around Blake and hugged him.

"Thank you, Blake," she said. "I am sure if anyone can bring Tuesday home safely, it will be you."

And with that, Blake turned on his heels. Tossing his backpack over one shoulder, he hurried out of the hospital and to City Park. It was a blustery day. Blake sat on a bench, took out a notebook and a chewed pen. He realized Serendipity had not tried to stop him. In fact, she apparently had complete faith in his ability to bring Tuesday home. Well, he wouldn't disappoint her. Within a few moments of writing, he had liftoff and was arcing across the city sky, invisible to all below him, following a silver thread.

The tree was delighted to see Blake hurtling toward it. All week it had felt rumblings from deep in the earth below, and this was very disturbing, for trees do not like change. Also, writers had been few and far between, and the tree had been lonely.

So Blake's arrival, accomplished by his familiar midair forward roll to a standing finish, delighted the tree. It rustled its leaves in a hearty welcome.

"Adventure, of course," Blake said, and bowed deeply to the tree. "Hero by the name of, well . . . Blake Luckhurst, actually."

The tree rustled its leaves again.

"I'm guessing a helicopter is out of the question?" Blake asked.

The tree did not respond.

"Horse?" suggested Blake.

The tree shimmered its leaves and a small white goat appeared from behind its ancient trunk. The goat stared at Blake through its amber eyes and gave a high-pitched *maaaaaaa*.

"Ha, ha. Very funny," Blake said.

The goat gamboled away and began munching on the lush green grass of the hillside. Then from behind him, Blake heard a low whickering noise. He turned to see a magnificent white horse, saddled and waiting.

"Nice," he said to the tree. "I am always, forever, at your service."

Then, in true hero style, Blake mounted the horse in a single, coordinated movement and galloped off through the mist toward the Library.

Cantering up the stairs, Blake observed the extensive damage that had been done to the Library's stonework and balconies. He glanced up at the gigantic word—IMAGINE—carved above the entrance and was relieved to see it was still intact. He was no stranger to chaos; all his novels relied on it.

He left the horse to take a drink at the fountain and walked toward the entrance, pushed open the huge doors, and strode inside. He could hear that the dining room was packed with writers, and all of them conversing noisily. But louder still was the argument that was going on in the Librarian's study. Blake approached the slightly open door.

He heard the Librarian in her unmistakeable voice saying, "She said she would do anything. *Anything!* So I took her at her word."

"She's a child," said a deep, gnarly voice with a distinctive twang.

"Well, we were all children once," said the Librarian.

"She has the right to grow up, doesn't she? Before such things are asked of her? What about the things she'll never do if you leave her there? Never finish school. Never have her first dance. Never fall in love."

"Well, we might be sparing her there," said the Librarian drily. "And you act as if this is something I can fix, Silver Nightly. Well, I cannot. She went of her own free will. I cannot undo what has been done."

Blake pushed open the door. "Hello, Madame Librarian. Mr. Nightly. I am Blake Luckhurst."

He reached out and shook hands firmly with the older writer.

"Pleased to meet you, son," Silver said.

"You two wouldn't happen to be talking about Tuesday McGillycuddy, would you?" Blake asked.

The Librarian was distinctly uneasy, and Blake noticed her stained purple tracksuit and untidy hair. On her desk was a messy circle of crumpled tissues. He noticed her eyes were red-rimmed and her cheeks puffy as if she had been crying. Then he noticed stains on the couch that might have been blood. Through the study's french doors, Blake saw that most of the balcony railing was missing. Beyond it, a huge globe loomed in the mist.

"What the hell is that?"

"Mr. Luckhurst! Language, please. We are a writer, and we have vocabulary. But to answer your question, that is a world that recently collided with my library."

"A what?" asked Blake.

"A world. And it's happening all over," said Silver Nightly. "Worlds crashing into one another and throwing us writers to goodness knows where in the process. It's chaos, and I'd say you're a fool to be coming here, except that you have the look of a man on a mission."

"I am here to rescue Tuesday McGillycuddy," Blake said.

"Oh, not you too," grumbled the Librarian.

"Her mother is very worried," Blake said. "Her father is in a coma. I have to get her home."

"Dang . . . ," said Silver Nightly, shaking his head.

"You cannot take her home, Blake Luckhurst," said the Librarian, raising herself up to her full, diminutive height. "Neither of you can. Nor would she agree to go. She's staying here. She has made a choice to stay here forever."

"But that's impossible!" exclaimed Blake.

"Unfortunately, it's not," said Silver Nightly. "Though what Madame Librarian is failing to disclose is that she created this here problem. She sent Tuesday on a mission to write a story to stop the worlds colliding."

"And why *are* they colliding?" Blake asked, glancing again at the surreal image of the world hanging outside the Library.

"Because of someone called the Gardener. He has, only a short while ago, passed away," said Silver Nightly, causing the Librarian to reach for more tissues and again wipe her eyes. "Young Tuesday was tidily set up to become his successor."

"His successor!" exclaimed Blake.

"Someone has to do it," cried the Librarian, impassioned. "There must be a Gardener. The last Gardener could never have died if Tuesday had not fully accepted her fate."

"Fate?" Blake asked. "You mean she was meant to be this? Chosen at birth or something?"

"No, Blake, it was a little more practical than that, actually," the Librarian said. "Tuesday came to me with a story already begun and a Winged Dog by her side. A Gardener must have a creature that can travel between worlds. There was no one else. In that sense, perhaps it was fate. Certainly that is how most of us find our most important adventures, wouldn't you say?

"Without a Gardener, all this would end. The only reason you and every other writer can come here is because the Gardener tends to these worlds. Tuesday is doing you all the greatest service. You only have to look around, or hear the stories in the dining room, to understand the chaos, the utter chaos, of a world without her."

"Tuesday's too young to have to take on all that," Blake said.

"My point exactly," said Silver.

"Do you know how young I was?" said the Librarian mildly. "The Gardener was a writer, like both of you. I watched him come and go. He was older than me, but only by a few years. In fact, sometimes you remind me of him, Blake. Of course he wasn't nearly so famous as you think you are, but he had ambition. And he loved it here. He came more and more often. There was a time of chaos, much like this, with the passing of the previous Gardener. Garnet took over. He sacrificed his writing career so that all of this is here for all of you. Such a long time has passed, and now he is gone. We wrote to each other, of course. His dog carried our letters, and I sent him books. Sometimes, he would send me a plant. But we could never . . . and we will never . . . oh, what have I done to that girl?"

She stopped and stared again at the broken balcony.

"Blake Luckhurst, did you bring a white horse?" she asked in a much more familiar imperious tone.

Blake looked out the window and grimaced. "Yes, Madame Librarian," he said proudly.

"That's a fine horse," said Silver Nightly.

"Perhaps, but of absolutely no use to you," said the Librarian.

"Use for what?" asked Silver.

"For reaching Tuesday," said the Librarian.

"You mean, there is a way?"

"There may be. How are you both with heights?"

"Heights?" asked Blake.

The Librarian moved to the edge of her rug and began to roll it up. Silver and Blake rushed to help her pull it back to reveal polished floorboards and a trapdoor. The Librarian indicated the handle, and Blake heaved the door open. Beneath them was nothing but a dark sky, swirling with worlds of every color and design.

"Where is she, exactly, in all of that?" Blake asked.

"Right at the very bottom, naturally," the Librarian said.

"And how do you propose that we get there?" Silver asked.

"Blake, go into the book room and bring my platform. You remember the one?" the Librarian asked.

"How could I ever forget?" Blake replied, remembering the day the Librarian had first showed him the Library, zooming up and down aisles and taking corners at hair-raising speeds. He had been intimidated by her ever since.

"Not that dang flying thing," Silver said.

The Librarian smiled for the first time that day.

"So we are going to rescue Tuesday?" Silver asked her, as Blake disappeared momentarily.

"We are simply going to visit," said the Librarian.

When Blake returned, he was dragging the platform behind him.

"Mind the floorboards, Blake!" said the Librarian. "I forgot. It takes a special touch to make it glide."

In a moment, the Librarian had locked her office door and the three of them were on the platform hovering above the open trapdoor.

"I'm not sure I'm going to like this," said Blake, forgetting for a moment to be heroic. And then they dropped into darkness between millions of floating worlds.

Chapter Twenty-Six

Tuesday sat at the workbench, wearing the Gardener's glasses—no, she kept reminding herself, they were *her* glasses. For quite a while, she had been working away with her tiny shears, carefully pruning the outermost branches of a tree that took up almost all of an entire world. The tree was occupied, not only by squirrels and birds, but also by some folk who lived in little circular houses within its trunk. Up at the top of the tree trunk, leaning out of a window—frozen in time—was a red-cheeked woman in a dirty head scarf. She had a bucket of sudsy water in her arms.

"I see," Tuesday said, and then hunted around on

the bench until she found a minuscule umbrella of the sort you sometimes get in expensive drinks, but even smaller still. Then, with the help of a pair of tweezers, she unfolded it and put it into the hand of a girl standing directly underneath the window.

"There you go," she said, satisfied.

Through her magnifying glasses, Tuesday gave the world of the tree and the girl and the umbrella a final once-over. As she was about to allow the world to be closed and returned, Baxterr trotted out to the middle of the Conservatory and pricked up his ears. He tilted his head from side to side, watching as three people crammed together on a silver platform zigzagged down through the sky.

"Ruff," he said to Tuesday, and he said it in the tone of bark that he used when someone was about to ring the doorbell at Brown Street.

Tuesday swung around on her stool, and there, descending to her floor on a platform she recognized— looking positively enormous through the lenses of her microscope spectacles—was a tall young man in an inside-out T-shirt. Was she seeing things? She whipped off the glasses. No, he really *was* there.

"Blake!" she said.

"Hey, Tuesday," he said, jumping down as the platform came to a halt. She might have hugged him, had he not been accompanied by two other people whose presence was entirely unexpected.

"Silver Nightly? Madame Librarian? What are you doing here?"

"Some people," said the Librarian, "are under the rather old-fashioned impression that you are in need of rescuing, Tuesday McGillycuddy. Is it true? Are you incapable of doing this job that you have taken on? Is Baxterr?"

"No, Madame Librarian," said Tuesday, in a very poised manner. "Quite the reverse. I have been catching up on the backlog, and we'll soon be up to date."

The Librarian swept up the Gardener's glasses and slid them onto her face. *My* glasses, thought Tuesday, feeling a little annoyed. She watched as the Librarian peered into the world Tuesday had just completed.

"Hmmm," she said. "Tweezers, please."

And Tuesday, despite herself, handed over the tiny pair of tweezers and watched as the Librarian reached in and plucked the umbrella out of the girl's hands.

"I can't help it. I laugh myself silly every single time she gets a drenching. We mustn't interfere. Only assist," the Librarian said, setting the umbrella back down on the bench and removing the glasses.

"You see, Silver? Blake? Tuesday is doing a remarkable job," the Librarian said.

"And you, Tuesday? Are you sure this is what you want?" Silver asked. He was taking in all the instruments and books, the tools and tubes. He hadn't said a single word as they had descended through all the worlds, so startled had he been to realize what writers had been creating for so long.

"Well . . . ," Tuesday began. "It *is* pretty amazing." Silver nodded.

"Quite a place you've got down here. Don't suppose you'd care to show me around?"

"Oh yes," said Tuesday. "You see, over here, this is where the worlds come in for routine—"

"Whoa," said Blake. "Tuesday, are you nuts? You cannot seriously be planning on staying here for the rest of your life."

"Oh, Blake, it's not just here! Baxterr and I can travel to any world we want. And the worlds are amazing. Every one of them. Look at them! I mean, in any day we can travel into the world of any book, meet the characters, be part of their adventures, eat food with them, feel snow, or go swimming. I mean, think of all the places we can go!"

"Except home," said Blake.

"Home?" said Tuesday. She frowned. "This is my home, Blake."

"No, Tuesday. It's not," said Blake. "You have a home at Brown Street. I've seen it. You've got a mother and a father who need you to come home."

"You've been to Brown Street? You met my parents?"

"Yes, Tuesday, and I know exactly who your mom is."

"Then you understand. If I'm not here, doing this, my mother won't be able to write anymore," said Tuesday. "You and Silver and all the other writers—your worlds will collapse and die."

"You see, Blake, Tuesday understands perfectly what her duty is," said the Librarian serenely.

"Come, Silver," Tuesday said, picking up the boat-hook. "Let me show you how to catch a world."

"Tuesday," said Blake, "I know this is going to be hard to hear, but you really have to come home. Your dad, he's really sick. He's in a coma."

Tuesday turned and stared at Blake, and it was as if a mask dropped from her face. Suddenly she looked younger.

"What did you say?" she asked.

"Your father, he collapsed. He's in the hospital."

"Well, he's clearly being well cared for," said the Librarian.

"No, Madame Librarian, that is not the point," said Blake. "He's incredibly ill. Tuesday has to get back to him."

"Dad?" Tuesday asked. She felt bewildered. "My dad is sick? He needs me?"

"Yes," said Blake. "And so does your mom. Do you really think if your mother had to choose between writing and you, she'd choose writing?"

Tuesday was trying to clear her head, but it was still full of worlds and planets. Her heart was beating too fast, and every beat was hammering out one word. *Dad. Dad. Dad.*

"Silver, tell her," said Blake. "Would you want a girl to give up her life so you could be a writer? Would any of us want that?"

"The boy makes an excellent point, Tuesday," said Silver Nightly. "It's not that you won't do a fine job.

A fine job, indeed. But this is a job for someone who's lived all their adventures. Who's made all their choices. I'm imagining these Gardeners, like Librarians, are pretty long-lived, eh, Madame L?"

"That is correct, Silver Nightly," said the Librarian, and to Tuesday's surprise, she sat down on the couch where the Gardener had so recently evaporated into golden dust. She ran her hand over the fabric and sighed. "We live a very long time."

"But I am just getting things back to normal," said Tuesday softly. She sat down on the couch beside Madame Librarian. "I promised Garnet. I didn't know . . . I . . . It overtook me. Something about being here . . . it made me forget so much. I *can't* leave."

"Unless we find another Gardener," said Silver.

"Well, it's not easy," said Tuesday. "I mean, you have to use the boathook. And then there's maintenance. And all the repair work. And you have to have the right dog . . . and it's not . . . I mean, it's a wonderful job. There are so many worlds to visit and so many adventures to be had. But my dad. What about my dad?"

"Well, why don't I continue?" suggested Silver Nightly.

"You mean while I go home and explain everything?" said Tuesday.

"Oh, I was thinking a little longer term than that," said Silver, rubbing his chin. "I mean while you're busy growing up and doing all that your young life has ahead of it."

"You mean, you would . . . become the Gardener?" asked Tuesday.

"I think this might be the best job there is for an old boy like me," Silver Nightly said with a grin.

Blake and Tuesday stared at him, and the Librarian raised her head and smiled.

"Ah, there it is," she said. They all stared at her. "You see, sometimes the way is not clear. And then, suddenly, it is! Silver Nightly, that is an excellent solution. Tuesday can go home and be whatever Tuesday McGillycuddy had in mind before all this came along. And you, Silver, can stay right here."

"Silver, what about your family?" said Tuesday.

"Since my wife died, there's been only me. And my books. Well, there'd be no shortage of reading here, of a slightly different kind, I'll warrant. But look at all that," he said, gazing into the worlds above him. "Look at all that!"

Blake sighed. "Well, that was unexpected."

"As will be the necessity of giving up Baxterr," said the Librarian to Tuesday.

"Giving up Baxterr?" Tuesday frowned.

"Well, of course," said the Librarian, "Silver will be needing a dog."

"No, no," said Silver.

"You can't," said Tuesday. "No. No. I can't!"

"That's the choice, Tuesday," said the Librarian. "Go home, by all means, to your mother and father. Your dog, however, will be required here."

Baxterr erupted in a fierce outburst of barking.

When at last he finished, Blake said, "Quite a speech, Baxterr. I agree entirely."

"Well, then," said the Librarian, "there can be no exchange. The Gardener must have a familiar. A creature to travel between worlds. The best are always the dogs. Dragons are so moody."

"Okay," said Tuesday. "I had better find their world. Garnet told me he hid it. Did he tell you about it?"

"The world of the dogs?" The Librarian was amused. "No, I do not know. Don't look at me like that, young lady. I've not the first clue where he might have put it. I much prefer cats."

"There's a world?" asked Silver Nightly, peering into the swirl of color and movement above them as if he might spot a Winged Dog at any moment.

"Yes," said Tuesday. "If we can find it, we can get you a dog of your own."

"Knowing Garnet, that world is bound to be in a very obscure place indeed," said the Librarian. "Personally I think the Baxterr option is quick and simple. Is no one up to the hard decisions anymore? Whatever happened to sacrifice?"

"It went out with quills and ink, Madame Librarian," said Blake.

"And the classics, I fear," added the Librarian drily.

So Tuesday, Silver, Blake, and Baxterr searched the sky for the world of dogs. The Librarian, meanwhile, retired to the primrose-yellow couch and chose a book from the pile on the small table beside it. From time to time, she coughed meaningfully, as if she thought her companions were wasting their time.

"Exactly what is it we're after?" Silver asked, his head thrown back.

"A world," Tuesday said. "But I haven't got any more clues than you."

"Hurrrrrr," said Baxterr, tilting his head from side to side.

"Surely, if he hid it, it wouldn't look anything like we expect," Blake said, gazing at pearlescent worlds and silver worlds, worlds that were tangerine and worlds that were fluorescent green. Some were like soap bubbles and others like steel. Some glowed brightly, and others were darker than the sky itself. There were worlds that were round and worlds that were any shape but round.

Tuesday thought of Mr. Tumnus's world in a cupboard. Perhaps the world of dogs would be like a tennis ball? Or a bone? She searched for a long time before she turned away from the sky.

Blake had decided it was easiest to study the sky while lying on the rug. And Silver had taken to one of the wheeled chairs from the workbench and was leaning back on it, world-gazing as if he might never tire of it. As for the Librarian, she had fallen asleep on the couch with a book open upon her chest.

Tuesday rubbed her sore neck and thought back over the time she had spent with Garnet and tried to remember every last thing he had said to her about the world of dogs. She thought and thought, and she then remembered one thing he had said, though not to her. To *Baxterr*.

"Doggo," she called, and Baxterr trotted over and sat in front of her.

"Ruff?" he said.

"Do you remember what Garnet said: 'Friends are never so very far away. Not if one uses one's *nose* . . .' And how he said to you specifically, 'Baxterr, remember the nose.'"

"Hurrrrrr," said Baxterr thoughtfully. He began to sniff in the particularly determined way that dogs sometimes do. He sniffed first at the sky, but then, not finding anything of interest to him there, began to nose around the Conservatory itself. He ran his wet black nose along the floor beneath the workbench and all around the table where the Gardener took meals. Catching an interesting scent of something rather like goat, he shook his head disbelievingly.

Over by the yellow couch, he smelled something very interesting. He gave a strange whine before redoubling his sniffing efforts until his nose was drawn to the table beside the couch. Upon this table was a pile of books and a porcelain teacup with a saucer resting on top of it.

"Ruff," said Baxterr, very sharply and clearly.

"What is it, doggo?" Tuesday whispered.

"Ruff."

Slowly and carefully, Tuesday lifted the saucer away from the teacup. No sooner had she done so than she hurriedly let it drop back into place. Whatever was inside the teacup began to flutter and buzz. But Tuesday had seen enough of it to realize that it was not a large moth, or a bumble bee. It was, when she peeped under the saucer again and saw it quivering, a tiny round world with two beautiful, furry golden wings on its sides.

Tuesday grinned at Baxterr, and Baxterr grinned at Tuesday.

"Hey, Silver," Tuesday called. "Are you ready to catch a world?"

Silver Nightly jumped up from the chair. "The secret to success is to be ready when opportunity comes."

Tuesday blinked and smiled. "Hello, new Gardener," she said as she held the boathook out to him.

"Well, ain't this something?" he breathed, gazing at it with a serious and slightly dazzled expression.

"You're absolutely sure you want this?" she asked. "Because once you take it from me, it'll be yours. Forever."

"If you look closely," said Silver with a wink, "you'll find that this here boathook already has my name on it."

There was the briefest moment in which Tuesday didn't want to let go. Being the Gardener had been the most extraordinary adventure. But she knew what she must do.

As Silver took hold of the boathook and her hand fell away, Tuesday saw him fill with pride. Tuesday stepped backward, swaying a little. She felt exactly the way she did after getting off a fast ride at a carnival—a little sad that it was over, but mostly relieved to be back on solid ground.

"The world we're looking for is over here," Tuesday said, leading Silver to the couch, where the Librarian lay, murmuring softly in her sleep.

"Where?" asked Silver, puzzled.

"Get ready, Mr. Gardener," Tuesday said. "It's in this teacup, and it's going to fly fast."

"In the *teacup*?" Silver asked.

Blake got up from the floor and came over to see what was going on.

"Did you say 'fly'?" he asked.

"It's got wings," Tuesday said. "I'm going to let it go, Silver. You'll need to hook it by a loop on the side."

"I'll give it my all," said Silver.

Baxterr barked.

"Okay," said Tuesday. "One, two . . . *three*."

Tuesday lifted the saucer, and the world darted up into the Conservatory. As soon as it was free, it began immediately to grow. Within a heartbeat, it was the size of a soccer ball, and a second later, the size of a hot-air balloon, its furry wings beating the air.

Silver lunged at it with the boathook, but it zoomed away from him, rising up into the dark sky.

"Dang!" he said. "I've missed the darned thing."

The world had grown to the size of a small moon.

"Don't worry," Tuesday said, "Keep reaching. The boathook knows what to do."

"Oh, my giddy aunt," the Librarian said, waking up to the sight of a colossal winged world directly above her.

"Here I go again," Silver said, feeding the boathook up into the sky. The hook extended and extended.

"Do you see the loop, Silver? There, there!" Tuesday cried.

"I see it!"

"Ruff," said Baxterr, who was practically prancing with excitement.

With a swipe that was not especially elegant, Silver snagged the winged world on the end of his boathook. He beamed.

"Excellent. Bring it in to that jetty, over there," Tuesday said, pointing to the narrow walkway. At first the world strained against the hook as if it wanted to fly away and be free, but after a moment, it appeared to change its mind and submitted to being towed down to the platform. With a magnetic click, it was secure, and its furry wings came to a gentle standstill.

"Well, hooley dooley," said Silver, resting on the boathook as if it were an oversized cane. He mopped his brow with his handkerchief.

Though it was not a large world, it was a beautiful one, its surface marbled gold and pearl.

"So what happens next?" asked Blake in almost a whisper.

"C'mon," said Tuesday. "This is the best bit."

The Librarian, perfectly awake again, said, "Well, this is something I have to see. Before I go home and chase that horse of yours out of my roses, Blake Luckhurst."

And so the Librarian, Blake Luckhurst, Silver Nightly, Tuesday, and Baxterr walked the narrow walkway to the world at the end of the jetty. When they opened the pearly door that presented itself, they found a world so bright that for a moment they were blinded. A rush of salt air washed over them, a breeze stirred, waves broke, and Baxterr barked.

"Oh, doggo," said Tuesday, patting him, "it's exactly like I always thought it would be!"

It was a world of wide, white stretches of sand and stepped cliffs that rose, ledge after ledge, into a blue sky full of puffy white clouds. Creeks snaked down over the sand toward a blue, rippled sea. Waterfalls tumbled in the crevices of the cliffs. And everywhere there were dogs. Huge dogs. Winged Dogs flying the currents of air, gliding, wheeling, leaping, and tumbling.

"This is where they all went," Tuesday breathed. "I can't wait to tell Mom I've seen them. Oh, Silver, you have no idea how much I want to go home."

Baxterr barked. "Yes, doggo!" said Tuesday. "Of course you can run!"

She watched Baxterr bounding away, and then he grew. He spread his wings and took flight.

"My, that's a wonderful sight," said Silver, blinking. "I guess he doesn't get to do that at home too often."

"This would have been his home," said Tuesday quietly as they strolled together along the expanse of sand, leaving Blake and the Librarian behind.

"I guess that's true, except it isn't," said Silver. "Anyone can tell that home for that dog is you."

"Perhaps we can come and visit sometime," said Tuesday.

"Sounds like a mighty fine idea," said Silver.

Tuesday gazed at all the dogs in flight, the dogs bounding along the beach, tossing their heads and frolicking together, rolling in the sand, and splashing in waves.

"How will you choose one?" Tuesday asked.

"You mean how will it choose me?" Silver smiled. "I guess we'll have to wait and see." And so they walked the entire length of that beach while Baxterr flew and landed and ran and flew again. Until at last

he came bounding along the beach with a friend. She was white, with a brown patch over one eye. She was bigger than Baxterr, with shaggier fur.

"Ruff," said Baxterr.

"Is that so?" said Silver Nightly, eyeing the white dog. He held out his hand and the white dog sniffed it, and then she licked it and barked.

"Are you sure?" Silver asked.

"Ruff," the dog replied.

Tuesday nodded. "So that's how it's done," she said.

"I think I'll take a stroll with my new friend, if you don't mind, Tuesday," said Silver Nightly. "I'm guessing you need to be getting home, and I'm sure this won't be the last time I see you."

"I'm sure it won't, Silver Nightly," said Tuesday. "Or should I say Mr. Gardener?" She held out her hand, and he took it, and as he did so a curious rush of energy ran between them. Tuesday and Silver both stared at their hands. The green had gone from Tuesday's nails, while Silver Nightly was chuckling.

"I'll be! I grew a green thumb!"

"I think you're going to be wonderful at gardening. But I haven't shown you anything."

"Oh, I'm sure Madame Librarian will get me

sorted," he said. "You get yourself home safely, and remember, you did a great thing for all of us, taking over in a crisis."

Tuesday walked back to the Librarian and Blake.

"So, it's all turned out quite well, Tuesday McGillycuddy," said the Librarian. "A second visit is always difficult. There are so many options. I mean, you might have refused the thread when it came to get you. You might have said no to Vivienne and no to me. You might have said no to the Gardener. Yet you did not. You have said yes and yes and yes. True imagination takes great courage. And you have worked a small miracle, in your own way. You have saved this marvelous place of worlds for writers and readers everywhere. And found your way, I think, almost to The End."

"And if I'm right, I'm never going to need my thread again," said Tuesday. "Because of Baxterr I can travel between worlds."

The Librarian sniffed. "Well, go on, then. You'll both be back, I'm certain of that. Whatever way you come."

With formality, she shook hands with Tuesday and Blake.

"I do like young people," she said. "You have so little fear. Now, off you go. Please don't get sensible too soon."

"Ready, Blake?" asked Tuesday.

"You don't mean . . . ," said Blake, grinning. "On Baxterr? Really?"

It was Sunday morning in City Park, and the earliest of the birds were scouting the lawns for worms. Night creatures were making their way home to their hollows in the trees, preparing to sleep out the day. On the grassy slopes and lawns, daisies were unfurling their petals, but there were still hours to go until the shutters on the ice-cream kiosk would rattle open for business. The only people about were some joggers, two City Park officials in their green uniforms, and a newspaper boy.

The newspaper boy always got to the park early, to claim his favorite spot. It was beneath a tree that shaded him from the sun on hot days, kept the worst of the rain off him on wet days, and made a good stand to lean his bike against. Best of all, though, the tree was at the junction of four pathways, which meant that plenty of people went right past where he stood calling out the headlines of the day. Last Sunday it had been "Seven Writers Abducted! J. D. Jones snatched in her sleep! Read all about it! Read it right here!" Barney had sold out of papers by lunchtime. He'd done well all week, actually, with that girl called Tuesday missing, last seen right here in City Park.

On his head was a bright red cap, and around his waist was the leather pouch in which he kept his change. At his feet was a huge stack of fresh newspapers, still wrapped in plain newsprint and tied with string. He sliced through the string with his pocketknife.

Taking up most of the front page was a picture of a man with a curling black mustache. He was on crutches, with the lower part of his leg swathed in white bandages. The headline read JEFFERSON LOSES FOOT.

The newspaper boy read through the details of how Cordwell Jefferson—a writer and, by his own admission, not always the most practical of men—had run over his own foot while mowing the lawn. "It's always a risk to tangle with things you don't fully understand," Jefferson was quoted as saying.

As his head was bent over the paper, a gigantic Winged Dog came soaring in over the treetops heading for the open lawn beside a bank of public telephones.

The newspaper boy heard a noise and jerked his head up. Where a moment ago there had been nothing and nobody about, there was a smallish golden-brown dog and, sprawled on the grass beside him, a teenage boy and a girl, slightly younger. It was never too early to make the first sale of the day, so the boy cried out, "Cordwell Jefferson maimed by lawn mower! Read all about it! Read about it right here!"

Tuesday picked herself up and brushed the leaves and dried grass from her clothes.

"A lawn mower," she said to Blake, raising her eyebrows as they walked away.

"Seriously?" Blake said.

"A crocodile," said Tuesday.

"Ouch," said Blake.

As they exited City Park, Tuesday caught the first of the notices bearing her face and the words: HAVE YOU SEEN TUESDAY?

"Oh, dear," she said. On every lamppost and telephone pole, in every window, there was her photograph staring out at her.

"Blake, how long has it been?" she asked.

"A week," he said.

"Thank goodness. It feels like months."

Tuesday began to hurry. As they were about to turn the corner into Brown Street, Blake slowed to a stop.

"Tuesday, I think you should know there might be a media posse outside your house."

"Blake," Tuesday said, "promise me you won't ever tell anyone that I really considered never coming home again. I think it was the world . . . I think . . ."

"I get it," said Blake. "And I think it might be best if you go home alone. Your parents . . . they don't want to see me."

"Are you sure you won't come in?"

"Nah. Can't stand soppy scenes," said Blake.

"Thank you, Blake," said Tuesday. They smiled at each other, and then Blake suddenly hugged her.

"Your home is right there," he said, pointing. "You think you can make it on your own?"

Tuesday ran. She ran with Baxterr beside her. She was almost to the front gate when a reporter, a young woman with a lemon-colored scarf knotted at her throat, turned around and cried, "There she is!"

All at once the reporters were around her. There was the clicking and whirring of cameras, and everyone was calling out to her.

"Where have you been, Tuesday?"

"Tuesday, can you tell us what happened?"

"Were you abducted?"

"Were there aliens?" asked the reporter with a badge that said *Universal Chronicle*. "Tuesday, can you describe them?"

"Tuesday, did your parents have anything to do with your disappearance?"

Tuesday, quite terrified, picked up Baxterr and held him tight in her arms. He growled at the reporters with the special, deep sound that he reserved for protecting the people he loved most.

Suddenly the front door was thrown open, and there stood a woman with bright pink hair and a furious scowl on her face. For a moment, Tuesday had the horrible feeling that she had come to the wrong house. She read the street number that was screwed into the wall beside the front door. Yes, it was definitely her own home.

"Clear off, you vultures," the pink-haired woman said. "Let the girl inside, will you?"

The reporter with the lemon scarf caught Tuesday's eye and held her microphone out to Tuesday. "Tuesday, you've been gone all week. The entire city has been waiting and worrying. *Where have you been?*"

"I wasn't anywhere," Tuesday stammered. "Baxterr and I . . . we went for a walk in the park."

Then the woman with the pink hair opened the gate and marched Tuesday up the steps and into the house, slamming the front door behind them. The light in the hallway was dim compared with the bright sunshine outside, and Tuesday had to blink several times before she understood.

"Miss *Digby*?" she said. "Is that really *you*?"

But before Miss Digby had a chance to answer, Serendipity Smith came flying down the hallway with tears of relief shining on her cheeks, and wrapped her daughter in her arms as if she would never, ever, ever let her go again.

Chapter Twenty-Seven

They sat, Tuesday and Serendipity, on either side of Denis's hospital bed. Tuesday had hold of one of his hands and Serendipity the other. The room had no windows and lots of machines that beeped and sighed.

Denis's skin was the palest gray, and he had a misty quality about him, as if he might fade away at any moment.

"Dad?" said Tuesday. "Dad?"

But Denis said nothing.

Tuesday blinked back tears. She realized that she had believed her arrival would make a difference.

That Denis would somehow sense her presence and magically awake.

Perhaps Serendipity had thought the same, for she had been loudly enthusiastic when they had first arrived, telling Denis how Tuesday was home at last, that she was safe, and how she had been on such extraordinary adventures, and didn't he want to hear all about them?

Both Serendipity and Tuesday had kissed his cheeks and forehead, but Denis had not stirred. His quiet breathing hadn't changed. Tuesday and Serendipity came to a sort of standstill then. Neither of them knew what to say. Tuesday observed the flowers in the vases all along the shelf above her father's bed and on the table at the end of his bed. There were roses in every color: lipstick pink, deep red, vivid orange, buttercream, vanilla cream, snow white. The ones Serendipity had brought this day, their petals not yet open, were a gentle shade of mauve.

Serendipity explained to Tuesday that it had become a daily habit to bring fresh roses to Denis's room. Along with balloons. The balloons, bought from a street seller outside the hospital, floated about the ceiling with messages of "Get Well," "We love you,"

"Congratulations!" and "Happy Birthday!" and "It's a Boy!"—which might have seemed strange to some people, but which Tuesday knew Denis would find hilarious, when at last he woke.

Not all of the balloons had words on them. Others were just one color, and very sparkly, or else they had stripes or spots, rainbows or stars. The room could easily have been depressing with all the tubes and drips and monitors about the bed and the beeping noises and ticking clock and the gray chairs and pale lemon blanket. But Serendipity had managed to fill it with color. The bright balloons over her head reminded Tuesday of the worlds she had left behind, spinning above the Gardener's Conservatory, and she wondered how Silver Nightly was doing and how his new dog was settling in and what he was going to name her.

Denis slept on, if being in a coma was anything like sleeping. Tuesday had no way of knowing.

"Is he dreaming?" she asked Serendipity.

"Maybe," said Serendipity. "I hope they're lovely dreams if he is."

"Do you think he hears anything?" Tuesday asked after another stretch of silence.

"Well, if he can't hear us, I hope he hears the sea. Or you laughing. Or all of us playing cards. Or the breeze in the trees at City Park. Or the birds . . ."

Tuesday heard the crack in her mother's voice as she said this.

"He's going to be okay, Mom," she said. "He's going to wake up."

"I'm sorry. But now that you're home, I feel even more desperate to get him home again too."

"Maybe he needs a story," said Tuesday.

Serendipity wiped her eyes. "Perhaps you're right. And that way I could get to hear it as well. I mean all of it this time—not the rushed version."

And so Tuesday began at the beginning. Holding her dad's hand and telling it to him as if he were awake and listening, she talked of her walk in City Park a whole week ago and how the thread had zoomed in from out of the blue and caught her up. Then she told him how she had met Vivienne at the tree and how they had visited the Library. She described the packed dining room and the pots of chili beans and meeting Silver Nightly, not forgetting the bit about how Cordwell Jefferson had actually lost his foot. Then she described how Vivienne, who had not been able to visit the Library, had waited as if frozen until Tuesday and Baxterr returned. She described the hike to the Mabanquo River and the night they had spent swimming in the hot pool, the picnic they had made, and how good it had been to sleep under the towering ferns. Then she told of *Vivacious* doing its magical thing of growing from a tiny boat into a dinghy and the night they had spent on the Mabanquo River, and the torrential rain and discovering, at daybreak, that the world had been crushed against another world that was pouring its ocean down on top of them. Next she described the terror of being grabbed by the vercaka and being flown higher and higher so that she thought at any moment she would become vercaka bait—or get dropped from a great height and end up like a splodge of strawberry jam on the ground.

Serendipity shook her head and chewed her lip but said nothing.

Tuesday continued, describing her fall instead between the worlds and waking up on the Gardener's couch with all those worlds, floating like the balloons around the hospital ceiling but thousands more, and all spinning and all different shapes and sizes. And how the Gardener was very old and fragile and terribly forgetful. How he had all manner of strange sayings that made no sense, and quite a lot of sense all at once when you stopped to think about them.

Serendipity's eyes had grown very large, but she did not interrupt, only squeezed Denis's hand and nodded to Tuesday to go on.

Tuesday described what it was like to be the Gardener. She neglected to mention the part about accepting the role of the Gardener *forever*. She had heard her mother refer to it as "poetic license"—when the truth required a little massaging.

Tuesday went on to relay all that Vivienne had told her about the battle of the City of Clocks and finally being reunited with Baxterr and Vivienne. And how at last Blake, the Librarian, and Silver Nightly arrived. Tuesday talked about how she had heard Denis was ill and how urgently she had wanted to come home and how Silver had become the Gardener. And finally how they had visited the world of the Winged Dogs and Silver had found his own dog, and Tuesday and Blake had flown home on Baxterr and arrived this very morning.

When she was done, Tuesday watched Denis's face expectantly, but there was no change. She laid her head down against his hand on the blanket. Everything was very quiet. And then the hand twitched. It moved. It patted her head. She sat up, startled. She stared at Denis, and Denis stared back.

"Dad?" said Tuesday, wondering if this was simply a strange phenomenon.

"Denis?" said Serendipity, also gaping at him as if he were an apparition that might disappear at any moment.

Denis smiled at both of them and blinked.

"My," he said, "that was a good story."

Chapter Twenty-Eight

After that, several weeks passed. They were nice, regular weeks, all with seven days, and all of them in the right order. Denis was at last allowed to come home, with strict instructions to relax and take things easy for a while. In her writing room on the top story of the house on Brown Street, Serendipity Smith began her next book, and from his vantage point in a great circular room, the new Gardener had the pleasure of seeing a world being born. The Librarian spent the week putting books back on shelves, and by Sunday she had got as far as trying to remember whether MacMiniman came before McMaryborough, or after. "Mc" names, she thought, ought to be banned.

Baxterr spent most days either sleeping in Tuesday's room or watching over Denis to make sure that he didn't overexert himself. In this, Baxterr had an ally in the pink-haired Miss Digby, who had taken to coming to Brown Street every day, and who would elbow Denis out of his own kitchen and tut at him if he so much as hovered near the ironing basket. Baxterr didn't mind, for Miss Digby had excellent taste in cheese.

And as for Tuesday? Well, she wrote. That is, she went to school and ate breakfast and walked her dog and read books and had at the very least her regulation eighty-seven minutes of fresh air each day. And whenever she wasn't doing those things, she wrote. And then, one Sunday, she had a late breakfast, took a bath, and dressed carefully. She brushed Baxterr until his golden-brown fur gleamed. Right at two o'clock, the front doorbell rang. Tuesday flung it open to see Blake Luckhurst standing there wearing pressed black pants, a shirt with orange stripes on it, and very shiny shoes.

"Ready?" he asked. A taxi waited behind him in the street.

"You bet," Tuesday said.

"We're off. See you later!" Tuesday yelled down the hall toward the kitchen, and she heard her parents call back their good-byes. She grabbed her very best coat off its peg, snuck a quick glimpse at herself in the hallway mirror, and dashed out the door behind Baxterr.

Blake got out of the taxi first and, in a very gentlemanly fashion, held the door open for Tuesday and Baxterr. The footpath of Gallery Street—one of the fanciest thoroughfares in the city—was invitingly wide, and Tuesday, in her very best sneakers, couldn't help turning a pirouette to make the skirt of her butterfly-patterned dress fly out in a circle. Baxterr, wearing his finest collar, shook himself joyfully, feeling the breeze in his well-brushed coat.

On either side of the street were buildings both old and lovely, each one with something to recommend it. In front of them were the imposing steps of the Hotel Mirage, the sometime home of prime ministers and film stars, musicians and artists, ballet dancers and cricket players. And, as it was widely known, the permanent home of Serendipity Smith, the most famous writer in the world.

"Tuesday McGillycuddy, take my arm," said Blake.

"All set, doggo?" said Tuesday, looping her arm through Blake's.

Baxterr gave a confident wag of his tail, as if strolling into the city's most exclusive hotel was something he did every day.

"And remember, doggo, we have to pretend that we don't know her. Or at least, that we don't know her any better than anyone else does," Tuesday said, and Baxterr gave her a look that showed he understood perfectly and was a little put out that she had felt the need to remind him.

Tuesday held Baxterr's leash lightly as they stepped onto the soft, pale gray carpet that had been rolled down the center of the marble steps. At the top, they met two doormen, identical in immaculate black-and-gold livery, who swung open the silver-and-glass doors and ushered Tuesday, Blake, and Baxterr inside.

The lobby was immense, with a splendid staircase that went up and up and up. Through the middle of this broad flight of stairs poured a waterfall intercepted by a series of fountains until the water arrived in a great shimmering pool on the ground floor. The ceiling high above, Tuesday noticed, was encrusted with crystals that glowed and sparkled. And there was the most delicious smell, as if someone had captured the scent of happiness and sunshine.

Tuesday took a deep breath. "Wow!"

"I think we go up there," said Blake.

And so, ignoring the bank of lifts, they began to climb the stairs with the central waterfall bubbling and sparkling until they reached the fountain on the café level. Guests were having coffee and tea from patterned china, and everywhere there were tables with tall-tiered cake stands bearing sandwiches and cakes. The tables were laid with white linen, and the chairs elegantly upholstered in striped red silk.

A waiter in a silver bowtie materialized, and Tuesday, feeling suddenly nervous, swallowed and said, "There is a table reserved under the name McGillycuddy."

"Certainly, mademoiselle," the waiter replied, in a voice that sounded as silky as the chairs.

A cushion of red velvet had already been set out for Baxterr, and Baxterr—once Tuesday had unclipped his leash—leapt up onto it neatly and curled his tail tidily around his feet. The waiter shook the folds out of three linen napkins, laid one across Tuesday's lap and one in Blake's, then tied the other loosely about Baxterr's neck.

"Are you here for the event?" the waiter asked.

"Oh, what event?" Tuesday asked innocently.

"Serendipity Smith is arriving at any moment," he said, nodding toward the double doors with large brass handles beyond their table. "She's finally back! She'll come through here, then take the elevators over there up to her own floor. Whenever she lets the press know she'll be arriving, we call it an event."

"Really?" said Tuesday. "How exciting. Do you think we'll get a glimpse?"

"Oh, most certainly. You have the perfect table. I see that your party is not yet complete," the waiter said, noting the empty chairs. "May I fetch you a refreshment to start?"

Blake and Tuesday felt the need to be unusually formal and polite.

"A chocolate milk shake for me, please," said Tuesday.

"And a root-beer float for me, please," said Blake. "If you have them."

"Indubitably," said the waiter, with a slight bow. "And for the furry fellow?"

"Milk, please, a little warm," Tuesday said.

"My pleasure, mademoiselle," the waiter said, and glided away.

Tuesday was pleased to see that Baxterr was far from the lone representative of his species in the hotel. There was a tall white-haired man sharing a plate of fruitcake with a bassett hound. And at another table, a young woman kept company with three greyhounds, all eating biscuits with foie gras. Beyond them sat a man with a pair of Chihuahuas on his lap, tiny bright flowers behind their ears, turning up their petite noses at their ham-and-cheese croissants.

When the drinks arrived, Tuesday's was piled with ice cream, cream, and grated chocolate, and Blake's threatened to froth clean out of its towering glass. Baxterr's milk was served in a sensible but beautiful bowl and—to Tuesday's immense pride—he lapped at it with absolute decorum.

Then an audible wave of excitement swept through the room. There was a sense of some kind of activity taking place below, perhaps at the hotel's front doors, and all the people in the café turned toward the gilded waterfall. A whisper rippled almost visibly through the entire hotel. Suddenly guests were arriving from their rooms, people in the café were standing, wait-staff were appearing in their whites, and even kitchen staff in white caps and striped aprons were emerging through swinging doors. There was a buzz coming toward the café. Everyone was craning to get a first glimpse of the event.

Someone called out, "There she is!"

Someone else said, "She's here! She's coming up the stairs."

"It's her!"

"I think she's here," said Blake to Tuesday.

"I can't believe it!" said the white-haired man eating fruitcake.

"Oh my goodness," said the man with the match-ing Chihuahuas, clasping them to his chest. "It's really SERENDIPITY SMITH!"

And indeed it was. The double doors were thrown open by a pair of liveried doormen. And then the flaming-haired figure of Serendipity Smith strode into view, accompanied by a flock of media people, cameras on their shoulders or microphones in their hands.

Serendipity wore a coat in plush tangerine velvet

lined with paisley silk, and her high-heeled crimson leather boots came up above her knees. Today, she had worn her russet-colored curls loose, and they rambled wildly down her back and around her shoulders. Upon her face was a pair of Lucilla La More glasses with bright gold, yellow, and white sunbursts at the temples.

Reporters pushed in closer, while hotel visitors scrambled for paper, napkins, bills, hats, dog collars, or indeed anything at all that Serendipity Smith might be able to autograph. Serendipity moved gracefully yet determinedly through the crush, pausing here and there to shake hands and to scribble her name. For the tiniest moment, her sunburst-framed gaze alighted on Blake, Tuesday, and Baxterr at their café table. And was it Tuesday's imagination, or did one of Serendipity's eyes flicker closed in the briefest of winks? Tuesday couldn't be certain. She could only try to behave like everybody else in the room, as if she were seeing the most famous writer in the world.

"What are you working on?" someone called out.

"Yes, what's next?" asked another.

And then the elevator doors opened, and Serendipity Smith stepped inside. The media wailed and cried out, begging for another photo, more answers, more time, but the doors closed. Two footmen stood impenetrably before the elevator's doors. The crowd sighed. She had been with them for mere moments, and now she was gone. Tuesday realized she and Blake and Baxterr had all stood up, and they sat down again.

"Hello, you two," said Serendipity, arriving with Denis and sliding into her seat at the table.

Serendipity wore her usual short hair, a simple black shirt and pants and, because it was a special occasion, a striking pair of short red boots. Denis wore a black beanie to cover his shaved head and looked incredibly stylish, albeit thin and pale. The waiter materialized again.

"You didn't miss it, did you?" he said. "She was right here. Serendipity Smith!"

"How incredible," said Serendipity, smiling at him.

She ordered afternoon tea for them all, and soon a tiered stand arrived, laden with food. There were miniature egg-and-bacon pies, thumb-sized sausage rolls, and the thinnest cucumber sandwiches. On the next tier were lemon tarts, strawberries coated in chocolate, tiny éclairs, squares of jelly topped with fruit, and caramel clusters. On the top were macarons in six different colors and flavors.

Tuesday felt like she was in a dream. She was here, together with her dog and her father and her mother and Blake, having afternoon tea at the Hotel Mirage.

"Did you see her?" Tuesday asked Serendipity.

"We did," said Serendipity. "We stood on the footpath and watched her arrive, then we followed along as she came into the lobby and up the stairs."

"And what did you think of yourself?"

"I think Miss Digby is a marvelous me," said Serendipity. "What did you think?"

"She was very . . . famous!" Tuesday said.

And they all laughed.

Tuesday, popping a last crumb of macaron onto her tongue, thought for a moment, and said, "Will Miss Digby be you from now on, Mom?"

"I hope so," said Serendipity. "But of course I may be required to be myself from time to time."

"Do you ever think of having a disguise, Blake?" Denis asked.

"Nah," replied Blake. "I am always happiest being my own magnificent self."

Tuesday shook her head, smiling, and put her hand on Denis's arm, saying, "Just like you, Dad."

Serendipity put her hand on his other arm and said, "You are magnificent, my love. I would be utterly lost without you. Promise me you'll never, ever get sick like that again."

Baxterr ruffed, and Tuesday said, "Dad, I'm still so sorry I wasn't here while you were so ill."

"What matters is that you're both home—that we're all home," said Denis. "Maybe one day I might get to see some of those other worlds you've all visited . . . Tell me again about it, both of you."

"All right," said Tuesday.

"Well," said Blake, leaning forward.

Baxterr ruffed, and Serendipity poured more tea.

In the middle of that night, when the house was quiet, Tuesday woke. She couldn't say quite why she had woken. There hadn't been a noise, and there wasn't a thread floating about trying to catch her, although there was a streak of moonlight coming through her curtains.

She got out of bed, went to her desk, and turned on the lamp. Tuesday knew she had something important to do, and so for a little while, she sat down and typed away on her pale blue typewriter. Every now and then, her eyes strayed from the page to gaze abstractedly at the curtains or the wall. When she was done, she reread her words.

"Vivienne is going *love* that," she whispered.

Then she turned off her lamp and went back to bed, and if you could have seen her face in the darkness, you would have seen that her eyes were shining.

Epilogue

I t's an old tree, tall and strong, with a thick pale trunk and branching arms that end in bursts of narrow purple-green leaves. Although it grows on a cliff edge, its roots run deep. Some of its branches reach right out over the Restless Sea, and the longest of them forks into an outstretched hand. In the palm of that hand is a tree house with walls made from planks of sea-washed driftwood and windows that drink in the view.

The roof of the tree house is a dome, shingled with scallop shells on the outside and painted inside with scenes from a great battle. There are cats with their claws dug deep into vicious ugly birds, and fish that fly through the sky like arrows. The birds snap their beaks at a Winged Dog who soars over them all, and a small girl shoots arrows from her seat on his back. This roof has a secret, though, and it's this: on the wall is a lever, and if you pull it, the dome will slide open and let in the sun, or the starshine, or the buttery fingers of a full moon.

The inside of the tree house has all the things a girl might need, and not much more. The veranda that rings the house holds a table and two chairs, and a potted garden of herbs and medicinal flowers. There is also a hammock where a girl might rest. And rest she does, sleeping soundly as a pearl dawn starts to spill onto the surface of the Restless Sea. The girl would deny it, but she snores, just a little.

It's not snoring that you can hear right now, though: it's a sneeze. A sneeze as dainty as the little pink nostrils it came from. And as the girl wakes, her ears prick, most especially her right ear, the one with the pointed tip. She hears it again: sssnizoo! Vivienne looks all around her but sees nothing. Then she feels the soft tickle of long whiskers against her neck.

"Ermengarde," she whispers, hardly daring to believe it.

Grinning, she reaches up and draws out a small, black rat.

"How did you get here?"

The rat merely yawns, showing sharp yellow teeth, and makes a tidy leap back onto Vivienne's shoulder, where she can nestle once again into the warmth of the girl's hair.

"Hang on," says the girl, partly to Ermengarde and partly to herself. "How did I get here? And where exactly is here?"

Vivienne tumbles out of her hammock, and the view over the Restless Sea momentarily knocks the air out of her lungs.

"Oh!" she gasps. She leans on the rail and smiles. She laughs and runs the full circle of the veranda, marveling at the timberwork and peering inside. It is, she thinks, the strongest and most beautiful tree house ever built.

Now she sees that in the middle of the table on the veranda, there is a package. It's wrapped in shiny red paper and tied with brown string. A label reads IN CASE OF RAIN. The girl tears off the paper without ceremony and finds a glass bottle. Inside the bottle is a sailing boat with a red hull and a white sail, and—she grins—a cabin! Written on the stern in tiny letters is Vivacious II.

There is one more thing, and she feels it as an itch in the tips of her blue wings. She wriggles them, but the itch *grows stronger. She notices it first in the shadow she casts on the wall of her tree house. But it's not until she sees it out the corner of her eye that she believes it. Her wings are growing. They are still leathery, still blue, but they grow and grow until they are large enough and strong enough to let her truly fly.*

Vivienne Small gives a whoop of joy and leaps up onto the railing of her veranda, spreading her wings against the shimmering sea. A breeze comes skittering over the water, and in a moment it will reach her, rush into her wings, and fill them like sails. Her nose will catch the scent of adventure, and in that moment, something new will begin.

GO FISH

Angelica Banks is not one writer but two. Meet Danielle Wood and Heather Rose, the two halves of Angelica Banks and the authors of *Finding Serendipity*.

What did you want to be when you grew up?

DW: I remember sitting in my mother's VW Beetle, outside a bookshop, when she asked me that question. I was eight years old, and I said, "I want to be an author."

HR: I wanted to be a writer. I seemed to know this innately before I even learned to read. I also wanted to be a teacher at one stage and would set up a blackboard for my younger sister and try to impart my vast seven-year-old knowledge.

What's your favorite childhood memory?

DW: My grandfather had a yacht called *Alathea* and we used to go sailing on it during the holidays. My father and I used to sit up at the bow, even when it was really windy, and we would make up new words for the things we could see. We called cormorants "dive-down-fishy-din-din-birds." And, to tell the truth, we still do.

HR: We had a boat called *Miss Wiggs*—a little white clinker dinghy. My grandfather and I would row out very early and watch the dawn wake the sky, fishing lines over our fingers. He would look about at the land, the sea, and the sky and say, "That's what beauty is."

What were your hobbies as a kid? What are your hobbies now?

DW: I liked to knit and sew, and I had a *lot* of small furry animal pets. Perhaps I have never really grown up, because these days I like to knit and sew, and I still have a great many rats, mice, and guinea pigs (although our family pretends they belong to my children).

HR: As a kid my hobbies were reading, baking biscuits and cakes, walking on the beach, writing, and sailing every weekend with my best friend in a dinghy his dad built for us. Nowadays my hobbies are still reading and baking cakes and walking on the beach. I also love gardening and spending time with my children, and my newest hobby is painting.

Where do you write your books?

DW: I write in a wagon in the garden. I had one especially made for me as a writing studio, and I think my love for wagons is related to my love for Roald Dahl's book *Danny, the Champion of the World*. Danny lived with his father in a wagon, and Roald Dahl wrote his books in a small aqua-blue wagon that he originally bought as a cubby house for his children.

HR: A couple of years ago, we moved to a house at the beach not far from where I grew up. My writing room is upstairs overlooking the sea. Every night I stand out on the balcony and feel enormously grateful for this house and this wonderful place to write.

What challenges do you face in the writing process, and how do you overcome them?

DW: I have three children and I teach writing at the university nearby. And I have a lot of pets, and a big basket of knitting yarn, *and* a spinning wheel that I really want to learn to use. I like a good game of Scrabble, or Bananagrams, so there are *always* distractions. I overcome this by reminding myself how terrible I will feel if the stories inside of me don't get *out*.

HR: Hemingway said, "There is nothing to writing. All you do is sit down at a typewriter and bleed." I think my greatest challenge is that every novel is like a marathon and sometimes it's hard to find the energy, courage, and discipline to open up my heart and mind to the characters and the plot and the sheer craft and time required for writing. And, like Danielle, there are always many other things to pull me away from the desk.

Where do you find inspiration for your stories?

DW: I don't think there's anywhere that I don't find inspiration. Inspiration is everywhere, and the ideas part of writing is dead easy compared with the hard yards of getting the right words in the right order on the page.

HR: I find life inspiring, too! I am always looking and listening and considering people and how they go about their lives. But even if I lived in an ice cave in distant Antarctica, there would be characters in my head and words they want to say to each other that I would have to write down. Some people sing and some people dance, and I seem to have to respond to life through writing.

What is your favorite word?

DW: This week, it's *haptodysphoria*, because it's a word that describes something I often feel, but I didn't know until very recently that it even had a name. Next week, I'll have a new favorite word: I look forward to meeting it.

HR: I think *hello* is a wonderful word. It's an everyday word, easily overlooked. But it's a word of warmth and connection, full of possibility.

If you could live in any fictional world, what would it be?

DW: I think, today, that my answer is this: I'd like to spend some time in the fictional world of Doctor Dolittle, as his assistant.

HR: Right now, I do like the world in *The Name of the Wind* by Patrick Rothfuss. There's a university you can go to where you can learn the true name of things for magical purpose. I do find that fascinating.

What was your favorite book when you were a kid? Do you have a favorite book now?

DW: My favorite book when I was a child was *Carbonel*, by Barbara Sleigh. And also the sequel, *The Kingdom of Carbonel*. It played into my (ongoing) fantasy of being able to hear what animals say.

HR: In grade three, our teacher, Mr. Viney, read us *The Hobbit*. I think it was the first fantasy book I ever came across, and I have been enchanted by it all my life. (Not the films!) My newest favorite book is *All the Light We Cannot See* by Anthony Doerr. Exquisite. But my eternal favorite is *Anna Karenina*.

Baxterr is more than just a family pet; he's Tuesday's best friend. Do you have any pets? And what are they like?

DW: I have Scout the dog, Lily and Oliver the alpacas, seven chickens (Julia, Effie, Strawberry, Penny, Bones, Thunderbolt, and Gwendolyn), five rats (Hester, Vivienne Small, Eepersip, Reepicheep, and Eowyn), one mouse (Toffee), sixteen guinea pigs (Coco, Milo, Chino, Honey, Sprinkles, Leia, Obi Wan, Arwen of the Elves, Teacup, Belladonna, Morgan Le Fay, Puck, Prickle, Daenerys Stormborn, Marmalade, and Casper) and many thousands of bees. What are they like? Oh, it would take so long to tell you. Suffice to say, they fill my heart with joy.

HR: Danielle is amazing with all things small, and she bred us two beautiful rats called Miko and Komiko that have totally ful-filled my yearning for a pet rat. And we have a fabulous fat and talkative cat called Chaplin because we are also quite film-mad.

Tuesday is a writer. What advice would you give to writers at the Beginning?
DW: When you write, don't try to sound clever, try to sound like *you*. No one else in the whole, wide world is *you*. No one else can tell your stories and no one else can use your voice. The best stories you will tell are the ones that come out of your tru-est heart (but that doesn't mean you have to, or should neces-sarily, write about yourself—imagination is very important).

HR: Write something every day. Even if it's a thought or a sentence or a line of a poem or a bit of conversation you heard—the way the sky looked or lunch tasted or how you feel as you're going to sleep. Fill whole notebooks with these thoughts. You may never reread them, but you're training your writing brain. And read! The more you read the more you'll learn about writing (and life!).

When all seems lost, Tuesday must set out
to save her friend—and herself.

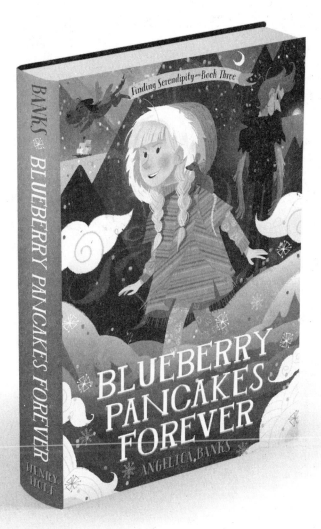

Keep reading for an excerpt.

Along a rocky stretch of coastline, where cliffs soared to the sky and seabirds soared even higher, there stood a lighthouse. Perched on a grim knuckle of stone, it was the loneliest of places, lucky to be visited by two or three ships each year. And yet, on this particular day, it was surrounded by a flotilla of fishing boats. On their decks were photographers and reporters with their camera lenses trained on the red door of the lighthouse. Right at midday, it opened.

Out of the lighthouse stepped a woman dressed in a vivid blue coat and carrying a bucket. The buffeting wind made her long red hair fly about as if in a blender.

The long skirts of her coat flew up, revealing a pair of spectacular red boots. After waving to the assembly of fishing boats, the woman made her way along a rough, sloping path that led to the water's edge, where she crouched to carefully fill her bucket. With that done, she caught up a thick cable of rope and began to haul on it, hand over hand.

The fishing boats attempted to edge closer, but the crashing waves and maze of half-submerged rocks deterred even the most valiant skippers. Several of the journalists put megaphones to their mouths and began calling questions over the wind:

"Serendipity, can you tell us what you're writing?"

"Serendipity, is Vivienne Small going to feature in the new series?"

"Serendipity, when are you coming back to the city?"

"Serendipity, do you know that *Vivienne Small and the Final Battle* is now the bestselling children's novel of all time?"

"The Mirage Hotel is keen to have you back. They're asking, do you need crème brûlée shipped in?"

"Serendipity, do you have a message for your young readers?"

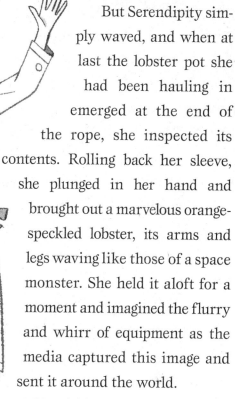

But Serendipity simply waved, and when at last the lobster pot she had been hauling in emerged at the end of the rope, she inspected its contents. Rolling back her sleeve, she plunged in her hand and brought out a marvelous orange-speckled lobster, its arms and legs waving like those of a space monster. She held it aloft for a moment and imagined the flurry and whirr of equipment as the media captured this image and sent it around the world.

Then she lowered the lobster into her water-filled bucket and clipped on the lid. Walking more slowly this time, and leaning slightly from the weight of the bucket, she made her way back to the lighthouse. At seventeen minutes past midday, she gave a final wave to the assembled fleet, then disappeared inside.

Several of the journalists shook their heads.

"We *must* be able to get onto the island," one said to the ship's captain.

"Not likely," the captain replied, shrugging her shoulders and shaking her head. "It's simply impossible to visit until we can send a rowboat across, and that is only possible on the lowest of tides."

"Well, when will that happen?"

"They come once a year. The next one's only six weeks away."

"Six weeks! We can't wait *six weeks*."

"Take it up with the moon," the captain said.

The journalist thought for a moment, stared up at the dull gray sky that showed neither sun nor moon, and sighed.

"She's been out here alone for months and months," he mused, trying a different tack. "It must be hard for her, not having anyone to talk to."

"She speaks to Constanza, by radio," said the captain with a wry smile.

Constanza was the proprietor of the only shop in the tiny village that clung to the mainland's cliffs and overlooked the lighthouse. It was Constanza who took Serendipity's weekly grocery order and organized the helicopter to make the delivery.

"Constanza is hardly a conversationalist," the reporter said. He had used every tactic imaginable to convince the taciturn Constanza to let him travel on the helicopter, or at the very least use the shop radio to contact Serendipity at the lighthouse. But with no success.

"Have you considered that maybe Ms. Smith doesn't want to talk to you?" said the captain.

"But surely she misses her fans?" the reporter said.

"My own mother was a writer," said the captain, somewhat wistfully. "She used to say that you could never be lonely with your characters beside you."

"So that's it? She won't come out again until . . . until when?"

The captain shrugged.

"There's got to be something we can do," the journalist said. "The whole world is desperate for news!"

"Well," said the skipper with a sigh, "if you want to, you can pay me, and we'll sit here all day, every day, watching and waiting. It's your money. But I assure you, she's gone for today."

And so, one by one, the fishing boats turned away from the lighthouse and made their way back to the village in the distance.

On the rocky outcrop, the wind continued to blow, whistling through a narrow crack under the lighthouse door and between the windowpanes. Inside, a red wig lay in a tangle on a table and the electric blue coat had been hung on a peg. The red boots had been unlaced and discarded.

At the sink stood Miss Digby in a pair of sheepskin boots, her usually tidy hair ever so slightly disheveled from being tucked up under the wig. Through the thick glass of the narrow window, she watched the retreating fishing boats. Each day, they were edging closer, becoming bolder. She knew they'd eventually find a way onto the island. That simply wouldn't do. She could lock the door, but sooner or later, she'd have to come out and face their probing lenses and endless questions.

Miss Digby shuddered at the thought, then turned her attention to the bucket in the sink. She removed the lid and was greeted by a host of coral-colored claws and legs, all waving.

"I am sorry, Gerald," she said as she gingerly lifted the lobster out of the bucket and lowered him into a large aquarium tank full of seawater. "I know it's inconvenient, but you needn't fear. We both know the drill."

Gerald landed on the pebbles on the tank floor and scuttled behind a large frond of seaweed. There he would hunker down, in a mild sulk, until darkness fell and Miss Digby would pop him back into his bucket, walk down to the shore, and release him into the sea. They had been through this catch-and-release routine every few days since the media had discovered her whereabouts. Miss Digby thought Gerald would have learned to avoid the lobster pot, but it seemed that he found her oyster and tuna baits irresistible. Truth be told, she was grateful for his company, even if he was given to sulking.

Miss Digby fixed herself a cup of tea and a cheese-and-pickled-onion sandwich. She ate, all the while feeling troubled. When she was done, she walked a circle around the tiny room, then slumped into a chair beside the aquarium and peered into its watery gloom.

"Why isn't she answering my calls, Gerald?" Miss Digby said. "Gerald? *Gerald?*"

But there was no reply.

Miss Digby sighed and reached for the radio. Not that she expected to get much more of a response from the radio than she did from the moping crustacean. She cleared her throat and, in her best Serendipity Smith voice, said, "Good afternoon. Constanza, are you there?"

"*Sí,*" came a flat voice.

"Constanza, I wonder, could you try the Brown Street number again?"

"*Sí, Señora Smith,*" said Constanza, pronouncing it *Smeet.*

Miss Digby could hear the phone ringing. The ringing went on and on and on. But no one answered. She sighed.

"I'll try again tomorrow, Constanza," said Miss Digby, trying to not sound too despondent. "*Gracias.*"